WHITE CRANE STRIKES

Ivy Ngeow

To Mimi,
All the best with writing
and publishing.

Ivy x

ISBN: 978-1-913584-11-5 PAPERBACK

ISBN: 978-1-913584-12-2 HARDBACK

Copyright © 2022 by Ivy Ngeow

A Leopard Print book

First published in Great Britain in 2022 by Leopard Print.

"Work is love made visible."
- Kahlil Gibran

CHAPTER 1

April 1971

The tingle of starting a new job drew him closer to the cabin. He was hit by the cloying reek of rotting drains, damp and mold. Not the metallic dried-up stink of a pond, like at his grandfather's farm, but that of the city. Dark, rank, rich. But decay *is* growth. Without it, there could be no change.

As he threaded his way through the gloomy path, his breathing turned short and fast. Dappled sunlight cut through the thick overgrown bushes like glints of glass. Anyway, there was no such thing as an "overgrown path", he reminded himself, because all paths started off overgrown before they became paths.

The stench filled him with a heady mixture of delight and revulsion. He remembered it from only the day before, but it still seemed an assault, an intimacy. Hadn't Grandpops once said, *paths are what we take, not what we make*?

The old brick-built cabin sat squarely and at ease at the end of the garden.

He opened his fist exposing the two gold-colored keys he'd been given. One for the house and the other for the cabin.

· · ·

"Ever done anything like this before?" he recalled Mr Alfred asking during the job interview.

"A little," he'd lied. "I am good with electrics, plumbing, heating, carpentry, gardening. I can fix most things." That was a slightly bigger lie but he would learn damned quick as he was only 22 years old and he'd learnt so much already. He'd had no choice. Since they shut the factory, he had to take anything. Odd jobs. Temporary jobs. This was the big one. A permanent gig. Dallas was gonna have her fancy wedding, about which they'd talked enough. The girls at Marshall Field's department store where she worked were excited, she said. Always the wedding, the wedding, the wedding. Those were her three Ws. His were wallet, wallet, wallet.

He hesitated before inserting the larger of the keys into the lock. From working at the steel plant, he'd assumed the smaller the building, the larger the key. He was right. It turned. He nudged the creaky door open. Even after it'd rained, the cabin seemed dry. Gloves on, he tested the windows in the main room first to see which needed fixing. The sashes were stiff from being swollen and covered in the thick veins of twisting creepers, yet, like muscles which had been forgotten, they moved. He whisked off the torn, dirty and probably candy-sticky curtains with a single flick of his wrists, like a conductor of an imaginary orchestra. The less he touched *those* the better. With his claw hammer, pliers and chisel, he stripped anything that was loose or tangled. He hammered in protruding nails which you'd catch yourself on. Day One of a new job meant safety first, trash next, trust last.

"Let me show you your office, work room," Mr Alfred had said after the interview the day before.

Office. The very icy hiss of the word brought a sense of seriousness about this job. Mr Alfred might even consider him to be of mild importance. Jay Jay had not been made redundant for nothing at the steel plant. Bud, his supervisor then, had patted him on the back and said to him on his last day, "there are no wrong turnings in life."

"I have an office?" Jay Jay said.

"Course. You're gonna be working here, aren't ya?" Mr Alfred chuckled.

"Yessir."

Then they'd crossed the terrace and headed down the wide, curved Indiana stone staircase into the gardens with sweeping views of Lake Michigan, beaches and the navy pier. "Should've seen the parties we had here back in the day." Mr Alfred had gestured at the tangled forest that used to be the gardens.

"Well, we had a gardener and a caretaker once," Mr Alfred had added. "Oh, and a driver too. I don't know how long they used the cabin for as their staff room but they did."

THE CABIN WAS WAY BIGGER than the entire apartment Jay Jay shared with Dallas. It had two rooms, the one he entered first, and another off it. An inner room. The main room still had a desk. Jay Jay was planning on turning that room into the workshop and the inner room into his office. Everything was like a mini version of Mr Alfred's grand old home. Moldy, filthy, rotten. A lot of work would be required to get the place going again and he couldn't wait to start.

MR ALFRED HAD ALSO SAID that if he had any equipment he could leave it in there. "I am sure there are already tools here," he waved vaguely at the floor, "but I can't say if you could still use them."

Jay Jay had thought, surely not. "Probably rusty or broken by now," he'd said tactfully.

"If you want to buy new tools, I'll pay you back for them."

Everything would work out fine. Jay Jay could see that Mr Alfred was a reasonable man, still sharp and quick, despite his age, whatever that figure might be.

"When do you think you can start, Jerry?"

"I... I have the job?"

"Course you do. The Professor sent you."

"Thank you, Sir. I really appreciate that."

"If you want to make a list of the stuff you'll need, or to make some notes, do that. I have a nurse appointment in half an hour. She'll want me back in my cage." Mr Alfred had laughed his crackly-wireless laugh.

IT WAS NOT a question of what Jay Jay needed, more one of what he had to trash. Old beer tins, cracked plates, broken cups. Excitement bubbled in him like a soda. He could make this place real nice, especially as it had to be his workshop. His studio. His "office". What should he call it? He'd never had one or needed one before. Living in a poky apartment and working at the steel plant before they shut down was all his knew. He could simply call it his cabin.

He tried the door of the inner room and with a little force, it swung open. An old bed sat in the middle. Both the bed and the floor were covered in a geometric-patterned vinyl flooring, now all cracked and torn at the edges.

At his grandfather's farm, he'd seen this kind of 'Fifties spotty design with random little shapes. Jay Jay moved the bed aside, which came apart with the movement. He wanted to check if the floor was concrete or wooden. If it was anything like the garbage he'd found and removed already, the latter would be also rotting now and he pulled up the vinyl to check. A corner was missing making it effortless to lift the sheet up. Once lifted, it was easy to pull away. He rolled and put it outside with the rest of the demolition trash.

Concrete. In the floor center was a double trap door in wood.

The frames were encrusted in its icing of grit and dust. A laundry chute-type of latch padlock was recessed into the wood so that the flooring sat flush. The padlock was fat as an apple and already black with rust. Between the paneling was zero to half an inch of gap due to shrinkage.

Jay Jay paused, considering breaking the lock, but his initial reaction was that even more junk awaited. He checked his watch. Still time. He had only been going forty minutes. He reached in his pocket for his flashlight, which he shone through the central and widest gap. The space was deep, possibly 7 feet. Just rags, a small cage, pieces of wood which might have been broken furniture. And something else.

"Oh shit," he gasped. He reeled as though he had been struck by some unseen force. The shock caused him to drop the pocket flashlight which rolled away and fell through the gap. His mouth went dry and his mind blank.

When he caught his breath, he crawled on all fours, peering again through the gap to make sure of what he had seen.

CHAPTER 2

He pushed open the rusty wrought-iron gate, its creak loud as a cat's cry. The front yard was darkened by shadows from excessive trees and shrubs. Rain came down, at first like needles and then in big slaps, making him squint as he looked up. He saw it. Three floors high, in Indiana limestone as smooth and creamy as his young face. "Oh my," he whispered. Turrets and wings framed a blue-black slate roof gleaming like scales on a dragon, the steep slope punctured with porthole windows. If this mansion was a monster, it might fly. About fifty yards away, he parked his '69 Chevy Camaro SS his Grandpops had bought him. Jay Jay had been nineteen at the time.

Assembled in GM Norwood, Ohio, with a bright Le Mans blue paint job, his car had black bucket seats, an 8-cylinder engine and Jay Jay's favorite bit— the signature white hockey stick stripe from the front of the fender to the door handles, certainly not a workman's van, he laughed. And not ready to be seen. Not yet. Not until he got used to the place.

After he'd walked a short distance up the grand tree-lined North Lakeshore Drive, he felt he might get used to working here. He walked tall, straighter; his chest expanded, shoulders risen. The path was covered by strangling weeds. Insects swarmed out of the lumbering thorny bushes when he disturbed the prickly undergrowth. The paving tiles, once ornate, colorful and geometric, were now missing or cracked.

He knocked and waited. He observed an old bell with the engraved word 'press', so he did. He listened. There was no sound. That'd be the first thing he'd fix around there. The once-polished oak door was formidable, its stained glass panel still intact. The door opened.

"Well, hello and good morning," said the old man. The 'well' made him sound friendly. He was frail, with sparse, fine white hair, a little stoop and his voice was thin. He was wearing clothes from at least a hundred years ago. No, maybe thirty, but at least he was well-dressed. At least he was *dressed*. You heard of old people who wore what they slept in all year round. "How do you do? You must be—"

"Jerry. Jerome Siracuse Lee. You can call me Jay Jay. Everybody do. I mean, does." Jay Jay lost the ability to speak, not that he was a great speaker in the first place. He had always been the quiet type. Lord knew how many got into trouble for opening their cake cave.

"Well, which do you prefer?"

"Jerry, Sir," he answered, which sounded better than Jay Jay in a job situation. Jerry was what the guys at the steel works called him. His great-grandparents had been alive when he was born, and they nicknamed him Jay Jay, a doubled-up American version of his Cantonese name, 謝. *Tse*. Like many Chinese words, it had multiple interpretations based on context. 謝 meant thanks, apologies and also the withering of flowers. That pretty much summarized one's entire life and its enigmas.

"Alfred Sutton." He held his hand out which Jay Jay firmly shook. "You can call me Alfred."

"Yessir."

"Eyetalyun?" Asked Mr Alfred.

How to explain this, thought Jay Jay. Siracuse, his mother's surname, gave away that he was Sicilian and one from New York, yet his origin wasn't easily explainable. His father was Chinese. He liked that Lee could be American *or* Chinese and no one could tell, which meant that depending on the situation, he was indeed both.

His great-grandparents had been from Canton. Coincidentally, they had the same surname, Lee. Marrying someone with the same surname was believed to be a curse, bringing bad back luck to the whole family. Jay Jay's great-grandmother's name was 李 茶, Lee Cha. She didn't have a name. Just a practical use. Cha meant tea. They called her *Cha! Ah Cha ah!* when they wanted tea. Jay Jay was a true American, from everywhere. Sharing the same surname as Bruce Lee was a source of pride for a kung fu guy like Jay Jay.

"I'm from Beecher, Illinois," he replied, as plainly as facts allowed.

"Robert Ellesworth," Mr Alfred said, then elaborated when Jay Jay blinked. "The Professor. A good friend. He sent you."

"Yes. No. My girlfriend, fiancée," he tripped over the word. " "Fiyawnsay"," she'd told him. "Not fiancy, hon. It's "for'n"." And small talk was "for'n" to him too. He left all that to Dallas. The art world and so on. "She told me about the job."

"Come on in. Let me show you around."

"I have my ray-zoo-may here, Sir." Jay Jay reached into his black leather and chrome briefcase, now redundant. Brand new and bought by Dallas for him from Marshall Field's. Mr Alfred smiled, showing his false teeth, white and straight, and then he shook his head and waved as though waving an insect away. Dallas said she'd easily return the briefcase for a refund since he'd never use it again if Mr Alfred did not want his resumé or if, by some insane chance, Jay Jay *wasn't* hired.

The old man already trusted him. Dallas found out about the job through the Professor at the art school. The Professor, she'd said, trusted her in return. He was probably sweet on her. They all were. She was a work of art. He went in and slightly bowed his head. He shuffled and cleaned his wet shoes on the door mat. He wasn't sure what to do with the briefcase, now as awkward as a dog who was dragged around but didn't want to go anywhere. He decided to set it down in the hall on a very long narrow table covered with paper, cartons, jars, so much stuff Jay Jay's eyes were unable to focus on a single thing.

"This is the hallway," said Alfred. The dark mahogany staircase was carved and sweeping. The stair carpet, which looked like it could have been blood-red, was now worn and faded. Once grand and in dark alternating stripes, the wallpaper was torn and peeling, stained at the top where there must have been a leak. This was a grand home once, thought Jay Jay as he stared at the huge monkey-tail handrail starter at the bottom step.

"There are things to fix in every room," said Mr Alfred. He continued to wander around the rooms, opening and closing the heavy polished oak doors and Jay Jay was already swimming in the information he had to take in. He didn't even write anything down. How was he going to remember all that? Should he go back to the briefcase? Dallas had packed a notebook in there the night before. A smart black hardback one from the art school.

"Don't think too much. This is to give you an overview," Mr Alfred said, as if answering Jay Jay's worried thoughts. "I don't want to go into a home. My family wants me to. But I was born and raised in this house. Your job as a handyman and caretaker is to help me fix everything here. I am capable of living on my own."

"Yes, I understand, Sir."

"Basically, I need your help to fix this damn place up and we haven't even got to the grounds yet. Are we good? Have you got green fingers?"

Jay Jay glanced at his hands in mock horror. Mr Alfred laughed, a thin but loud squeak which sounded like an old basement door's hinge.

The enormous front sitting room had its couches and chairs covered in white fabric. Everything was covered in dust, sheathed in an opaque blanket of cellular particles — hair, skin cells, insect carcasses, clothing fibers and all the detritus that life made and was made of. The chandeliers were coated in cobwebs like icing on a cake. You hardly were able to tell they were made of crystal drops. This joint would need a good clean, maybe that was all that was needed first. Jay Jay might have said that aloud.

Mr Alfred replied, "You are being straight with me, and I like that. If you need me to hire a roofing guy or a cleaning team, you book them in. I'll pay. You will find the right people for the right job. I am sure you are well-connected."

Jay Jay wasn't but he sure wasn't gonna let on. He'd find a directory, he would check their references, he'd ask around. The girls at Dallas's work might even know good people. No way did he want to screw this up. They toured the kitchen, various rooms, including a vast library with floor to ceiling oak bookcases. In the middle of the room sat an old-fashioned banker's desk which was double-sided as on one side sat the banker with access to all the drawers, cigars, drinks, ledgers and so on, and on the opposite side the customer, the small businessman asking for a loan with nothing but the cap in hand. The desk was the only spotless thing in the entire house, so it must be in use. The top was still covered in green leather, smooth, dust-free, polished.

They headed out of the library, and there was a piano room with a bar, the bathroom and then the levels upstairs. The bedrooms began to blur together. He had no idea what each room was. "This was my mother's room, also the room I was born in," Mr Alfred said. Each bedroom was similar, and all with the same problems of torn and stained wallpaper, rotten floor, rising damp. The cracked ceilings and broken lights topped the rooms.

"Sir, do you intend to do this place up to live here alone?"

"I like that." He stopped and peered at Jay Jay. "You're asking the right questions." Jay Jay had only asked one. He wanted to do the best job, so it was the most important thing to find out today. "I am not sure yet what I'd like to do. Either sell or keep and run as a mini-hotel and I'd still be able to live here." He waved randomly. "Medical care does *not* come cheap, I'll tell ya that." He paused and vaguely pointed to the heavens. "We're lucky it's morning, Jerry; most of these rooms have no working lights. At night it's black. I live in one room at the top. The smallest room."

With that Mr Alfred waved to the narrow staircase. Jay Jay was impressed that an old man like him was still able climb the stairs, though he wouldn't be for long. Once he'd smartened up these bedrooms on the second story, Mr Alfred might even move downstairs to be in more comfortable surroundings. "Well, for years, since all my businesses started to go kaputski, this house is all I have. I rented out some parts as offices and that didn't work out. It's only recently I secured some funds to start the works. Never too late, right?"

Didn't seem right to Jay Jay for him to live the remaining few years of his life in that grand home in a dirt- and clutter-crammed attic room with a sink and a toilet, like a prisoner. He deserved way more.

"No, Sir."

"I know what you're thinking but I can still do this because I did it every day. I've crawled these stairs before I could walk and I have kept my health going. That is what poor people in Greece, China, Russia, and all those places, do. Every day they are up and down mountains and hills. If you sit around all day, you're gonna turn old. I am not old. It's this house that's old. I'm not hiring you to care for me." Jay Jay nodded, although he disagreed as the man appeared vulnerable. He kept *that* to himself. One fall was all it'd take. Did Mr Alfred just say he wasn't old? Did he mean he was not ill? Because illness was a sudden unexpected hit. At any age. He'd seen it. Papa Moriarty. One minute he was eating a wafflewich. Next minute, bang. On the floor. Cardiac failure and he didn't know it. He thought it was bad indigestion. The pain was not in his heart. It was way deep in his guts. And that's the body for you. The mind had nothing to do with it.

"And know what? I'm kind of tired of living like this."

Jay Jay could immediately see what he meant by "like this". A hobo, prisoner, in a near-derelict cage infested with roaches, mice, poison ivy and other pests. They wouldn't go so he might as well

be friends with them until now. It was time to call in help.
"Someone like you."

Jay Jay was quite inexperienced. But he was qualified, trust-
worthy and hardworking. Young, too. For sure, Mr Alfred's was a
big family and Jay Jay might get to meet them if he got the job, if
they came round. If, if, if. He was daydreaming about being in
charge of this entire property five days a week.

They went out to the rear terrace through grand, arched
French doors.

JAY JAY WAS BORN in the spring of '49 in New York City. His
grandfather spoiled him, a little too much, hence the '69 Camaro.
An only child, his early childhood started off great. He remembered shiny new toys every Christmas and birthday. A glossy black
bicycle one year. Trains with lights another year. Kung Fu Club
with other Chinese kids on Saturday afternoons. Far as he knew
his father could still be alive, though he had no idea where. A
stockbroker at the NYSE, his father was doing well before some
business deal went wrong. A gang went after him and he had to
"leave New York in a New York minute". Jay Jay and his mother
went to live with her father in Beecher on a pond farm less than an
hour's drive away from Chicago. He always remembered that
every time something went wrong, his grandfather would put his
fingers on his temples, shaking his head and saying, "don't do
business, it'll do you".

The hard life made his mother very sick and she passed away
when Jay Jay was 10. She was a city girl, unsuited to farm life,
broken by it. She'd had to give up the things she loved: shoes,
handbags, a teaching position in a college and even a favorite hair-
dresser in Queens all because she feared that the gangs would be
back for them too. It seemed dangerous for them to stay on in
New York.

After she passed away, Siracuse was added to Jay Jay's full

name. At that point, Jay Jay thought it sounded rather grand and he decided he didn't want to be a farmer.

Grandpops Siracuse convinced him to go to the city. He was welcome to come back anytime he'd like to. Being a seventeen-year-old semi-educated farm boy, Jay Jay decided to train in engineering drafting while doing odd jobs the instant he arrived in Chicago in '66. That was how he got hired at the steel plant. Dallas would be so proud of him, now. She'd tell all the girls at work. The customers too.

"Now, I will leave you to think things through," said Mr Alfred. "We can talk before you leave."

Jay Jay wondered where he should start when he remembered he had to get back to the house to retrieve his briefcase with the notebook in it. When he turned around, the old man had vanished. He was alone. Jay Jay left the cabin and forced the door shut. He wandered back to the arched French windows but it was now shut. It was the kind that wasn't openable from the outside. It had no knob to turn, just a keyhole. Mr Alfred must have forgotten and shut it automatically. He walked the narrow passage along the side of the house. Mr Alfred was talking to someone, and it was only his voice, so he must've been on the telephone.

"I know what I'm doing. And you know damn well I do. Stay out of it. No. You stay out of it."

Mr Alfred slammed the receiver down with a loud thunk, and a dinging ghost of the sound echoed long after. Who was he talking to? Jay Jay shrugged. It did not bother him. Nothing much did, not after seeing Grandpops' new wife, Carmelita, and her son, Ernesto. Going by his instincts, he felt a little concerned for Mr Alfred, who so far seemed like a great guy. *Shuddup, sharpen up and shoot straight*, was what Bud said before the factory shut.

Dallas was older only by a year but she was wiser by about 30. His instincts had told him she was way smarter. Women always were. They told you that. And if you disagreed, you were wrong. So it must be true. Now, Nesto went against his ex-girlfriend Sofia's wishes and became a cop. And that was a bad move. Look what happened to *him*.

He got back to the front door and pressed the enormous bell again. He waited. "I forgot my notebook," he said to Mr Alfred, who had reddened, probably from the conversation. "I'm gonna need to write things down."

"You do that." He stepped aside and handed Jay Jay two massive brass keys.

"One for your workshop and one for the house. I know you will look after them."

"I will, Sir."

"You can come and go as you wish."

"Yessir. Thank you." Jay Jay leaped to the hallway table where his briefcase stood like a wet tombstone. He picked it up and went back via the path again rather than through the house. Since the nurse was coming to see Mr Alfred, he didn't want to be in the way. When he got to the cabin at the end of the garden, for the first time, he felt excited about opening the briefcase to retrieve the notebook. He slid out the new 2B pencil which Dallas had fitted neatly in the briefcase's leather pen slot. He held it in his right hand and tapped the eraser end on his chin. Before long, he'd filled the first two white pages with a table of categories and a list of items he had to purchase for electrics, carpentry, plumbing and cleaning. Then, quietly he left. When he reached his car door, he realized he had forgotten to answer Mr Alfred's question as to when he was starting.

CHAPTER 3

As soon as he got home to his red brick apartment block on North Kenmore Avenue, he took out the notebook and re-read what he wrote. He knew the tool stores where he'd need to stock up. Hadn't he spent more than enough times looking at the store displays, spending money he knew he'd never have? He checked the white plastic clock over the yellow tiles in his cramped kitchen. Only 12 noon and 6 hours to go before Dallas got home. When he peered into the fridge for something to eat, the tele-phone rang and he jumped.

"How'd it go, big boy?"

"Doll, I made it."

"Ya made it?"

"I made it."

An audible but tiny scream. She was at work on her lunch. She sounded strangled. "Yer. A. Genius."

"No, you are. I'm doing this for us. For the baby." Uh-oh, he said the B-word and now she'd be blown off site.

"If it's a girl, I'm gonna call her Jennifer," her mind was scat-tered. "If it's a boy, John."

"Okay," he agreed, unable to contribute a thing.

"When do you start?" She said, suddenly back on track, somehow.

"Unfortunately, he was on a call and I left too quickly to find out."

"Oh no, sweetie. Maybe you can 'phone him."

"I don't have his number."

"I do."

"Oh you are an angel. You know everything."

"I'm a woman."

He laughed. She never got mad at him — not until she was real mad. Her heart was made of gold, which he kept shiny and polished.

"The cutlery drawer, honey? There's a piece of paper where I wrote down Mr Albert's address and phone number when I was in the Professor's office. Ya got that?"

"Yeah."

"I gotta go. Love you. Mwah."

What a lucky man Jerome Lee was, had become. He made a sandwich and grabbed a beer. He lay down on the faded couch with the flowery print. The musty odor of the mansion still filled his nostrils. Was that ominous? He felt "knocked out", foggy, drugged. Something was not right and he could not put his finger on it. He'd replace the couch as soon as he had money. Saggy and broken, the couch had springs that made sure you never slept more than 45 minutes straight. When he woke up from his snooze, he picked up the hand-set twice before calling Mr Alfred.

"Sir? You were busy with your appointment and I had no chance to leave you my number. I have a list of items I need to purchase and the cost is too much for me to bear upfront."

"No problem, Jerry. I appreciate your honesty. You can come back tomorrow. I'll advance you the money."

Jay Jay hung up. Through the lounge window, he noticed someone walking on the far side of the street. Uh oh. Was that who he thought it was walking towards his apartment? Nesto. What was he doing here?

"Hey, ssup." Ernesto waved and called out. Seconds later, the doorbell rang.

"What do you want?" Said Jay Jay into the buzzer.

"Hey! No need to be all coy. Is how you talk to family?"

"Ernesto. I ain't gonna ask you to come in."

"Just found out you might have a new job. Now I need a job too."

Jay Jay sighed and buzzed him in. He eyed the rotund ex-cop, in a T-shirt that was way too small with pockets and buckles, making it look like a restraining jacket. Nesto got Jay Jay into trouble once. He was a smooth operator. Even the Police Department had no idea he had a team running a "protection racket" planting evidence and making up false charges against South Side residents while dealing their own drugs and supplying the bangs to gang bangers. Did he do a day's work? Pah! He was in no fit state. He still thought of himself as important. He was carrying a gun.

"I thoughtchu moved to LA," said Jay Jay. After jail-time, he didn't add.

"Ya thought wrong. After 2 years being a 'private resident' at Cook, y'know, now I decided, I'm gonna stay. The Hills ain't for me. Headed back to Beecher, and I ran into your Grandpops."

"You went to see him?"

"Not *that* weird. My mom married him last year, dja forget? I called on him yesterday. He said chances are you'd be in. Dallas can make things happen." Ernesto wriggled his fingers like a magician before the bunny was pulled out of a top hat.

"I don't wantchu here, Nesto."

"Hey! What's up widya? Man! I can't believe we're related."

Jay Jay shut the door, resisting the urge to slam it. Unbelievable that they were related, he had to agree. He craved a whiskey. But they'd been out of it since he lost his job. He folded his hands together and rested his elbows on his knees. He thought about his grandfather's sudden wedding to Carmelita the year before. He preferred not to, in general. A few heys and cuss words blasted the air, but when he went to the kitchen window to check, Ernesto had left.

———

"HONEY, I kinda like the look of this light blue dress. Whaddya think?"

"You look like a movie star."

"Aww. But do you think light or dark blue?" She held two dresses by their hangers and lifted each as she announced the color, as if Jay Jay wasn't able to tell which was which. Her eyes were bright with curiosity and expectation as to what his verdict would be for their celebration meal out.

"I think light," he said after a long while. Only two days ago, she had made sure that he understood her explanation that dresses with high empire waistlines were necessary to conceal the baby bump. He was unlikely to forget that detail.

"OK. I'm getting ready now. Honey, please hand me the pearl necklace? The one on a gold chain."

While she was getting changed, he opened her vanity drawer to find the chain. Underneath all these bottles and jars of cosmetics was his gun. Seeing Nesto that day had reminded him that a tiny breeze was blowing trouble his way. He left the gun, he picked out her necklace — real gold, freshwater pearls — which he bought her last birthday. He shut the drawer. Jay Jay picked a seafood tacos place in South Ashland Avenue on West Side that was the kinda 'fancy' his wallet would stretch to. They also had margaritas which she'd enjoy. Her favorite food was Mexican, anyhow.

"Baby, I wanna thank you for getting me that job-"

"Chickens? Hatch?"

"Naw, I'm 89% sure I start tomorrow."

"What about the 11%?"

"11% of not starting tomorrow."

She smiled. "You ain't got a contract. What if tomorrow he says Ciao?"

"He's not Eyetalyun. Anyway, if he says that, I'll go look for someth'n' else."

"Cheers," she stuck her tongue out and licked the salt off her margarita glass. She glowed with innocence and health, all lashes and lips.

"Cheers."

———

THE NEXT DAY, he calmed down when his eyes floated up. *Catherine*, the name was gold painted on the glass over the paneled double-door entrance. What was it called? Something that sounded criminal. Transom. That was it. He had not noticed that name sign yesterday. You could hardly see it, he thought. Who was Catherine? Most of the gold paint job had disappeared, like those word puzzles where you had to fill in the missing letters. A touch-up job was all that was required. He mentally made note of 'gold paint' as an item to add to the list. He pushed the wooden door-bell. Déjà vu. Mr Alfred descended the stairs after a long time.

"I gave you the keys, son."

"Sir, I am sorry, I did not want to intrude."

"Intrude away. You're starting today. Now. Come into my office and we will sort out the accounts."

Jay Jay went into the library with the banker's desk and its green leatherette covered top. Mr Alfred opened a drawer and took out $250 cash and a $250 store card, a lot more than he ever had in his hand. Dallas had wiped the briefcase down and checked its condition was still brand new for the store refund. No point keeping expensive items which would never be used again.

"If ya need another for a new job, I'd just buy again, honey. No sense havin' someth'n' to keep only to look pretty."

"Naw, sweetheart, I got you for that, don't I."

Mr Alfred wrote something down in a ledger and said to keep the change. "I have a bookkeeper, don't worry about anything. We can do running accounts." Jay Jay pictured the two of them running, a ledger in their hands. With the list in his work pants pocket, Jay Jay went to the stores for reels of cabling, tubes of plumbing pipes, electrical and manual tools. Everything was shiny and clean. To be trusted with so much money and to buy the right stuff was a new, enormous feeling. He remembered what Dallas had said, to be trusted was greater than to be loved.

But she also said luck was just a feeling. If you felt lucky, then you were. If you felt fat, then you were, so you might as well feel skinny.

He parked his Camaro, no more than fifty yards away. Mr Alfred would not even be looking out from his study or his bedroom. For a start those faced the back of the house and besides, no rooms to the front were even occupied. Jay Jay was allowed to use the telephone and he called a company that Dallas used at work for doing commercial cleaning. They also stretched to larger domestic properties. They might well take on cleaning *Catherine*, which was huge as a hotel. Jay Jay's plan was that he worked on the workshop in the garden while the cleaners started with the rest of the house. Once he'd finished setting up his work-shop, they would switch over, after weeks or months. He was here for as long as Mr Alfred wanted him. He was a keeper, in both senses of the word. Mr Alfred left him alone. Jay Jay wanted to impress him with the level of activity and organization. Maybe one day he'd be as organized as Dallas.

———

HE WAS ON ALL FOURS. His heart thumped as he peered down the crack, turning his head left, right, left, right, to give each eye a chance to look. Seven foot down, his flashlight was still on.

The air was cold as winter, thick. Outside of the flashlight's cone of light, it was so dark he could not see his own fingers.

White bones. *Bones.* Should he even mention anything to Mr Alfred? Or Dallas? But then came the doubts. No, wait. Maybe Mr Alfred already knew about the bones. Could be animal bones, even. He flicked the thoughts away like they were cobwebs.

Jay Jay stood and dusted himself off. He went to his pile of new purchases and searched for a crowbar or a claw hammer to break the padlock. He moved the extendable ladder near the trap door. He decided to crowbar the loose and damp paneled doors through their many gaps. The wood came apart in loud pops like firecrackers. The splintered shards of wood shot out. He leaned over and looked into the deep, dark hole. He extended the ladder until it reached the ground. He descended slowly and picked up the torch. All the time his attention was drawn back up at the hole. He did not want to be trapped in here though... no reason for him to be. Just something he learned from the movies. He shuddered as he studied the bones.

No. Not one skeleton. A dog's too. He'd seen these on the farm, reminding him that he wanted to telephone Grandpops to inform him he'd started a new job, but

a) not until he was home tonight and

b) that might not be such an awesome idea now.

Who started a job looking at bones unless you were in a morgue or cemetery? He shone the flashlight at the rest of the room, which was about 10' by 10'. His breathing was shallow and the air was cold, pungent with thick mushroom odors. Jay Jay was shivering while the warm April sun was beating down outside.

What was that? He strained to hear. A faint voice, getting nearer. *Oh no.* Mr Alfred was calling him. For a few minutes he had forgotten where he was. His mind spun. He had to get out of here quick. He mounted the ladder, the flashlight between his teeth to light his steps. Now the gaping hole was exposed as he had removed the vinyl.

"Jerry," the voice was audible now. "Would you please come in here for a minute and give me a hand?"

"Yessir! I'm coming, Sir." The wealthy said "would" and not "could", Jay Jay suddenly thought as he jogged.

"Good, cause I am waiting. Where are you, Jerry?"

"I'm here." Jay Jay appeared at the French window on the terrace, panting. "How can I help you?"

"A few things I need moving. The cleaners have started on the front, so thank you."

"My pleasure, Sir. They'll do a great job."

"That's good, then. Come with me." Mr Alfred took him into the kitchen. "Well, first, would you like some coffee?"

"That would be swell, Sir."

"Milk?"

When Jay Jay saw the milk, he thought of calcium and the creamy white bones again, making him nauseous. "Yes, Sir. Thank you."

Cool, he thought, Mr Alfred was not coming into the cabin. He'd return to hide the hole later. He didn't want Mr Alfred to know that he had gone into the basement. He wasn't sure why but he had a strong hunch that he should not mention his discovery.

"So how's today going?" Said Mr Alfred.

CHAPTER 4

"Yeah, so I got no thanks. This customer came in. He wanted perfume for his wife, tried on everything. I swear, 40 minutes went by."

"Doll—."

"Hang on, wouldja let me finish? He tried on at least 8 lipstick shades on his hand. Now I can see another customer was waiting, you can tell I have a seventh sense for customers. The moment they walk through the door-"

"Sweetheart?"

"Honey? When you say things I nod and uh-huh until you're done."

Jay Jay smiled and bit his tongue.

"Three customers came and went. Now I am losing commission with each of these. But I forgot what I was gonna say. What are we having for dinner?"

She opened the fridge. "I have some lasagne from two days ago, we can heat that up. Was gonna do that last night but we went for fish tacos instead. So worth the trip. Don't you just love seafood? Really spells out special occasion for me. That and margaritas. Lord, it was perfect, was it not?"

"It was."

"Whyuntcha say it like you mean it."

Jay Jay didn't love seafood. He grew up on a pond farm and that had something to do with his indifference. But he kept that to himself.

"I mean it, honey."

Dallas leaned over and kissed him. "Jay Jay," and she looked all serious. She paused. "I have seen *the* dress."

Since he proposed two months ago, she had been looking for the perfect wedding gown. After that he lost his job. Wasn't great timing, but much in life wasn't. He did not feel he was ready. He just felt he had to be. Tying the knot was called that for a reason. The Professor who taught her at the Art Institute did her a favor and had got Jay Jay a "class act" job. She was an enabler, a street-smart broad. To Dallas there was no such thing as "can't". Both her mom and her absent dad had grown up during the Depression and had been artists. A tremendous force and energy took over their minds, no matter what. A vague clutching at the ideal. Dallas rebelled, without rebelling and without a cause. She worked in a store so that she could still be an art student and in the future an artist. Her mother approved. Success was a matter of time and dedication, not talent, according to her mother. Dallas was okay with that. She put the lasagne out on the worktop and switched the oven on.

"I hate this. I wanna move. We need a new apartment. The landlord ain't fixing anything."

"That's cause he's got all these apartments to fix and he will get to our turn soon."

"Yeah, and? I still hate it. I can't wait." Jay Jay didn't want to hear the W-word. And the "I can't wait. I can't wait. Oh I am so excited." He didn't bring up that he was a little anxious about the job, nervous, after what he'd found that day. What if it was the previous caretaker? And his dog. He changed the moving images in his mind from dress, to death, to drink.

"We're outta beers. This is the last one." He showed Dallas like she'd never seen a beer.

"Yeah, it's Friday," she replied, putting the lasagne dish into the oven. "You can do the groceries tomorrow while I am at work." She shut the oven door and looked at him.

"You can have it. I don't want any. We had a big treat last night. Probably too many margaritas for my waistline."

Jay Jay slumped on the couch after dinner with his empty bottle. He stared at the telephone, absent-mindedly picking at the label on the bottle. He put it down and whipped the telephone receiver off like it was the lid of a trash can. He jabbed his finger into the finger holes, dialed each digit with deliberate slowness and waited for the tone. "Grandpops?"

"Ya don't sound too good. Whatsamatter? Last time I heard ya got an inner-view. Dja get it?"

"Yeah." He was troubled by the dank, deathly odor still in his nostrils, the job, the bones. All of it. He went cold just thinking about his recent 'good luck'.

"You're gonna tell your news or what?"

"Well, yeah. But today was only my first day, GP. I go back Monday."

"And? Nesto said-"

"No! GP, I want him to stay out of my life."

"That's not fair now. He was a cop."

"A bad cop. Remember, GP? Or you forgot? Cause you were in on it?"

"Jay Jay, sonny, you listena me. I'm not ringing you to hear this bullshit again. Let's talk about you. Not him."

"I don't want you to tell him anything. Yeah. So I got the job. Who knows how long it'll last."

"You'll be fine. It came from the Professor."

"No. From Dallas."

"Whatever. Nesto needs your help now. Once he did help you or have you forgotten that too? You almost became a manager at the factory."

"Bullsh—."

"Jay Jay. Hey."

"They were scared of him. It was one of his victims. Of course he was gonna make me manager."

"Jerome Lee, please. Please stop that now? You come back soon. Some weekend when you're not working, I am gonna need you up in Beecher."

"Listen," sighed Jay Jay. "I gotta go, Grandpops. I was just calling to say I am okay and I started work and I am earning good money and I am a stayer."

"You are. Good for you, sonny Jay. Your daddy would be so proud of what you're doing. Always said you were the hard worker in the family."

"Yup. Bye."

"Bye."

He didn't like the tone of his grandfather's voice now because Nesto had been there poisoning him against Jay Jay. He wished they'd kept Nesto in the slammer for a bit longer. He only got 2 years. It was a mystery to Jay Jay why. Maybe he had been an okay cop the rest of the time, when he wasn't doing his shakedowns.

"What was that about?" Said Dallas.

"Nothing," he replied. Dallas didn't have to find out Nesto had been coming to quake up his apple tree and he wasn't falling for that again. Nossir.

"Thinking of driving up to Beecher tomorrow."

"Why? Your Grandpops asked for you?"

"He did, sweetheart. I figured I'd give him a hand before this job got too busy."

Already his first day had been tiring. But a satisfying tiring, as was any physical labor. He just didn't fancy the cemetery bit. What Dallas's reaction would be, he'd rather not see. "Jay no quit", he'd said, when he was only 3. Anyway, she would not let him. Nothing *bad* bad had happened, so why would he quit? He bit the loose rough skin on this thumbnail, tearing it. He sucked the blood away and soothed the pain he inflicted on himself.

Dallas switched on the television and got one of those art-y magazines out of her bag. Probably picked it up on her way home. *Art in America.* Some bright jungle painting on the front. Like there were tropical rainforests all over the States. He watched her reading the journal intently like it was a manual, or something. He glanced at the articles over her shoulder. "Rothko's Black Paintings". "New York: the Visual Riches and Recessionary Blues". The large-font titles meant nothing to him. He didn't dare mention painting a wall black, and then having to add, "joke".

Work should not feel like working, she'd always said. She *was* a hard worker even when — or especially when — she was relaxed. She gave up both studying art and modeling to work full-time at the store. The guilt always scratched at him like a rough wall you accidentally brushed past. After he lost his job, he found nothing for six months. Two months ago, they'd discovered she was pregnant but she was still unable to tell her employers yet. They both had to hang on to their jobs. He didn't want to lose her. Could there be a more terrifying thought? Why didn't nobody teach you that in school? What's the point of being the class math maven if you fail at keeping a beautiful woman you loved? Made no sense. If he took care of Mr Alfred's estate, Mr Alfred would take care of his.

"I don't feel too good, honey," said Dallas suddenly as she looked up from her magazine. "I don't want to watch anything on TV."

"Why? Whatsamatter?"

"I... I just need to... get out of these clothes and go to bed early." She pointed at her tight, Estée Lauder nautical-style uniform. Its buttons, epaulettes and wide-legged pants could have been worn by any uniformed female from receptionist to airline stewardess via registered nurse.

He hadn't noticed until then that she was in her maternity work clothes, while heating up the lasagne and making herself a Negroni.

"I suddenly feel... I don't know what it is... a strong smell, a gloomy awful feeling... is it just me?" She sniffed at herself, turning from shoulder to shoulder.

Oh no. He thought, surely it wasn't contagious, whatever "it" was? He did stink like a grave, so how would he know?

"See anythin' different?" she said, changing the subject.

He stared.

She gave him her huge smile and showed her white straight teeth. He'd only say the wrong thing. To give him clues, she patted the back of her blonde head and then turned to show him. Facing him again, she grinned and stuck her chin out, pleased as a child with a candy bar. Oh. He saw. A new haircut, gradually increased in length in a seamless curve to the back, shiny as a helmet. Her bangs had been cut blunt and long, nearly reaching her huge lashes. He hugged and kissed his little sailor.

"Would you be a sweetheart and do the dishes?" she said.

"Of course," he replied. "You go and lie your pretty head down."

Jay Jay thought about going to his grandfather the next day while Dallas was at work. He'd spend the whole day giving a hand on the farm. He would go first thing and he'd be back in the evening. Dallas would not miss him at all. On his way home, he'd bring something tasty for dinner and some cold beers. Plans made, he turned off the TV and the lamp to get an early night himself.

———

SATURDAY MORNING, they were both up early. "I'm going to the stores to pick up some food. I will be back very soon, honey bunch." He pulled on his leather jacket. In the car, he sang along. The radio was playing The Doors' *Love Her Madly*. So apt that he sang along. Before he got back to the apartment, he had a smoke outside. He took in the street scene. A removals truck moving a piano. Children on bikes. Old people sitting on their front steps.

He liked the Lincoln Park area, particularly this Sheffield corner, and would be sad to leave. He took in short puffs and stared at the brown paper bag of groceries. After picking them up, he climbed the stairs.

"Hi, honey!" Jay Jay said, as he came through the door. "I'm gonna make us something to eat now."

"Wow, whatchu got?"

"Tomatoes, eggs, bread, whatever you want. As long as it's a bacon omelet?"

"Right."

She smiled. She wasn't gonna disagree. She was no dumb broad. No chance of discussing the basement discovery which he nicknamed Bones 1 and 2, or even his present reluctance in working at Mr Alfred's. His heart sagged like a sack of potatoes but he kept his head straight and steady while he smiled back at her.

He decided to drive up to Beecher once he had dropped Dallas off at the store. He hoped her manager wasn't gonna be too hard on her as she *was* a little late.

———

ON THE BRIGHT SATURDAY, and "still fish harvest o'clock", as Grandpops used to say, he arrived at the familiar white clapboard farmhouse in Meadow Lane. Set in 20 acres of water and ponds the place was a "high-value asset" in land-locked Illinois. Top quality soil and ground water made Grandpops plenty of money. He'd been raising fingerling fish and adult fish for pond stocking for years and had no intention of retiring.

The dogs Terry and Suzanne ran out and jumped on Jay Jay.

"Down! C'mon guys. Down!" Said Grandpops. He was looking as thin and tired as his ripped cable knit sweater, and he had more gray hair. He was not as old as Mr Alfred. His grandfather was 66 and in need of retiring, whatever he said.

"Jay Jay you know I needed you to—."

"That's why I am here, Grandpops."

"You see, Luis is down with chicken pox, can you believe it? Damn! The timing is just the pits. I got nobody else working. I had to let Cruz go."

Jay Jay waved to say, "don't matter".

"Whatta we gotta do?"

"Seining. Moving catfish. You drive the tractor, I'll pull the net in. Gonna take about 2 to 3 hours and then we're gonna have a beer. I just have a big order I gotta take care of. I gotta do this. Without your help we wouldn't be able to do this by Monday."

Jay Jay had done some seining since he was a boy. The process of transporting the fish from ponds to the holding shed and then to the stock ponds was as familiar to him as his own hands.

"How's things, Grandpops?"

"They'd better be better, sonny." He liked his word play.

"What'samatter?"

"Vietnam. Competition. Lower demand." He sighed. "I don't want to go into it. Or sell up. You know?"

Jay Jay nodded but he didn't really. He left this place after all as he couldn't stand the agricultural life. He couldn't understand what the fuss was. Where were the fancy drinks, records to play or movie nights?

"D'you wanna a sandwich? Sum'n to be getting on with?"

"Naw. I'm good. Let's do it." At "do it", the dogs started jumping again. To them the phrase meant "play time!" Kinda was for them. He patted them with both hands.

Jay Jay, his grandfather and the dogs walked to the tractor park.

Jay Jay climbed in the tractor seat. He remembered how to start the John Deere. He'd been driving one since he was 14. He turned the key over and dropped the throttle slightly to warm up the engine. He saw from the corner of his eye someone with a crooked beehive coming out of the white ranch house.

Grandpops' "new" wife and Ernesto's mom, Carmelita, was

54, young enough to make Grandpops look good. There was nothing exceptional about her except her huevos rancheros eggs, John Wayne swagger and her Romeo y Julieta cigars from Havana. She called out in her mild accent, waving, "Hey Jiay Jiay! *Sì, tu! Como—.*"

He ignored her and continued to push the stick shift into first with the handbrake down. His grandfather had gone to rig up the seining nets with the dogs. Once he'd seen her tripping over stairs, somersaulting and landing flat on her back with the pink platform wedges dropping down on her like two bricks.

Carmelita de la Rua was probably angling for his grandfather to sell the farm because she was too busy spending money. He wouldn't put it past her. He thought of his own parents and the one tiny little luxury they could afford back in New York City. A gold-tipped fountain pen that was his dad's. Jay Jay still had that somewhere in his drawer. His mother's jade earrings from Macy's. His parents enjoyed experiences more than "things", unlike Carmelita. They took him to art galleries and children's theater. His father, if he was still alive, would be so heartbroken, as Jay Jay was, to see her and Grandpops. She was not keen when Jay Jay visited, though she obliged with a generous show of hypocrisy, now. She'd turned up from nowhere 3 years ago. Okay, not nowhere. Somewhere.

The dogs jumped into the pond. They were trained to guide the edges of the net with Grandpops.

He lifted foot off the clutch and drove steadily, trying not to think about Bones 1 and 2 even though they kept popping up every few hours without warning or triggers. It was shit. Unseeing them would be nice.

He hadn't mentioned anything to Dallas and certainly not Grandpops who was under pressure and too busy to talk non-fish. The sight of Carmelita just brought back the unpleasant memory.

The seine net was dropped around the edge of the pond and once 15 foot in diameter, then you'd haul the fish in.

If Jay Jay told his Grandpops anything, he'd tell Carmelita

who would then tell Nesto. Place was overrun with double douche baggage. Ernesto was now "dropping in" on Jay Jay. She had filled him in, easy. Now Nesto would know everything.

Almost everything.

CHAPTER 5

He'd been working for a month. On Monday, May 17th, Jay Jay went to the store for some timber before he got to Mr Alfred's. He left before Dallas was up. While the weather was holding up he wanted to fix the windows and doors. This would take a while. Some amount of adjustment of the window cord and weights and the hinging on the doors after cutting out the rotted wood was required. In some he had to replace the glass too. He went straight to the cabin to place the wood for sawing up later on.

What had been an exciting and private work-hideout and hangout now gave him the creeps. He put the radio on to drown out the noise in his head. If he wanted to keep his job, he'd better not bring up the dead to anybody, not Mr Alfred, Dallas, not Grandpops and least of all, Nesto. The problem with Grandpops was Carmelita. She was a terror as was the night his dad was shot by the gangs in '59. Jay Jay was only 10. He would never forget the look in his father's eyes. The radio had been playing Elvis Presley's *Now and Then (There's a Fool Such as I)* when the cops came with the news. Every time that song came on since, he froze, thinking of that day.

After checking that the sink tap was working, he made himself a cup of coffee.

Back in the house, he cut out with his knife where the bay windows had been painted shut.

His priority was the first floor front bay windows, then the rear. He placed the two ladders in the right positions before climbing them. Taking out the window sashes from their grooves made a noise like an enormous firecracker. The rotted wood had expanded and split. Even the sliding made gigantic crunches like a guillotine. The plaster was damp and weak in many places and came away like a moist cake. He hoped Mr Alfred was upstairs in his room as this was a disruptive task. Although he had lain tough drop sheets on the floors and he was wearing eye protection purchased that morning, he saw splinters fly off like shrapnel.

He downed tools after taking out a full set of 6 panels. He needed to fully fix another set from the other bay window, so 12 in total. But due to a lack of space in the cabin, he could only do 6 at a time. As he came down the ladders, voices became audible. Harsh tones. One of them was Mr Alfred's. He crept to the hallway outside the library. The door was slightly ajar and he glanced in without getting too near in case he was seen.

The back of a young blond man appeared. Jay Jay guessed he was young because of the hair, posture and build.

"I don't want you coming round here again," said Mr Alfred.

"You can't say that to me. I wrote to you. I called you."

"Well, you can stop calling and writing."

"Things are getting very hard now, Uncle Alfred. My father has—."

"Your father knows nothing."

"My father needs to complete these projects. This is a family project, Uncle Alfred."

He was probably around Jay Jay's age, judging by his voice, though of course he wasn't sure. Jay Jay noticed that the man was well-dressed. He was in a white polo knit sweater with zigzags like maybe a Ralph Lauren or something. The kind that would always stay white because they never did anything dirty. Dallas sold clothes like these in the store.

"Those buildings were using up wasteland in the—."

"I didn't agree with the plans in the first place." Mr Alfred started shuffling around the man to avoid him, who turned around to follow him in the room. Jay Jay was astonished that the man was not that young, looking like he was in his thirties or forties. He was tanned, with nice hands and his face was healthy-looking like a rich guy's oughta be.

He clamped his jaw and frowned. "We were making use of steel plants which have shut down. Seemed a good idea."

"Bad idea," snapped Mr Albert. "When the South Side steel plants shut down, so did banks and gas stations that relied on the business of the people who worked at the plants. Who will buy these apartments your father is building?"

"Landlords," the man put his hands down on the green leather covered desk. "The University is new. Students need accommodation. But he needs your help. Funds are seriously low now and we cannot complete."

"I must ask you to leave now," said Mr Alfred, not looking at him. He sat down in his chair at the desk.

Mr Alfred sighed. He took a second, pulled his drawer open and got a check book out. A quick zip, the satisfying tear of a perforated sheet. He scribbled something, signed with a flourish and half-threw, half-slid the check at the man, where it sailed towards the floor like a feather from a dying bird which the man caught.

"For your engagement party," he said.

The man put the check into his pants pocket.

"Why, thank you, and here is your invitation card, Uncle Alfred," the man said, withdrawing a small white envelope from the same pocket. He slid it across the desk but Mr Alfred didn't even look at it or say anything.

The man removed from his brown document wallet a sheaf of paper which he pushed across Mr Alfred's desk. "Would you please sign?"

That word again, thought Jay Jay, "would".

"I will not." Mr Alfred's hard blue eyes kept staring back at the man.

"The wedding is next year."

"Congratulations," muttered Mr Alfred sarcastically, sounding more like constrangulations.

"And year after that, your big Eight-Oh."

Mr Alfred glared at him.

"We will celebrate with you at your 80th birthday, Uncle?"

"I'm not doing anything."

"We must. It's family."

Mr Alfred sighed and grimaced at the same time. "You got your check. Now go," he said.

"Goodbye, Uncle. It was nice to see you too."

Jay Jay slithered back into the front bay window area to move the 6 panels. The front door slammed. From the window he saw Mr Alfred's nephew leave. He descended the stone steps, brushed his hair back roughly with his hand and strode down the broken tiled path.

Mr Alfred's nephew looked back at the house and spotted Jay Jay framed by a hole where the window had been. "And fix the fuckin' doorbell, will ya?" He said.

Jay Jay did not like the man's tone. He immediately clenched his gloved fists over the panels he was carrying. He was so surprised he could not reply. And even if he would have, the man would not have liked the language that Jay Jay woulda used.

After working on sawing and filling gaps in the timber frames in the cabin, Jay Jay reached out for his lunch box. He hummed to the chorus of *Bridge Over Troubled Water* playing on the radio. He had worked damned hard and achieved his aim of fixing all 6 panels before moving on. He heard the front door slam. That was the second time today. Mr Alfred must have gone out. After his sandwich, Jay Jay needed milk for his coffee so he went through the back French windows to the kitchen where the refrigerator was. Mr Alfred was out. There was no sound. "Mr Alfred?" He called. No reply.

He tiptoed into the library. It was a terrible mess. Mr Alfred had torn up that document, whatever it was, and left it all over the floor. Should he clear it up? It was a difficult choice since the doorbell control panel was in this room. But if he did not clear it, then Mr Alfred would wonder why he'd come in to fix the doorbell and yet not swept the pile up.

He made his coffee. He found a dustpan and broom and went to clear up the mess.

The typewritten words were now in fragments.

After the day was over, he went to say goodbye and that he'd finished fitting the sashes and the place was all good, secure. Well, to be straight, he wanted to check if Mr Alfred was OK. Mr Alfred was not in his study so Jay Jay called out on the grand staircase. "Mr Alfred? Mr Alfred? See ya tomorrow?"

"Oh. Wait there."

"I'm good, I'll be here," he called back up the staircase. There was shuffling, after a minute Mr Alfred appeared at the top of the staircase.

"Good. Thank you for waiting. A very good friend and business associate of mine needs your help."

"Oh? I'd be glad to help, Sir."

"Mr Chan, who owns the Jade Palace Garden."

Jay Jay nodded and said, "Yes?"

"Well, somebody's blown a fuse or something. Now the air conditioning is not working. Be a good man and do whatever it takes to fix it."

"Sure, I'll take care of it." Jay Jay said.

"And don't worry, they'll pay. Parts, time, whatever. You know where it is?"

"No, Sir." Jay Jay figured it was time to own up that he didn't know where Jade Palace Garden was after all, despite nodding earlier.

"Write this down. *W. 23rd and S. Wentworth Ave.* Now. That job is urgent. Don't come here tomorrow. You go straight there. "

CHAPTER 6

"Can I help at all? What are you looking for exactly, Sir?"

"Well, something for my wife."

"She's a lucky lady."

"Oh yeah." His eyes darted over the glass counter. "She is," he said absent-mindedly, distracted and unaware of what he was looking at.

"Lipsticks for her? Maybe a perfume? Is it her birthday?"

"It's her birthday. Now how did you know?"

The man was tall, maybe around 40 or 50, in a modern gray suit and he wore big gold square wire-framed glasses. He was attractive in an old-fashioned Hollywood way. He was tanned and there was something refined about him despite the cheap suit. Dallas wondered what his wife looked like. The man was looking at her and not the counter.

"I guessed." She looked at him back. "Let me show you our new spring-summer colors." She slid open the glass drawer and got the lipstick samples out, all in a variety of exotic pretty names. Orchid, hibiscus, peony.

"So you like the pink? The Rose d'Or."

He didn't reply. She tried again. "What color is your wife's hair? And eyes?"

"Ohh, err, she's... she's ginger and she... is brown-eyed."

"She sounds priddy."

He looked at her without replying. Did he or did he not agree his wife was pretty? She scratched the back of her earring and started to look serious when she thought about his reaction. In retail you must keep your hands off any part of your head, stop thinking immediately and smile a big smile instead.

"What about your feller?" He asked brightly.

"Well, thanks to me, he's recently got a great job." Dallas grinned, replacing the lipsticks he was clearly not interested in, and getting out the different powder compacts, some modern and some traditional.

"Oh yes?" He looked at each powder compact carefully, picked one up, the silver one, and examined it like a museum object.

"Yes. He's a handyman." She'd had to give up being an art student to work full-time in a store because he lost his job. Now she was pregnant *and* had left art behind. She couldn't tell that to a stranger, a customer. Her grin sank into a thin line.

He triggered open the push mechanism to spring open the mirrored lid like a switchblade. Then he repeated the action with four of the other compacts. He looked like a boy excited about new toys which "did things".

"A handyman?"

The man was impassive. He had to put down the last compact he played with.

Dallas's face cracked and fell like a plate. He was still a customer so she bravely tried to hold the face plate together. Could he have acted more shocked if Dallas would have referred to being a handyman as a great job?

"I'm sorry," the man said. "I was actually thinking I — we — really need a handyman for some jobs which need fixing at home—"

"Oh?"

"Yes."

Dallas knew the store was not a place to talk about Jay Jay. She was at work herself. Jay Jay was already busy and the man seemed to understand.

"Do you work around here?" Dallas glanced at the clock on the top of the high walls of the store. Her lunchtime was almost over and here she was, having not even made a sale that morning.

"You know what?" He ignored her question, like he hadn't heard. "I'll have a lipstick, a powder compact and a perfume. Any. You take a look and pretend you are shopping for yourself."

Dallas got busy as she knew this was gonna be a sale of more than one item. Her commission would rise after a morning of no sales. She kept thinking, quick, hurry, brown-eyed, ginger, pink with yellow, not blue undertones, satin not gloss, and perfume... she actually grabbed the biggest-sized bottle of Yves St Laurent Rive Gauche, and the powder compact. Oh, silver with diamanté, most definitely the silver and not the gold. Choosing for others was easy. Being blond herself she chose what would be the opposite of what she chose for herself. Plus the man appeared to not care at all.

"I got your wife Rive Gauche, from *Pairs*. She'd love it."

"Pairs?"

"In France. Means left river bank."

"Oh. Paris."

She went red. "Lots of artists here have told me that's where artists hang out in Pairs. Some day I'd love to go. I love romantic cities. New York, London, Rome, just like the movies."

"You're an artist yourself?"

"Not a very good one. I'd been modeling and taking art classes—."

"I love romantic cities too. I have family in Yerp."

At the mention of Europe, she started wrapping his purchases with tissue and ribbons from under the counter.

"Oh. You're Yerpeen?"

"Not fully," he said. "My parents came from Spain. Not Mexico. Spain. Vineyard workers."

"Okaaaay," she said, not understanding why he made the distinction unless he was trying to indicate he was not Latino in origin. All wrapped, she tied neat bows, curling the ribbons and inserting cards as she had been trained to do. She was starving and pregnant. A shizzmizz combo. A little yelp or maybe a desperate gasp came out, hopefully not too audibly.

"You got any plans for the weekend?"

"Yeah. I got an engagement party to attend."

"Oh, whose? A friend?"

"No. No one I know. The nephew of the old man who my fiancé works for."

She saw he thought about what she said for a little longer than usual.

"What's the name of the guy?"

"The nephew?"

"Yeah."

"Carl Sutton. Why? See? You won't know him. Place has been amped up, or sure will be after my fiancé has been done with it for Mr Sutton. I've imagined the glitzy shattoh it used to be. It's why I am so agonizing about what to wear. 'Sgonna be the most class act party I ever been to, like going to the White House."

For a second, the color fell from his handsome and Spanish-looking face.

"Are you okay? Sir?"

He shook his head. "I'm fine, I'm fine. I— I'd better get back to work."

"No problem. I am almost done."

"You got the dress? Your outfit?"

"I saw one... a little out of my budget. In the women's section on first floor. Pink. Quant."

"Kwont?"

"She's a British designer."

"Pink?"

"Well, you know the rules," she said, a little tired but interested as he was in fashion.

"I don't."

"No purple or black." Jay Jay would never listen to a word when she talked clothes. He had a volume dial for her in his mind which went all the way down to zero.

"Why not?"

"I'd look like an eggplant. How wouldja like to pay, Sir?"

The man smiled his mysterious smile which started small but spread like a book. He observed she was pregnant when his eyes drifted down. He did not reply but he got his wallet out.

Dallas thought for a minute.

"Please come with me to the cash register."

He followed like a dog on a leash. She carried his gift-wrapped parcels and started to add them up. She announced the total.

He handed her a hundred and fifty dollars. "Keep the change," he whispered. "What about the earrings?"

"Earrings? Pardon me?"

"For your outfit. For the Mary Quant dress."

"Well... umm... I'd seen some Halston silver moon crescents," she laughed, not because of the humorous moment but because she was genuinely thrilled to recall the design detail, as a child was describing a toy. "Very cute drop earrings on a fish hook."

He nodded and she appreciated he listened to each word she said, like he was a friend.

"Thank you," he said.

After he left, she rushed off to the deli opposite and got the quickest pastrami on rye you could get in a New York minute. She found a bench, sat down and ate. Then she wandered around some other stores looking at clothes and shoes.

"Thanks for covering for me, Sherylanne," she said, gently patting down her formerly perfect helmet cut bob. Windy City was dead right.

"Hey no problem, Dallas. A customer came. But she didn't buy anything."

"OK," she set her bag down in the sliding closet behind the counter.

"This came for you."

"What is it?"

"I don't know. I'd better get back to handbags now."

"OK, see ya round."

The boys on first floor had delivered a gray polka dot box tied up in a fat yellow bow. *Oh!* Dallas was totally surprised. What was this? Must be for the baby. So far so good. No way was it from Jay Jay. He didn't remember anything, give anything, or buy anything, let alone wrap anything. They did say pregnancy did things to your mind but yep, and nup, it was *not* her birthday.

She opened the paper box. The pink Mary Quant dress. She gasped. On top of the dress sat a little black box which she picked up and opened. The silver Halston moon-shaped earrings. *Oh my!* She put them down and hugged herself.

She pulled the dress out of the box. Holding it up, she looked at the label. Her size!

A card fell out onto the floor, face down.

CHAPTER 7

J ay Jay found a spot to park the blue Camaro a little north of the Jade Palace Garden. He'd turned up to another job looking like he was on a date and "...unprofessional?" as Dallas would say. Grandpops had wanted him to feel proud rather than a bit guilty, but Jay Jay wished he had a van, more so than ever. Dallas seemed thrilled that he was getting more work contacts through Mr Alfred. "Well, honey, actually it's Mr Sutton," she said. "He's one of the patrons of the Art Institute. The whole family are."

"Yeah, I know."

"What didja know? That he's Mr Sutton or that he's a patron?"

Jay Jay shrugged. "Both, I guess."

"See, I toldja he'd like you," she said.

10:15 a.m. The Jade Palace Garden was not even open yet. He got out with his tool bag. He'd have to come back anyway, if he needed to go to the store for parts, materials or more tools. He rang the bell and looked in through the glass doors.

"Welcome! Welcome!" A slight Chinese man with a big smile emerged from the darkness and into the light with a bunch of keys. He unlocked the door with one or three of the keys, Jay Jay had no idea. He remembered a complicated system like this from his steel plant days. Didn't hurt for a commercial practice to be extra secure. Especially in Chinatown. Finally the door swung open, light as a page in a book, and Jay Jay was inside the restaurant.

"So Jerry, I'm Mr Chan," the man said, still grinning. "Mr Sutton is a big client. A great friend. We go back years." He offered his hand. "Pleased to meet you."

"Jerome Lee." Jay Jay broke into a big smile and shook Mr Chan's hand.

"You look a bit Chinese," said Mr Chan. "Are you?"

"My father is, was," Jay Jay replied, aware that he was olive-skinned, with glossy hair and dark, hooded almond eyes. "My great grandparents were from China."

"Really? How did they come to America?"

"She... well, my great-grandparents came in 1870, and my father was born 10 years later," Jay Jay replied, knowing Chinese Americans always wanted to find out how *did* one arrive in the States, because no journey was either identical, nor an A to B process.

"To Chicago?" Mr Chan asked.

"No. They went to California. They were Hakka, from Southern China. Laborers. My grandfather was born in San Francisco in 1901."

There was still so much to explain. The emigration process always went via somewhere or someone or something. He added: "Railroad industry. Thousands of Chinese laborers, including my great-great-grandparents worked on the transcontinental railroad."

"That's... wonderful. How did they end up in Chicago?"

He said *wunnerful*, like he'd learned English from gangster movies.

"Sir, who needs laborers after the job is finished? My great-great-grandparents left. California didn't want them any more and showed it in the usual ways. Everyone went east. Some went to NYC or Boston, but my ancestors came to Chicago."

"Well, you know a lot about your family history."

"I don't. 'S all I know." Jay Jay said, embarrassed, not mentioning the holes in the history on his father's side. For example, where was his father now? Jay Jay chewed his lip and looked down.

"Our ancestors worked so hard to survive and give us the stories we have today," said Mr Chan.

Jay Jay looked up at Mr Chan. "They sure did. It's all relative." Jay Jay noticed that Mr Chan didn't use the clichéd phrase that the generations long ago gave us what we have today. They didn't. Instead he said they gave us *stories*. Jay Jay and Mr Chan still worked and struggled to make a living, as their ancestors did, but in a less harsh climate.

"Ha, see what I did there? *It's all relative*," Jay Jay repeated his inadvertent joke, surprised at his own confidence. Mr Chan pointed at him and laughed with his eyes shut.

"Hey," said Mr Chan, "you speak Chinese?"

Jay Jay shook his head. He didn't want think of his father who'd left him when he was still so young, and took the language with him. He had had a tremendous ear for music since he was a child and could remember melodies after hearing them once. He chuckled at the thought of the Elvis songs that he grew up with that were about as Chinese as apple pie.

"You like kung fu? You like Bruce Lee?"

"Yeah. I learned kung fu in school with my Shaolin master, Mr Wu." He grinned. He remembered Saturday afternoons at the Spirit Dragon School of Wu Shu martial arts in West Cermak Street.

"Wow, you did? Jay Jay, I tell you we need your kung fu skills in this restaurant."

Jay Jay burst out laughing. Chinese boys back in school were all serious until they were joking with you. And then you knew you were suddenly in the 'in crowd'. They only joked with those who found them funny. They could detect the boys who didn't *get* their Chinese humor.

Mr Chan was a funny guy. He made Jay Jay feel like he was funny too. That hadn't happened since he was at school.

"I think I am pretty good! I still train every fortnight or month. I can do the moves." He started sweeping his limbs and holding his core for the Horse Stance but stopped, feeling self-conscious.

"What have you watched? *Marlowe*? *A Walk in the Spring Rain*?"

"No, I don't think so. I watched *The Thunderstorm*, *The Orphan*... when I was a boy."

"Yeah?" Mr Chan raised his eyebrows, nodding, impressed.

"Yeah."

"Have you heard? He's got a new one coming out this year. Fall."

He said *fawl*. Just *that* one word made Mr Chan sound real American.

"Really?" Jay Jay was a little excited for Mr Chan. He would love to catch a movie night but Dallas was not keen on martial arts. "Not tryna sound obvious, but do they ever stop kung fu fighting?" she'd said once, looking at her watch.

"Yeah. Called *The Big Boss*. 唐山大兄," he added in Chinese.

"Ah, like you."

Mr Chan's gold fillings shone when he laughed raucously, as if he'd never heard himself called that before. Clearly, he was the boss. He wiped his tears with his knuckles. "Come on, I'll show you what the problem is downstairs in the kitchen."

Mr Chan snapped on more lights, the two-way, three-way. The first two he switched were wrong, and then the third was the right one.

They descended a narrow staircase into the basement and again, more light switch tests. Mr Chan showed him where the exhaust fan was and explained what was not working. "Started going wrong last night and we reset the thermostat..."

Mr Chan's words were swimming. Joking aside, Jay Jay had little experience in commercial buildings and least of all commercial kitchens. He would have to learn and talk to somebody standing in line at the stores, hopefully some kind of heating and plumbing engineer or technician. As a handyman, everything he had learnt was from Grandpops when *he* was standing in line somewhere. Jay Jay also learned when he was chatting or when he was back of the counter at the steel works listening to customers' problems. Having no colleagues to "learn" from was tough.

Suddenly the briefing was over.

"I'm going to have to go, I have a very busy day with the kids today. Mrs Chan is back in Hong Kong," Mr Chan laughed unintentionally, at the very idea of even being with his kids.

"I can't stay," he said again, to make sure Jay Jay understood. "You'll have to figure all this out yourself and fix this for us by tonight or I am in trouble. I know I can trust you. Mr Sutton sent you." Mr Chan laughed again. And Jay Jay laughed along. From the boys in School, he'd seen that the Chinese laughed out of embarrassment and loss of words. One had to focus and listen for the context. Laughter was the punctuation for conversation. There was sad laughter, which was for sympathy. Huge laughter was for jokes, and little laughs were for covering up embarrassing gaps in conversation or for the just-in-case-it-was-funny kind of situation.

First things first. Jay Jay switched on every damned light in the kitchen. No point trying to work in the dark. Little rooms fed off a long corridor – probably store rooms, an accounts office and maybe a lunch room for staff, Jay Jay presumed.

He was surprised how much came back to him regarding basic electric stuff. Firstly he made sure, as Mr Chan did, the AC was turned off, but the mains was still on at the circuit. One point for point one! Jay Jay went through in his mind the other obvious things he had to do. He got his tool bag out and his screwdriver. He took apart the AC unit, taking mental note of the make and model. Checked the filters. He studied the capacitor, fuse, loose wiring, inspecting for any water damage. He cleaned the filthy fuse, hoping it was the right one after its service more than a year ago by the company. But who could say? Had it been correctly maintained, then debris would not have built up and blocked the connections.

Filters needed to be cleaned to allow the flow of air. Similarly, fuses, too, had to be kept clean to allow the flow of electricity. He started to enjoy himself. Jay Jay liked being on his own with "toys", to dismantle, explore, solve and resolve. But this was frustrating, particularly as after each step, he had to switch on the AC again to make sure the circuit breaker didn't trip, or the problem hadn't been solved and a completely different problem had cropped up.

Some time passed. A commotion sounded, coming from that staircase or maybe a different staircase? Was there another escape route to the street? This was quite likely, as street entrances into the basement were common. He listened hard and he was about to go into the stairwell to say "Hi guys, I'm working here today" but something stopped him. He put his tools down.

"I'm not... Please. I... " A girl spoke. She had the prettiest, sweetest angel voice. Like Dallas. But nervous and almost in tears.

"You listena me," a man's voice hissed.

"No, you listena me." Another man.

Jay Jay followed the voices, creeping closer to the corridor outside the room interconnecting the staircase and the street. He pressed his ear against the shut door.

"Gentlemen, gentlemen. All of you." Said a third man's voice, an American. "With due respect," he said. He sounded educated, Jay Jay thought, though anybody who said *with due respect* had no respect at all for the person spoken to.

"With due respect, Officer Chan," A clearing of throat, a light thud of documents or papers. The faint rustle of something card-like landing on what must have been a counter top or desk. Silence for a few minutes while the item was picked up. Another bout of rustling and swishing.

"This photo ring any bells?"

"No."

"You don't know her or it doesn't ring bells?"

"Both."

"What about this?" A light floppy sound.

"Never seen it. I don't know anything about this."

"That's what we looking for. Now. We see advertisement. For sale. But they cannot sell it. Know why?"

"No."

"Cos it's ours. They steal."

"Who?" Said the girl.

"That's what you have to find. You are cop. We gonna give face. We try Mrs Chan. But she back in Hong Kong. We don't ring that number on the ad. You help find what we want. No one get hurt. But if you don't? Someone get hurt. Capeesh?"

Jay Jay could hear the girl weeping. No further words were exchanged.

After a shuffle of footsteps, they all left via the staircase to the street and the front door clunked shut. He rushed into the little office room that they had been in. As the high level windows to the basement room were higher than the sidewalk, he saw their legs. Three suited men and the girl's slim legs in jeans and white sneakers. The men had standard men's leather shoes. He could not tell them apart. But she was not in uniform. They dispersed in different directions. The girl's legs seemed to hesitate, they turned as if she was about to return to the basement. She had a small red canvas shopping bag with her. It had made the fabric sound Jay Jay heard earlier. She had put the papers or cards, that thudded on the countertop, into that bag, for sure. Jay Jay could see how she dangled the bag almost at ankle level. The text and logo on it said "The Art Institute". Dallas's art college!

With the visitors gone, Jay Jay remembered his tasks. What was he in the middle of? Oh yes. He was about to check the sensors of the thermostat, and whether water had damaged the coils. He had been about to switch off the mains circuit when the commotion happened. What had annoyed him was having to keep quiet and not being able to see the looks being exchanged. Grandpops always said "don't do what doesn't do you". While something was not right, he should simply mind his own business, do his job and leave.

When he got back home, Dallas was watching TV.

"Hey."

"Hey."

"How was it?" said Dallas.

Jay Jay didn't answer. She stared at him, deciphering but there was nothing to decipher. She was having a baby; he should let her relax.

"You're back late," she said, changing the subject. "Jeet yet?"

He shook his head slowly.

"Thought you went and fixed up that Chinese restaurant. They give you a meal?"

"Naw. Well. Yeah. I got a takeout." He held out a paper bag to show her. "The kitchen opened after I fixed the AC and circuit breaker problem. Ya know? One night, let's go. Dinner is on him. Mr Chan was so pleased with the job I did. Real nice. You'll love it. Fish tanks, chandeliers, red carpet, gold paint. Just your style, doll."

"My word! Oh Lord! What'd I say? They love ya, I toldja they'd love ya. Tell me what they got."

"Why, Chinese food."

Dallas threw her arms over him. "We had nothing in for tonight."

"Was just concentrating on the new job. Sugar pie? I'm hoping for more work. Mr Chan is good with me. There're still things to be done, like fixing up the counter tops, more electrics and dividing folding doors, so they can have private dining rooms. And so on."

"Oh that is wonderful news Jerome Jerry Jay! What about Mr Alfred?"

"What about him?"

"Won't he be mad?"

"Why would he? He sent me in the first place."

"No, I mean that Mr Chan is taking up your time."

"I haven't got any more restaurant work right now, so we don't have to think about it yet."

He thought back on the girl in the basement again. Come to think of it, he never saw her face, but you could tell a lot from someone's shoes. And he didn't like whatever she'd had to agree to. Whatever it was wasn't good. And what was her name even?

"Let's eat! Have you got won tons? Have you got chicken chow mein? What've you got in that bag, Lord Jerome?"

———

THE NEXT THREE days Jay Jay worked on all the other sash windows at Mr Alfred's house. He planned to come back to the French windows on the first story facing the yard and the kitchen windows. He was working on the basis of the front first, then the back, and lastly the three side windows.

Mr Alfred's room had been tidied up slightly. "Oh, the nurse Nancy came," said Mr Alfred, almost apologetically. "We have a shouting match whenever she comes," he cackled his phlegmy laugh. "It's like having a wife you didn't know you had."

Jay Jay laughed politely. He had brought planks of wood up the stairs to fix the rotten parts of the timber, a few cans of paint and some sandpaper. The windows and doors didn't have to be fixed before the winter, so he had plenty of time. He also had to re-paper and paint each room but again, he had all year to do that.

"I heard that all went well at the Jade Palace Garden," said Mr Alfred.

"Yessir."

"That's good. You know something, son, I forgot to mention that we oughta finish the yard work by July."

"Oh, that shouldn't be a problem."

"What about June?"

"I am sure I can. After the sash windows are done."

Jay Jay wondered about the sudden deadline. People Mr Alfred's age usually didn't have any deadlines. "The deadline is when I'm dead," he'd joked ever since Jay Jay had started working for him. "Your deadline is my flatline."

Jay Jay decided not to ask: Mr Alfred would tell him in good time why June.

"I'll give you your check today. Don't forget to drop by before you go."

"Thank you, Sir."

Jay Jay worked hard and only stopped by in the cabin to grab his notebook and plan out what was required in the yard, ready for three weeks' time. Most of the work was weeding, clearing away and removing everything from the completely overgrown grounds. Same in the front yard. Sure, Mr Alfred could do with a few new flowering plants to pretty up the place. That would follow after the clearing away, then he'd know how much space was left. Some fancy parties in the distant past would have taken place in a yard of this size. The stone terrace and steps had to be cleaned up, all nice. Broken naked lady statues would have to be rubbed down, Jay Jay smiled at his own schoolboy joke.

Dallas would be very happy. Today was pay day. Chances are she'd want to be taken out, she'd want to buy new stuff for the baby. Always the baby, the baby, the baby. She had magazines she was reading, friends to talk to, her mother to telephone every day, all about the baby. The most important thing was the baby carriage. You'd think they were choosing a new automobile. He'd made note that it was the Maclaren, not *a*, but *the*, that they'd be ordering. *Lightweight enough for both aeronautical journeys and quick city trips*, said the brochure. Well, he sure was looking forward to space travel. She had outfits chosen for a boy and a girl and a new chest of drawers ordered. The excitement had left Jay Jay behind. She was racing forward and he was still getting ready. The only thing that they could still enjoy together was eating fancy meals. She'd transformed into... a mom. His mom.

At lunchtime he got in the Camaro and drove off to a sandwich stand on East Bellevue Place and North Rush Street. He came back to his cabin where he ate, surrounded by his tools. He looked around and was beginning to like the room, which was every bit as good as a workshop, studio or even a little outhouse on a camping trip. He visualized making a stool to sit on and a workbench from all the offcuts during the works.

Jay Jay almost fell through the floor. Hell, he'd have to replace the rotten floorboards he smashed up, and finish what he started. He could only walk around and sit at the edges of the room to avoid an accident. He had not forgotten Bones 1 and 2. He thought about his discovery again, while he was eating his lunch, perched on a broken tree stump that he'd found in the yard, now officially his "stool". He'd been caught up in the job recently, but now he was in his "lunch room" looking straight at the bulge of the latch under the vinyl flooring. He screwed up his sandwich paper into a ball and moved the vinyl out of the way. Armed with his retractable tape measure, he calculated the area of the floorboards he had to replace.

He paused. He wanted to and he didn't want to. Should he? He grabbed his flashlight and opened the wooden trap door where he had broken the latch. He switched it on. Yep, still there, why would they not be? Bones 1 and 2 were like old friends now.

Let's see, he thought. Clothes. You could not tell what they were as they had rotted into a dust practically as black as ash. Shoes? There were none. Where could they be? You could tell a lot from someone's shoes. He thought about that cop's white sneakers. He shone the flashlight around. It showed a fairly big space, which could have been used to store anything. Booze, firearms, drugs. Anything at all. The house had witnessed Prohibition after all. He shut his eyes and for a moment put the back of his hand on his mustache and imagined the Old Days. Those that Grandpops had mentioned. The music and the dancing. The cocktails. The shiny black and white spats.

He opened his eyes and sighed. "Well, Bones 1," he said aloud.

"You're not as bad as I thought. Yeah. You're dead and no one cares. But we're gonna clean up yer room. Yup, and you, Bones 2." And why shouldn't he? A sharp twinge of guilt bit into him, excitement, too. He always enjoyed transformations, not only of himself but spaces. Like the psycho from Alfred Hitchcock's movie, he was talking to skeletons but hey, it wasn't his mom. Also, there was no one else to talk to and what harm did he do? He was only talking himself out of loneliness and fear. People talked to their cats, dogs, budgies. Kids talked to their toys. No one said that was crazy. Bones 1 was a friend, yes a lil' creepy, but it was hard not to be creepy when you were dead. Jay Jay sensed he might be intruding into some kind of tomb. The sooner he "got over it", the sooner he could turn this room into something and the less creepy it would be. "See? 'S like a cycle. The more you're scared, then the more you're scared." He whispered.

A little round metallic object on the filthy floor caught his eye. A glint of some glass. He shone his flashlight. A single spectacle on a chain, which he picked up. He was fascinated, but didn't know what it was called. He'd only seen these in the movies and his Grandpops had never had one. Of course, he looked through it but the glass was scratched. He rubbed its once pebble-like smoothness. What did you see once, Bones 1? He smiled. In those few seconds, Jay Jay was transported to another world and he wasn't afraid any more. Finding the circular eye glass was part of the plan to get to know the hidden room and make the whole cabin his.

He replaced the eyeglass on a little brick ledge foundation wall, as though he was tidying up. Probably worth nothing but didn't seem right to throw it right back on the floor. Anyhow this room would be tidied up pretty soon and have lights, an exhaust fan for ventilation, electric sockets, shelves, and hooks. It would be a neat, usable space.

But not being able to tell Mr Alfred or Dallas.

Now that bugged him.

Chapter 8

"Well, I am glad you stopped by for your check." Mr Alfred said with a smile as he looked up from his desk.

"You did say to do so, Sir."

"Here is a little extra." He handed Jay Jay a second check.

Jay Jay took the $1,000 check. He knitted his brow, wondering if there was an error, as he did not remember the expenses being so huge and a round number too. "What's this for?"

"Why didn't you say you're getting married?"

"Sir, I... well, I mean, I... " Jay Jay lost his tongue. He had no idea. Dallas? No, couldn't have been.

"I only found out this afternoon when I had a telephone call from Robert."

"The Professor? From the Institute?"

"Yes! Now. You know he was calling to find out how we are getting on here, and I said, just fine. Jerome is a fine young man also known as Jerry. Now, he told me you are engaged! Didja forget?" He cackled, which turned into a cough.

Jay Jay beamed. He *had* forgotten until that moment. He was indebted to the professor and, yes, Dallas, for getting him the position here. Dallas had always had something to do with the art world. They loved her and she them. She was sharp as a painting.

"Thank you, Sir! This is so generous."

"You're very welcome."

What could possibly go wrong? It was the best first month anybody could have had in any job. Then he remembered he was getting married, the baby, moving apartment, more furniture, clothes and all the rest of it. Most of the check would go on the dress and the baby carriage, he sighed. Everything slipped through his fingers that she was holding apart.

After 6, he got home.

He went to the fridge and got a bottle of beer. She looked at him all suspish.

"Well, we oughta invite Mr Alfred, right?"

"Sure."

"I mean, we've got to. He's paying."

"Where again? What are we doing?"

"Dja forget already? I told you like 620 times."

"Well, I'm sorry... please. I've been... Tell me for the 621st time. And this time I will write it down in my notebook."

"First, we're getting married. I showed you the dress."

"Yup. Pretty sure I remember." He vaguely recalled something but all the dresses looked the same, though he didn't say as much. He scratched his head. What was he doing each time the conversation came up about the wedding or the baby? His mind must have drifted off like he did whenever someone spoke a "for'n" language.

"Well, secondly, we're super lucky to be doing this at Hotel Baker. The Professor got us room hire on a dirt cheap deal."

What did she mean dirt cheap? Nothing was. Jay Jay didn't like the fact that everything they did, were doing or about to do was "thanks to the Professor". He supposed he'd meet him soon. "You know?" Dallas said quietly as though answering his thoughts, "I wish I had a dad to give me away."

"Oh sweetheart! No, we will make this special." He came over and hugged her. She disentangled herself quickly.

"So thirdly, the cost includes catering. We don't have to do a thing. But the cake is not included. Something we'd need to look at together. Dja hear what I said? This Saturday we're picking the cake."

Jay Jay couldn't believe this was happening to him. It was like an exam and he was concentrating now far more than he ever did in school. "Yeeeeahhh... so we order the cake... this Saturday?"

"Yes, Jerome Jerry." She looked stern. Her mouth had turned into a line and she had that little crease between her eyebrows.

He noted she hadn't mentioned the cost yet. What point was there? A wedding was a bulldozer. Didn't matter what you thought. Your mind went into hire-purchase from the day your future wife took over your mind and body. He had just laughed whenever Grandpops used to complain it had happened to him, as it had to Jay Jay's dad, and it would happen to Jay Jay too.

Working at Mr Alfred's and Mr Chan's had transported him into another world. One strange to him, powerful, rich and alien. He'd forgotten all about everything going on at home, even getting married and being a dad.

After they cleared the plates, Dallas brought her notebook out. It was white leather, with embossed gold lettering which said My Wedding. She had a notebook for it too?

She said it was all in there: all her ideas and the dates everything was supposed to happen. Phone numbers for the dress and the cake. The venue. A dizzying array of photos and cut outs from magazines. His head spun like a 7-inch on a turntable.

"Here's the Waterfront Ballroom. I know you'll love the swinging' 1920s decor. 'S real pretty, with big windows. See. We'd have a romantic ceremony here looking out onto the Fox River."

"Where... Where is this?"

"I toldja. Hotel Baker. St Charles?"

"Oh, downtown."

"What do you think about an intimate romantic ceremony,

probably under a hundred guests—."

A hundred? He read the handbill. 100 W. Main St, looked at the photos. Grand, wood paneling, chandeliers, stained glass, right next to the Fox River. Just the kinda thing Dallas liked.

Did they even *know* a hundred people in their whole lives?

"Too few? You think maybe 200? Then we'd need the Rainbow Room—."

"Naw. Let's — let's — go with whatchu got."

"Well, I have got a guest list. I wrote down the people you would probably invite like your Grandpops, but take a look, lemon pie."

Naturally the list included the Professor and Mr Alfred. "S'pose you gotta invite them, Dallas."

"Well, I did."

"Good."

There was nothing else to add to the conversation. She'd thought of everything. Jay Jay shut his eyes and pinch-rubbed the area between his brows. He could not stop thinking of "other things". Bones 1 and 2. The Chinese girl. The argument between Mr Alfred and the nephew.

The next few weeks became a blur of cake, dress, dress, cake, lists, menus. Dallas started to repeat herself, reminding him like an alarm clock on snooze. "You didn't forget, didja?" Jay Jay longed for the simple moments relaxing in his cabin in Mr Alfred's yard. Or the old days, pre-Mr Alfred, when Dallas was working hard in the store and modeling on weekends.

The what-kind-of-cake became a thesis in itself. Surely someone could write a book on wedding cake. Or maybe some-one'd already done that. They visited the "back rooms" of bakeries and cake stores. Big commercial ones and little artistic kinds. Old-fashioned, modern. She definitely wanted a 1920s cocktail to go with the venue which had to go with the cake that looked like a fountain about to erupt. Then a modern kind like a cubist build-ing. An Institute of Art kind. A granny-style lacy kind. Everything was like choosing the dress but this time for the cake. Over and over again, they went through the options. Jay Jay was exhausted. Dallas's project had become bigger than her, than him, than them. If only Mr Alfred or Grandpops or anyone else knew what had happened in Jay Jay's tight little life. Suddenly his neat space had been slit open like an envelope and all this glitter and confetti had poured out, never to be picked up again.

After trying more than 20 cakes which all kinda tasted the same to him, Dallas finally made a decision. She fine-tuned the bakery to the number of almond essence drops. She went with the 1920s one. "Hey, a black wedding cake? Or white? Jay Jay? Are ya list'nin'? Black or white?"

Jay Jay came to his senses. "Oh! White. Honey. Let's not go for black. Seems... wrong."

"Okay! How about cream or ivory-colored and not just white-white."

"Okay."

"Which one? Cream or ivory?"

"Uhhh... wut?"

"Well, yellowish white or whitish white? Jay Jay. I need you to concentrate."

"Ohhh... uh... I'm sorry, I can't. I... can't." Didn't they already view 12 shades of white? Which one of the 12 was she referring to?

"Ivory," Dallas turned to the counter assistant and repeated, "ivory."

When they got home he went and got a beer. But the discussion wasn't over. There also had to be a debrief where they had to discuss if he could taste the fruit in the cake or not? What about the alcohol content? Too strong? He wanted to joke as he opened his bottle of Bud, *naw, ain't strong at all,* but he resisted. Maybe he shouldn't have resisted the urge to joke with her as she'd once considered him funny. They did say women got brain-damaged by fellas and pregnancy. He choked on his beer at the thought and started coughing vehemently.

"You okay? You okay, Jay Jay? Don't go and choke on me

now!"

She banged the palms of her hand on his back. He was still clutching his bottle.

He had finished all the windows and was only focused on the yard work for Mr Alfred, because the nephew was getting engaged in June. Suddenly Jay Jay sympathized with the man, who would be having a parallel experience with him, but on a much larger scale. He imagined at least 800 wedding guests. A cake which would sink the Titanic and a dress which used more miles of silk than the distance to the moon.

He would be glad when all this was over, but he had only just started. He had been back to Mr Chan's once to fix the flushing in the toilets and to replace loose tiles and rotten grout but he didn't see or hear the girl, the fellas or the attorney guy. Maybe he'd imagined it all.

―――――

THE DAY WAS GRAY, a little rainy, which hadn't put Dallas off. He teared up when he saw her dress. Sure, he'd seen — but not *looked* at — what was the most amazing, drop waist, beaded silk and lace ivory (it was ivory, right?) dress with a scalloped theatrical hem line. The 1920s theme Dallas was so passionate about was actually dreamed up because of her bump. No way was she gonna wear a regular dress with cut in waistline. Not when she had no waistline.

Jay Jay had fun writing the song list. That was *his* job, his favorite part of the wedding preparations which almost made him forget he was the one getting married. He chuckled to himself. He wrote 40 songs down. He was given strict instructions there weren't to be any "wrong" songs. She meant songs like Marvin Gaye's "What's Going On" or anything which reminded anyone there was a war going on. They opened the dance with an upbeat number, Three Dog Night's *Joy to the World*.

Dallas had to give the list to the hotel a week before and they did everything. They also had a smooth Stephane Grappelli style 1930s gypsy jazz but only for an hour before the wedding reception when drinks were being served because an hour of jazz, no, 15 minutes, was enough for anybody. Anyhow, a live band all night would simply cost too much.

———

ON THE BIG DAY, in the glittering ballroom with the enormous windows looking out over the river Jay Jay felt at ease for the first time. This was now his world, a new reality. And Dallas had made it all happen.

He looked at her when they began their dance. She had gone all the way with the 1920s look. He liked it. She'd had her eyebrows re-shaped and re-colored. They were straight, no arch, darkened like she was Pola Negri. Her rosebud lips were painted a reddish black which made her blue eyes shine with light. He touched his mustache for a moment.

He was such a lucky guy, to have a beautiful woman love him and do all this for him — for them.

"You look like Marlon Brando. Or maybe Jimmy Dean."

"Which one?"

"I pick Jay Jay."

He took her hands and they started to dance. The guests cheered. The photographer suddenly rushed around the dancing couple. A few flashes exploded before the guy disappeared back into the background. A burn of embarrassment burst in him.

He started to perspire. He caught his reflection in the gilt-framed mirrors shaped like the large arched windows opposite. The pale blue Little Italy suit, cut and made to fit at South May Street in Near West Side had not been an expense he'd welcomed. "Wut? He's a real Eyetalyun, y'know," Dallas had persuaded him. He wouldn't be makin' these suits forever, the tailor had told him. He'd been doing it back in Sicily since 1949. Jay Jay had listened and nodded like he was doing this Mario guy a favor.

Luxury had always been a vice he couldn't afford for something you'd use once. Was this outfit made to live in the closet after one day of wear? He winced with the pain of pleasure. He did look like a movie star, him, a guy who'd never bought any clothes or shoes for himself. He never spent anything and he was always so careful. Grandpops had taught him well.

There would be rainy days. Jay Jay considered himself fortunate Mr Alfred had rained a few dollars on him especially for this grand event. He looked across the room and Mr Alfred waved at him and smiled. His other hand held a silver-topped walking cane. Jay Jay thought Mr Alfred was a true gentleman: he'd rather have a stylish prop than a practical aid to walking.

He marched briskly over to Mr Alfred. "I only wanted to say hello and congratulations," said Mr Alfred to him, beaming. "But I am going now. I've stayed for the whole ceremony. Beautiful. I won't stay for the party. I am too tired, the music is a little loud and I've called a cab."

"Thank you, Sir," said Jay Jay. "For coming. For everything."

Mr Alfred waved the appreciation away. Jay Jay offered to wait with him in the lobby. He tried to insist. He'd feel guilty if he didn't, but Mr Alfred declined. "You go back to your party and your big day."

After Mr Alfred left in the cab, Jay Jay returned to the party, "his big day". Someone large and round was coming out of the men's bathroom in the breakout area. The bastard!

"Hey, hey, hey. Who's a lucky guy." The bastard said.

He could not remember seeing Ernesto earlier. Of course Dallas must have invited him. She had to have done.

"What're you doing here?"

"Now, Jay, I forgive ya. Your big day, and all dat. 'S what the old fella said if I heard right. But ain't no way to talk to your cuzzin."

"We are not cousins."

"All right, then I'm your step-uncle and you are my step-nephew."

"Cut the crap. Who even says that? And why were you listening to my private conversations?"

"Not exactly private in a room with a hundred people." Ernesto stared at Jay Jay, who frowned, seeing Ernesto had more to say. Ernesto ran his tongue along the front of his teeth. "Actually I *am* your family. And I am here to celebrate with you."

Then Ernesto gave a huge smile, fake as a game show host's. "Lookatcha. Now you look like a million dollars and you ain't talkin to your cuzzin no more."

Jay Jay shook his head and left. He went straight back in the ballroom and he did not look back to see if Ernesto followed. *Brown Sugar* by the Stones was playing and he saw the crowded room was getting into the party.

Jay Jay was looking for Grandpops. Was probably that tramp Carmelita who brought Nestosterone the Testosterone here. Now where was she? He cast his gaze over the room.

She was not hard to spot, she looked like a tropical bird in her deep-V pink dress feathered with sequins like she was a Vegas clairvoyant. She wore green jewels and some kind of gold headgear. Jay Jay wasn't sure what these things were called but he'd seen enough movies. He was about to stride straight to her when he was interrupted by Dallas.

"*Where* were you, darling, where *were* you? Time to cut the cake." Her blue eyes were imploring, huge, anxious.

He put his hands to his head. "Oh, doll, I am so sorry. I — I had to — say goodbye to Mr Al —"

Jay Jay wasn't able to think. Dallas was in her own world. They both were. His head swam. The country was getting poorer and poorer. Boys younger than Jay Jay were dying every day in Vietnam. Right here in this ballroom, everybody was enjoying the icing of Jay Jay's new life. The whole wedding thing was just cake. Life was changing, and the country too, and here he was having cake.

"Well, c'mon. We're waiting."

Chapter 9

The 100-year-old village of Elkhart Lake was the poor man's casino resort town. Hawaii or Mexico were out of reach, he told Dallas. She did have her head screwed on right on her pretty little neck. The new job, moving apartment, the baby, the wedding would make for an expensive year. Elkhart Lake was a three-in-one destination: Catskills, Vegas and Chicago where most of its money came from anyway.

They took a walk the next day on the crystalline lake shaped like an elk's heart, hence the name. "It's a kettle lake," said Dallas, reading out from the handbill. "In the depression a great chunk of glacial ice formed the heart shape of the fourth-deepest natural lake in Wisconsin."

There were all kinds of amusements around the Germanic Victorian-style lake front. They enjoyed watching sailboats and kayaks on the Sunday. "This isn't the real honeymoon," said Dallas.

"It isn't?" The comment threw him.

"Naw. This is just practice. Getting used to things. Married life. Family. We're gonna go to Cancun like I said."

"Wut? But when? After this?"

"No," she laughed. "I toldja. When the baby is here and we have more money."

He shoulda taken her camping at Kettle Moraine State Forest. That would seriously have been practice for Elkhart Lane, he snorted to himself. "Sure," he said. Would that day come? Surely you had less money when you had a baby, not more?

Elkhart Lake had to be too good to be true and whatever they had was not good enough to be true. His mind wandered at dinner after he chose the chipotle-braised pork cheeks in the floating theater pavilion. He would have been equally happy with a taco and a Modelo. He was kinda looking forward to getting back to his own heaven, the cabin in Mr Alfred's yard. He shut his eyes and stopped himself thinking. He put down his napkin and chewed, enjoying the sensation of chipotle in his own cheeks.

———

JAY JAY WOKE UP THINKING, "Was it over? Or just beginning?"

Dallas was packing and he realized he wasn't dreaming.

Hell, it sure *had* seemed like a dream: sunsets and all. They'd said goodbye to Chi-town. Jay Jay had driven the blue Camaro upstate for three hours to a resort in Elkhart Lake. Honeymoons a speciality. The first evening they'd had dinner looking out on the twinkling lights surrounding the lake. He almost *had* forgotten about work.

But he had not forgotten that his wedding was nearly ruined by Nesto appearing out of nowhere. Thankfully there had been no chance that he'd confront his grandfather. Was a man allowed to be married in peace, or not? He had wanted to wring Carmelita's neck but he'd been too busy getting married.

When he got back, he'd go out to Beecher. Carmelita had to stay out of things and keep it that way. She wanted Jay Jay to give Nesto a hand. Get him a job at Mr Alfred's, Mr Chan's, anywhere. No way. He was already very grateful that Mr Alfred had taken care of the wedding. He wasn't going to ask for anything else.

———

BACK IN CHICAGO on the following weekend, Jay Jay got a surprise call from Grandpops. He was glad because he wanted to talk to his grandfather too.

"Well, you had a beautiful wedding and I wanted to help you and you said no."

"No, Mr Alfred off —"

"Well, I am your grandfather. I will help you in other ways. When you're moving apartment, when the baby comes. Whatever. I have a check for ya. Don't forget. Ready whenever you want. Couple of months. Whatever."

"Thank you. And thanks for calling."

"I just wanted to check that you're okay. You seemed very disturbed at the wedding."

"Is that why you called?"

"No, but it's one of the reasons."

"We had a really awesome time," Jay Jay said, but he was thinking, "no, really, I'm on a break from sarcasm."

"And... ?"

"Well, I'm gonna shoot straight."

"You shoot straight."

"I didn't apprec... I wanted... Ugh. Why was Nesto at my wedding? Why do I have to help him with anything?"

Grandpops sighed. "Imma sit down now."

"Is it her? I know it is." He could not bring himself to even say her name.

"Look, you mean Carmelita. Now she had nothing to do with this. That new employer of yours. He can help poor Ernesto."

"No. He can't. I hardly know him."

"Honey, who's that?" Dallas called out. "Is that Grandpops? Can I say hi?"

"In a minute," he yelled back. "Look, I'll catch up with ya another time. Dallas will wanna tell you about our first betting experience. We won a total of $130. Yeah, right?" Jay Jay tried to cheer himself up. He didn't mean to upset Grandpops. Jay Jay's stomach was boiling, so he needed to change the subject. That was what rich people did. Mr Alfred, his old boss, and probably Mr Chan would too, if he got another chance with the Chans.

———

NOT LONG AFTER, Jay Jay settled back into his routine. He was always expecting the call from the Jade Palace Garden for his side hustle, but it never came. He would be so honored to fix that faded wallpaper. Maybe something in red and gold. Black with gold bamboo? Was that good or bad luck? He was just daydreaming. He knew very little about design. He'd better not screw up and offer any advice or tips. For now, he had to continue his work on Mr Alfred's yard. The tea party reception for the old man's nephew's engagement was in a week.

Today, he'd be putting in some plants which Mr Alfred had selected and written down in a list which he had then typed up. Why did we *write down* but *type up*? He wondered. The tinkle of the carriage return rung out in Mr Alfred's office through the hall doors. He knocked.

"Come on in," called out Mr Alfred, the tremor in his voice a little worse. "Now, I sorta know what I want and how much of it. I have been in real estate for a long time. Not that you can tell from the state of this place," he cackled and waved around him at the cracked plaster ceiling, the bulbless chandelier and torn wallpaper. "Welcome to the Addams' family residence," he dropped his jaw and made a ta-dah face. Jay Jay smiled politely and said "It's fine, Sir. That's what I am here for."

"I can tell you love buildings," said Mr Alfred, all serious. "You must think about them a lot."

Did he? Jay Jay had not given the matter much thought. Someone like Jay Jay did not *think* about buildings. There was nothing to *think* about. You only said that if you were all educated and smart. Buildings were just places to be used, to be fixed, to be looked at. You thought about other things. Money. Food. The baby. Grandpops. Bones.

"Now. It's important but not that important. If you can't make my nephew's engagement party, I understand. I don't really want him to have the party here, but we must."

"Yessir." Jay Jay listened.

"I want to show them that I am good. I am looking after myself and the place. My nephew and his future wife's family are trying to get their hands on this estate. I won't let them." He shook his already shaking fist.

"Naw, Sir. Imma make sure. You don't have to worry about anything."

"I know I can trust you." It *was* greater to be trusted than to be loved. Love was just the showpiece of the trust. The hard work was done. That was why people say *build trust*. They didn't say *build love*. Mr Alfred patted Jay Jay on the back and handed him the typed list. Jay Jay stared at all the technical plant names and the quantity of each.

Seeing his bemusement, Mr Alfred said, "When you get to my age your handwriting will be no good for writing in Latin," Mr Alfred laughed loudly at his own joke, actually holding his belly. "Hence the typing."

"When you come back with them I will tell you where they go." He dangled a key in front of Jay Jay's eyes.

"What's this?"

"You didn't think you're gonna drive all that back in your Camaro, did you?"

"Oh! I never thought. You mean? It's... ?"

He remembered seeing a shiny white truck a few yards away

from the house that morning, but thought maybe someone else was doing work in the street.

"Yes. Bought for your use. Anytime and anywhere and for anything. I figured I wasn't being fair on you. You're moving big things around. When you're done with this house, I can sell it on or you can keep it, whatever you want."

"But, I... Sir, I can't... this is so... "

Mr Alfred shooed him off. "You'd better go! Toodleloo."

———

JAY JAY STARTED to ease up after taking a while to settle in. Mr Alfred's generosity no longer surprised him quite so much and he could tell when the old man was cracking wise. The way he kept his movements precise, in spite of the thing. He probably had a long word for that too, but Jay Jay understood him better now.

He slid onto the still-new seats in the truck and brushed his hand over everything. The steering wheel and the dashboard and the vinyl. He checked the mirror and said, "aww man! You're one lucky guy!" He stuck the key in the ignition and turned. He looked for something on the radio. The happy clappy song *Knock Three Times* was playing and he felt like he was on top of the heap. He knew the words too: *pipe* was a strange word to squeeze into a song lyric. What songs had the word pipe? He wondered.

He forgot about Dallas and the baby, and that was something. Feeling guilty for not wanting to think about them, he thought about them, but he still felt guilty too. He did not like to keep secrets from her and yet he was. If he could only erase that part of him which met Bones 1 and 2 on the day he started working at *Catherine*, he would be so far over the moon, he'd be orbiting a different planet altogether.

That comment about the Addams Family had not been so far off. Why had Mr Alfred assumed Jay Jay would not find the bones? The floor was false, wasn't it? Or maybe Mr Alfred had ignored or forgotten the incident as something that wasn't even considered important, to which he would simply have a reasonable response. Jay Jay gripped the smooth edges of the seat and ran through the possibilities. This was gonna be the bugbear that caused a breakdown in their relationship. The more Mr Alfred trusted and rewarded him the less he trusted him. He slammed his hands on the steering wheel. *Damn!* He whispered.

He remembered the plant list on the passenger seat. The address to which he was going to seemed familiar. Englewood neighborhood, south of the meatpacking district, Back of the Yards, near where Nesto lived. Not the greatest area, then. The Garden of Eden was a large garden and landscaping center run by Polish emigres. Mr Alfred had an account there for his projects. Jay Jay chuckled at the biblical name, though of course he hadn't done that in front of Mr Alfred. He had no idea just how religious he was but he did have some priest coming every now and then to pray with him, and for him too, most likely.

He parked in the parking lot and jumped out. With a satisfactory thump, he shut the door and was about to lock the truck.

"Well, look atcha."

The hell was that? A voice he knew. He swivelled around. "What are you doing here?"

"I should be asking you what you're doing here."

"Well, I'm working."

"Well, I'm working too, now. Big fancy wedding, honeymoon on the lake your grandpa said and now a shiny truck? Wanna show me your new toy?"

"No, Nesto. I am not playing. I am busy."

"So you are now too important to play with me? You weren't when we were kids?"

Jay Jay didn't like to be reminded. His poor grades were mostly Nesto's fault.

"You did not," said Jay Jay knowing that he was hired to be a draftsman and he did the test himself without Nesto's help at all.

"'S not *my* fault they shut down the plant," said Ernesto. "How may I help you today?" He put on a fake customer service smile and voice. Jay Jay looked toward the store entrance, dying to get away.

"Show me your list, c'mon. Whatchu got?"

"Thank you, I'm fine, really." He turned to walk away. But Nesto snatched the paper away like a gust of wind, ripping it and leaving one half. He held it up, jeering.

"Oh shit, Jay Jay, I am so sorry," he made as if to hand the ripped half back. "Here! Was an accident."

"What do you want?" Jay Jay tried to grab the scrap back. Nesto snatched the dangled paper away as Jay Jay reached out for it.

"Well, I am *not* working shit hours for shit pay here for nothing, ya hear?" He hissed. "You gonna get me outta here."

"What? How?"

"I want you to help me get back in the CPD. I just wanna be a cop again."

Jay Jay shook his head. "No. No. I am just a handyman there. I don't even know him."

"You will." He gave back the missing half of the list to Jay Jay.

Jay Jay snatched it. "And if I don't?"

"Don't make me do this, Jay Jay. If you don't, I will go there myself to see him."

"He won't meet you. He doesn't even know who you are."

"Oh he will. And now I will help you purchase your list of plants and save you time. You can go back to the old fella and impress him. You're never gonna find that list yourself. It'll take you a month. Come on."

It was like being back in school again. Nesto always got his way and made Jay Jay follow him around like a ghost. But this time Jay Jay would not let him block the way. He was doing great on his own. No way was Nesto gonna screw him up like he did to himself, getting busted. He clamped his jaw. He didn't want to believe that Nesto recognized all the Latin words on that list, yet he allowed himself to be led by him. Nesto found a gigantic motorized cart to drive them in the enormous cave of a warehouse. "You want palms? We gotcha," Nesto waved around him in a grand manner, like he was a lord. "Succulents?" He guffawed and leered. "Suck you, Lens!"

The dense rows of plants, shrubs and even trees made the warehouse into a mini Amazon forest, one where someone had brought along caged lamps. Jay Jay checked the mark on one of the lamps. It had been made in a North Lawndale factory only 2 blocks away. They'd shut it down, just before Vietnam.

"Are you sure you don't need me to help you unload? I can come with you. Jay? Jay Jay. Hey! How about a thanks? Okay. How about a no thanks, then? Well, nice knowing ya. Bye."

Jay Jay jumped into the van and started the ignition like he was on fire. He did not want to listen to Nesto's monologue. He reversed and drove fast despite the weight of trees. He couldn't wait to be out of there. The very idea of working with Nesto repelled him. He was lucky he had found the job himself, and through Dallas. No way was Nesto sharing his pie.

The only thing good about this garden party for Mr Alfred's nephew was that Nesto would not be there. He shuddered at the thought of being unpleasantly surprised at his own wedding by this souped-up drum kit in a suit. Having Nesto anywhere left a stain and now he felt soiled (yes, he laughed at his own joke) by the experience of running into him at the landscaping center, and having to accept any help from him at all.

He set to work as soon as he got in. He did not even pop in to say hello and tell Mr Alfred that he had picked up all the items on the list but two. He drove in using the rear access lane and parked outside his cabin that, in its days as the grand home's garage, had housed a pair of Studebaker President Phaetons, according to Mr Alfred. With pride he remembered how he had refused Nesto's offer of help to unload, although he had to do this by himself now, with ropes. Possible but hell, it might be a little slow.

In a few hours he had moved a couple of trees, using the truck's own engine power, ropes and his steering and driving skills. Once upon a time the job would have taken three horses.

Jay Jay and his truck managed it all by themselves. He felt like he'd been trampled by three horses when he finished.

When he got back into the cabin, he found a blueprint plan on one of the benches he made, all laid out, not folded or rolled. He stared at it. He checked that the boards, broken padlock, vinyl were intact and they were. No way was Mr Alfred strong enough to lift and roll the vinyl, remove floorboards and climb a ladder down.

Jay Jay had bought new boards to fix and replace the hatch but he had been waylaid by the landscaping work in the yard first.

"Jay Jay?" The frail voice of said old man.

"Yes?" Jay Jay called back. There was no time to do any checking now. He had to study the blueprint with Mr Alfred.

"Jay Jay?"

"Yes?" He repeated. "I'm in here."

"Oh good," the voice became louder and Mr Alfred appeared at the cabin door. "Did you find... Ah yes, you did."

"Did you leave it here for me?"

"Oh gosh, no. My nephew did. He's a landscape designer. He went to the store and made a blueprint this morning. I wanted to discuss it with you."

"He dropped the prints off in here?"

"Why, yes, he did. That he'd do something I say is a miracle," he laughed but not in a happy way. A bitter, angry laugh. "Since he's been a boy he's done the opposite. But he knows this is for the engagement party."

"Okay."

"Do you understand any of it?"

"I haven't looked. But I should if it has a key of what goes where," said Jay Jay.

"I know you'll ask me, won't you?" Mr Alfred hesitated, inquiringly but not in a condescending way. Mr Alfred was innocently asking, probably assuming that Jay Jay wouldn't be able to read the "for'n" words or understand the visuals.

I was a draftsman, he wanted to say. *Not only did I read plans,*

I drew them too. Look at my handwriting in my notebook if you don't believe me. But he stopped himself. That seemed rude. You didn't talk to an elderly man like that. That was not how Jay Jay had been brought up. Grandpops was from that world. You might be bottom in class but could still be top class.

Instead he said, "Yes, I will."

CHAPTER 10

Jay Jay dreaded all parties but he had to go with Dallas. All Mr Alfred's Art Institute connections, patrons, donors, lecturers, artists and curators would be attending. The Professor he'd been looking forward to and yet dreaded meeting was not around. Dallas said he had a conference abroad. "Iddilly or somewhere in Yerp." Old "Yerpeen" families would be present. Jay Jay resisted asking "you mean like vampires? Families who are over 200 years old?" He couldn't see Dallas finding it funny. He kept his skull cave shut.

More anxiety had already crept up as to what she'd be wearing. Dallas was saved by the girls at the counter. At least they helped her choose her outfit and use her staff discount card. No purple or black. "Those are the rules," she'd said to Jay Jay. After all she was now 6 months pregnant, and increasingly *did* resemble an eggplant.

They had better weather in June than at their wedding, thought Jay Jay. The plants and trees transformed Mr Alfred's grounds, from front to back. Jay Jay was immensely proud. He liked Mr Alfred's taste. Kinda old world Florida. Yuccas, hibiscus, plumeria. The fragrance from the potted jasmine filled his head the moment he walked in with Dallas. He'd fixed the gate, painted

it in black gloss so it looked brand new, re-tiled the path, planted
roses and repaired the doorbell. He'd even repainted the gold-
letter "Catherine" in the glass transom.

Mr Alfred loved roses. Pink and white. Climbing, rambling,
shrubs, all kinds. The entrance alone was like a miniature castle in
Spain. He'd also installed an alarm system. The best you could
buy. You never knew these days in Chicago. He'd put the system
in for his own peace of mind as much as for Mr Alfred's security.
At first the old man was reluctant, but he was persuaded. Times
were bad due to the war. Work was hard to come by. Some,
inevitably, turned to crime.

"I have my own protection." Said Mr Alfred.

He didn't question that. He knew Mr Alfred meant guns.

There were guns everywhere. In every room. On the walls, in
drawers, in cabinets. Mr Alfred slept with a pistol under his pillow
and a Bible on the night-stand with a little jug of water, a cup and
all his medication, he was supposed to take morning and night.
When all this partying was over, he was expecting to have to do
the yard work too. Somebody had to maintain it all and Jay Jay
was still clueless about plants. He'd need to read up in the library
near home. There'd be more work. And he didn't want Nesto
involved. He thought back to their conversation in the parking lot
at the Garden of Eden.

He recognized Mr Alfred's nephew, the blond man he'd taken
a dislike to at first. "I don't think you two have formally met yet,"
said Mr Alfred, "this is my brother's son, Carl."

"Hi, I'm Carl," he said. Even his name was way harsh. The way
he said his own name, with teeth gritted made a menacing growl,
like Krrl. "How do you do," The man spoke without moving his
lips, like the ventriloquists Jay Jay had enjoyed watching on TV as
a kid.

"Doing fine, thank you," said Jay Jay, a little stumped for any
slick reply. The unmoving mouth must have been infectious as he
found himself not moving his either. Suddenly he felt all shy,
awkward, like he didn't belong there. Carl looked straight at him,

the way he first remembered him doing: this time with a false smile which cracked open the fixed expression, like a fault in a Ming vase. "You've done a great job here. Good to see you have your own office. I left you the blueprint in there."

"Yeah, I found it. Thanks."

"Come on," said Mr Alfred, "you must meet my brother, Ralph." He sighed and took Jay Jay's arm. "Ralph, meet Jay Jay. He did all of this great landscaping work."

"Well," said Ralph. "I would love to have you make my place over. It's in the Bahamas. It's a dump. Could do with some help."

Jay Jay looked a little blank. He didn't make small talk. Where was the Bahamas? Jay Jay hadn't looked at the inside of an atlas since Grade School.

The man was a little older than Mr Alfred though not much. Jay Jay found it hard to tell the age of elderly people. They developed a cloak of invisibility, faded landscapes you walked past and ignored. Young people were like lurid portraits. He looked around at the guests. The old men and women started to blend into each other. The women had very short gray hair like the men, which was why the elderly women in the Arts wore huge and brightly-colored dresses and jewelry. To stand out, to be noticed at all.

Mr Ralph had a strange colonial accent, like he was from TV. Yet another white-haired man in a white Ralph Lauren linen shirt, like every other elderly white guy here. He talked to Jay Jay like Jay Jay understood what was going on. The 4Ps. Property, politics, people, the President. Names were dropped. A bit of trade, business, the government. Vietnam. All the things that Jay Jay tuned out from. Jay Jay even started listening hard to the band. Music what what he loved. He spent all day listening. No radio, no work. Though this wasn't music that he was interested in, he still listened to the changes and the beats. The string quartet was playing 30s violin music, sounding like something from the gypsy campfire scene in The Wolf Man.

Something was going on with Mr Ralph. Mr Alfred had hardly mentioned his brother to date. Mr Alfred had shaken his head from time to time when he handed over the plant list to Jay Jay, like he didn't like the idea of having an engagement party at all, maybe that had something to do with it. The argument which ended up with a torn up agreement was also a clue to there being some kind of "situation".

Déjà vu, like his wedding all over again. The string quartet was playing on the lawn under a pole tent. Jay Jay's cabin was being used as a storage facility for drinks and surplus outdoor furniture. He was kinda attached to the room he thought of as his and had to stop himself from "helping". He was so used to always moving this in and that out, lifting this and dropping that, seeing others do it felt strange.

He wondered if Carl was aware the floorboards had been up in the room. No indication that he was. He'd have to be more careful next time. Other people had entered his "office". He'd finish and secure the floor by next week, no excuses.

Jay Jay was wearing his wedding outfit without the coat. "Not buying yet another shirt I'll never wear again," he'd said to Dallas when she was trying on her new dress. He'd left the jacket back in the apartment. For one thing, the weather forecast had been for warm weather and secondly, it was a day-time event. Even without the suit coat he felt damp and sweaty.

Some familiar faces jumped out at him. Mr Chan was there, with a young woman, most likely his daughter. She had long straight hair, center-parted in the current fashion, a structured black and white mini dress and she had that international spy look, like Doris Day in Caprice. Whenever he noticed the dress first and then the woman, Dallas would say that just made the woman badly dressed. The thought made him laugh. Was she the girl cop? Hard to tell without the white sneakers or the Art Institute cloth bag. She was as smart as the rest of the guests. He wanted to talk to Mr Chan but had seen that Dallas, on her way back from getting a cold drink, had wandered over to talk to Mr Chan and the girl. He quickened his steps and followed Dallas.

"Mr Chan," he said.

Dallas said, "honey, so glad you're here. Mr Chan has more work for you!"

"Oh hi, Jerry. This is my niece," he patted the woman on the shoulder like a pet. She did not smile once. She had a nervous, anxious look about her. She kept her eyes fixed on the ground, as though hoping not to be noticed.

"I have two children." Chan said. "They're here somewhere. Twins." He looked around. "Oh. That's them." He pointed at a pair of Chinese boys about 12 years old. They were tall and sullen-looking.

"I do need you back at the restaurant," Mr Chan turned to Jay Jay. "I've just been so busy."

Mr Chan led Jay Jay to a quiet corner under the palms near the kitchen, away from the music and the guests, from where the waiters appeared with trays of food. Jay Jay glanced back at Dallas and the woman talking.

"Now, as you know by now, Mr Sutton recommends the restaurant to the CPD."

"No, I didn't know that."

"I am proud to say we've hosted a few dinners at the Jade Palace Garden for the force."

"Oh really," said Jay Jay. Where was this leading? To more work, he hoped. Being informed that Mr Alfred was well-connected to the Chicago Police Department made him nervous about Bones 1 and 2. Ohhh-kaaay...

"We are going to have several meetings and banquets in the next month and I will require you to fix anything that needs fixing. Have you seen the state of the wallpaper? That's first." He paused. "The only thing is, you will need to leave your job here 'til later."

"Oh!"

"Yes. Oh. You see, several other businesses need to use your services. The whole street. The Chinese supermarket."

Jay Jay did not answer. He was aware that he looked glum, his mustache turned down. "Mr Alfred is not filled with joy about this. I did talk to him. He is my good friend. I know he wants this place done, but..." he waved around him at the word *this*.

"So you're saying, just so I'm clear, Sir, you... "

"I'm just saying temporary to him. This will save us all face. And we'll see how it goes. I know you'll pull it off. You just have to do all of the restaurant's work in 2 weeks and you will be back here. You won't have a workshop of course, just the room in the kitchen basement which you saw last time."

Jay Jay did not answer. He didn't like the idea of not being allowed to do both. What Dallas wanted was for him to be making more money. Doing the restaurant job would mean more future work. If he stayed at Mr Alfred's there wouldn't be because an elderly man's time was limited and doing up the mansion *involved* only a certain number of tasks.

"Times are gonna get tough. You know, Vietnam. Think about it."

Jay Jay did. The steel works. As an apprentice, he got draft deferment. Tool-making was considered essential. He had been in line for more technical training. He bit his nails and looked at his shiny shoes. These stupid clothes. He would never need them again. He kicked a stone, which scuffed the gloss finish of the brogues. The crowd made him uncomfortable. All those creative-types: Dallas's world, Dallas's people.

Mr Chan took out his wallet and handed him $400. "For materials. I want new wallpaper, paneling to chair rail height, red carpet. The whole joint just like a Shanghai club. Remember the kung fu movies? Think high-class gangsters," he chuckled a little too hard.

Jay Jay looked at the money in his hand, before ramming it in his pants pocket, sorry the suit-coat was still at home.

"I must go now, and look for the boys." Chan said.

"Bye," said Jay Jay. He held the palm of his hand on his fore-head as if everything in his head might burst out of it. Ever since the discovery of Bones 1 and 2, he had become uneasy with Mr Alfred, though he never noticed. At least he didn't say so. Maybe he was too happy with Jay Jay's work to mention it. "Okay," he finally said, but Mr Chan had already gone.

He did not want Dallas to find out about the bones. Ever. She was just wandering over now. He'd never seen her in that pink dress before: it was the exact colour of the blooms on the hibiscus he'd planted. She just would not be thrilled to find out he was leaving just because she wanted him to *moonlight* at the restaurant. Now the moonlight was turning into daylight.

"I've never seen that dress before. Is it new?"

"Of course it is!"

"How much was it?"

"Never you mind. Anyway, there'll be more parties here. Mr Alfred's nephew said the Institute—"

"You never wear the same thing twice."

"Honey, you didn't expect me to wear my wedding dress again, did you?"

He didn't find it funny but he laughed anyway. She *would* say that because she didn't want him to find out how many hundreds her dress had actually cost. He did not even look at the shoes or jewelry. He didn't want to. Scratch that, he didn't dare. He did not let her finish. She was going to go on about the Arts events. She did have a point about being seen in the same outfit, but there would be no more parties for him. He really needed to start that new job. She'd be happy he would be doing "commercial work". He yanked his tie undone and put his hand on the back of his neck to ease the pressure. The heat was intense even under the shade of the palms.

"Put that back on, honey."

"Okay." He did, but he didn't pull it tight.

When they got home, he had a call from Mr Alfred. Uh-oh. That wasn't good. What if he screwed up both jobs? Mr Alfred's voice was friendly, like he was going to tell a joke.

"I hear you got your Chinese takeout for 2 weeks!"

"You heard?"

"Mr Chan tells me you're gonna be at the Jade Palace Garden.

That's fine. I have known him twenty years. Ever since he arrived here from Hong Kong. We have no more deadlines here. I'd love it if you would fix all the electrics when you come back. While the days are long."

"Okay, Sir."

Having two bosses was making him hot again. Irritable. Like two-timing a girlfriend. Okay at first, then later... complicated. "Wh-when I return," he assured Mr Alfred.

"Hey, Doll, I got to work at Mr Chan's. 2 weeks. Maybe longer."

"Why, that's great news, lemon pie."

He bit his lip. *No, maybe I won't be back at Mr Alfred's. Will that bother you?* She wanted the status. The "shatt-oh", the Institute, modern art, "Yerpeens", Mr Alfred's old-world connections. Sure, it was pretty low-rent to be working in a restaurant basement, but he was only doing it for more money. She couldn't have both. You couldn't buy class.

Happy that he had Mr Alfred's "blessing", he got to the restaurant first thing on Monday. He was playing with fire, working with no contract and all that. The cleaning lady let him into the dark and quiet space. He had brought softwood pieces, boards, white paint, and drop sheets in the white van. He wondered how long it would continue to smell new. He set up doing the first task that Mr Chan mentioned at the party. Putting up temporary partitions. Stripping the wallpaper, half the restaurant at a time so that diners might still use the other half.

By Thursday, there was still no sign of Mr Chan. He had been using the $400 left for him by Mr Chan. It was running out, fast. He also needed to discuss the new wallpaper. Mr Chan had spoken about paneling too, at chair rail level. "To make the look old world, like a salon or Shanghai-club style". Jay Jay could research in the right art and design books. Dallas was a member of the Institute's library. It always came back to "the Institute", like saying "the Universe". The answers were all there, to the plenty of questions in this world. Such as... what is paneling? And polished wood or painted, and if so what color paint?

At lunchtime he decided he'd better ring someone or do something. The only person to ask anything was the middle-aged cleaning lady who came every day. The one time he'd tried to talk to her was on Wednesday last.

"Hi, I just wondered... do you know... where Mr Chan is—"

"Sorry I no speak."

For the first time, he regretted that he could not speak his dad's language. After so many generations of hardship, his ancestors had made him an American. That had been their dream. He was so disconnected from his culture that China might as well have been on the moon. Jay Jay sprang up and, taking big strides, left the restaurant, ran next door to the Chinese medicine store and asked the cashier what to say.

He came back to the restaurant and asked in Cantonese whether she had seen Mr Chan and if she knew where he was.

At first, she shook her head. Then when it hit her what he was trying to say, she smiled, he saw that she had gold incisors. Her eyebrows lifted. He'd always had a good ear, at least for music. He remembered every song he ever heard: the lyrics and the melody. And language was just melody with words you didn't understand. He could sing *Sukiyaki* by Kyu Sakamoto. In Japanese. And he hadn't heard *that* since he was a kid in '63.

Now he did dread the reply. He would not understand a word. Being a parrot was not the same as speaking the same language. But she pointed to herself, and then to the telephone behind the bar.

"Yes!" Jay Jay thought. He'd made himself understood. Jay Jay worked all day until the diners arrived at 6pm so he'd never seen anyone else in the restaurant. Except Mr Chan, of course.

There was nothing else to say. He watched her make an animated call. He had no idea what it was about. The harsh, spitting sound of Cantonese made it seem like you were having a fight even when it was a normal polite conversation. He got on with his work and waited for her to "tell" him. He needed to buy the soft-wood for framing so the sooner he knew about the paneling the better. He didn't like to make stuff up off the cuff. And it wasn't just him. Didn't everyone just preferred firm plans in place before starting anything? He sighed and sat down on his stool to think.

She finished her call and just repeated the gestures. She pointed at herself, the telephone and made the thumbs-up sign with both fists. She nodded to him repeatedly. He echoed the thumbs-up sign back to her.

She pointed to herself. "阿姨." She said. "Ah-Yi."

Jay Jay repeated, "Ah-Yi."

She smiled her gold-toothed grin and did the double thumbs-up again. Okay. He understood that much. 阿姨 meant auntie in Cantonese. They were all Ah-Yis. Any older lady. Cleaning finished, she left.

Later that afternoon, Jay Jay sat down on his stool. He looked at all the stuff and materials and started to wonder what he could do without Mr Chan's input. He packed up, folding the drop sheets first. No. He would *not* come in tomorrow. It was the pits: working should feel like not working. Wasn't that Dallas's philosophy? He was not enjoying this gig. Thank God he hadn't burned his bridges with Mr Alfred completely. He might be back there soon, after all. He set off for the van with the stool and the drop sheets. As he propped the restaurant's glass door open with his bag of tools, he saw someone coming towards him in hurried little steps. She was waving.

It was the girl from the party.

CHAPTER 11

During a quiet moment at the counter on a late Thursday afternoon, Dallas studied the card which she had stuffed into her purse when it had fallen out of the pink Mary Quant dress before the weekend.

ENJOY THE PARTY.

was all it said.

"Oh hi, Sherylanne! I didn't see you there." She quickly slid the card back into her purse behind the counter.

"How was it?"

"Was what?"

"The party. I haven't seen you since then."

"Oh. Yes," she said, not knowing why she whispered. Thursday was late night shopping, and the cue for that was the tinkly music which had just begun from the grand piano in the entrance atrium. The pianist started playing, distracting them with *Shall We Dance?* from some Broadway show. The Piano Girl from Singapore, as she was known, was a talented 14-year-old whizz. The store had a big sign painted for her, displayed on an easel:

PLAYING TODAY! FEATURING LI-AN DONOHUE

Reading her mind, Sherylanne said in a dull voice. "Oh yeah, the Piano Girl."

"Michael's daughter, isn't she? Look at all the customers crowding around her." Dallas half-listened to all the Liberace flourishes the girl was doing with her fingers. Since Sherylanne was dating Michael, the girl's father, getting Li-an the gig was the least she could do, in Dallas's opinion. The girl just had to play for a few hours on a Saturday afternoon and on Thursday nights. Nice work if you could get it!

"Oh yeah. I'm so proud." Sherylanne's mouth was screwed up in a tight line, her eyes dead.

Maybe they shouldn't talk about the girl any more because Dallas detected a tiny, acid spray of jealousy in her friend. Okay, that was an understatement. She hadn't kept up to date with the latest Michael-and-Sherylanne news and really she didn't want to. She was just a colleague and not-quite-close friend. Dallas changed the subject. She cleared her throat as if beginning a speech. "The party was really great. The music. The food." She did enjoy herself for a short while even if Jay Jay had wanted to leave early.

"Aww. You looked amazing in that dress."

"I am glad I tried it on in front of you. I could not stand too long, especially in the heat. I was okay to go when Jay Jay said so."

"I am glad too. So who is he?"

"Who?"

"Come on now. The guy who gave you the dress and the earrings."

"I don't know. Just... Just a customer."

"I didn't do the cash register. Must have cost hundreds easy. You're soooo lucky."

She bit her lip and smiled. Anyway, they might not meet again. Tall, dark and handsome and a guy who got what he needed, not what he wanted. It was his wife who was lucky.

Just then a group of ladies spilled into the store, laughing and talking loudly. Dallas recognized most of them. They worked in the offices nearby and looked like they already were already one or two drinks down, and up for a big evening out: probably for a celebratory birthday for Jean from the typing pool or Joan's undeserved promotion. They swarmed around the cosmetics counter eager to play with some gorgeous new treats, so it was show-time for Dallas and Sherylanne.

———

THE FOLLOWING MONDAY, Dallas had just finished a team meeting in the staff room and was about to head to lunch. She went down four flights and back to the counter where she was being covered by Duane from Men's Toiletries. The hair on his upper lip wasn't quite a mustache and he wouldn't be getting a five o'clock shadow after a week without a razor. Yet he was selling French soaps and Italian aftershaves like he'd already traveled the world.

"Thanks, Duane."

"Cool," he said, making some hand gesture that even Dallas couldn't understand.

She picked up her bag, noticing the scuffs and frays from use. She sighed. Already it looked like a man's old boot. How did it get so lame after only two years?

She wiped the bag quickly with the soft cloth used for polishing the counters. When she looked up, the man had appeared. "Oh!" She exclaimed. "I... I...Why... I am just about to go on my lunch break."

"Mind if I join you?"

She looked down, unable to reply.

"Look. I just thought... I wanted to thank you for helping with—."

"No, no, you already did," she lowered her voice. "That dress, and the earrings—."

He ignored her. "A quick bite. No restaurant or anything. I know you don't have long."

She hesitated. She looked at him for any hidden meaning. "Okay," she said.

They crossed State St and sat down at a table in Buddy's sandwich bar.

"You enjoyed the party?" He asked when they had ordered.

"Oh yes! Very much so."

"Would you like a coffee or something else with your pastrami roll?"

"Yes, coffee would be perfect," she said.

"What about a little cake?"

"No, thank you," she patted her rounded belly. "This little one is helping me lose my waistline already."

He grinned.

Lunch with a stranger: was it wrong to feel so excited?

"I bet you looked a million dollars in your outfit."

"Oh," she laughed, not quite sure what to say for a moment. "Thank you." She patted her hair self-consciously. He had clean, neat, if hairy, hands and slightly wavy dark hair, swept back. A Romantic. With a capital R. His angular chin with a pointed goatee beard gave him a refined profile like the painter Eduardo Rosales Gallinas. He was wearing a gold wedding band on the left hand, matching his gold square spectacles. She felt safe with him. He couldn't have wanted anything to do with her. She was going to have a baby soon.

"I'm very interested in the art world."

"Oh yes?" Dallas sat up straight. She had known this was coming. Here was someone with the same interest. She didn't want to bring up his resemblance to a 19th century Spanish artist. Or for that matter the Orientalism movement that he represented. He had said he was very interested in art, though. The slightest thing and her butterfly mind was thinking about art history and artists. Getting pregnant hadn't extinguished her passion for art, though all she did now was sell cosmetics. Still, that was a kind of art too. Makeup art.

"You see, I am an artist too," he said. She'd met types like him, men who announced themselves as art geeks.

"You are? What... What do... Is it painting?"

"I'm an amateur. I paint at night, weekends."

"What style?"

"Industrial landscapes."

"Oh, neat."

"What about you?"

"Well, I—" Dallas took a sip of her coffee. "I am into drawing. Pencil, pen and ink, that kind of thing. Figurative. People, hands, feet, architecture, animals. Painting? Well, not yet. I have only modeled for painters at the Institute."

"You'd be a terrific model if I ever did portraits."

She blushed. Portraits, he'd said. More than one.

"Well, I am very impressed," he added. "Hands and feet are the toughest subjects for any artists. I would love to look at your drawings."

She did not answer. Her mind moved fast again. He couldn't have meant that. Small talk. She was intrigued, all the same. "Have you had any success? Are you selling your work or have you had a show?"

"No, not yet. That's why I am trying to establish connections. I don't have much time to paint. I have three children."

"My baby is due in September."

"Congratulations." He said this like he was saying *okay-fine-whatever*. It just came out flat as a sheet.

"Who are your influences?"

"Primarily, I'd say Richard Diebenkorn."

"Northern Californian, bright industrial landscape art."

"You've heard of him?"

"I have."

He sat back and his eyes lit up behind those square lenses.

"Who else?" she asked.

"David Hockney."

"British. Pool art collages." she said.

"Excellent. You know all the artists." he clapped once, like a toddler anticipating a cookie.

"Oh yes, I do! Let's see. There's Max Factor, Estée Lauder, Yves St Laurent..." she counted each one off on her fingers, her eyes rolling back in mock impatience.

He laughed. "Yes. And don't forget Chanel."

She pointed upwards as though thanking him for the reminder. "Well, I... I would love to look at your paintings," she said.

"I'll take some photographs. Or maybe one day I'll take you to my ah-telly-ayr."

Dallas paused. A woman's alarm bells usually rang when a stranger offered to take you somewhere and he was not a cab driver.

"Where is your studio?"

"It's... at home." He chuckled, running his fingers through his hair. His frown lines deepened giving him a determined look.

Dallas imagined "home" to be a space he was sharing with his wife and three kids constantly stepping on tubes of paint which then squirted like toothpaste everywhere. She smiled at the chaotic image.

He smiled too, misinterpreting hers. She didn't care to elaborate.

"Did your wife enjoy the gifts?"

"She had a wonderful birthday. The best. Thank you so much. I wanted to say, you got it perfectly right. Unbelievable. She thought *I'd* chosen them all."

Dallas cackled like a child, easy and loud. "What is your day job?"

He coughed. "I'm an attorney in... a law firm."

"You're a lawyer?"

He smiled. "I do my best. At least I *have* a day job!" He threw his hands in the air in that Latino way.

"So do I," she said but he probably didn't hear her.

"I don't have a card on me," he said. "It wasn't meant to be a business lunch, so I didn't–"

"Speaking of which," she said, "Time for me to get back."

Dallas picked up her frayed and scuffed navy handbag. She'd seen him notice, though he'd looked away. She tried to hide the sight of the gold-colored rings, embellishments which had long tarnished to a bronze.

"Let me get you a new bag," he said. "Maybe in red for the summer."

"Oh, no, no. Thank you. I'm fine."

"I insist," he said, then changing the subject. "Where was the party?"

"What? The engagement party? It was... actually I'm not sure." She racked her brain trying to remember but Jay Jay and her had had a spat in the car on the way there and then there were all those turns and shortcuts he'd made. "The North Side. Why?"

"Nevermind. I wanted to picture you in your outfit right there. I'm a landscape artist remember? Context, context, context."

"Right." She smiled blankly. *What context?* She thought, or rather, her sarcastic, pregnant brain thought.

"I am so glad we have so much in common," he said. "Hope to meet you again. I enjoyed lunch with you."

"I enjoyed it too. Only—" she hesitated.

"Yes?"

"If ya don't mind me askin', what's your name?"

CHAPTER 12

"The auntie called me," the girl said. She was panting, and appeared to have rushed there. She was in blues, carrying her cap with the checkered headband under her arm.

"Oh, yes, Ah-Yi." Said Jay Jay.

He wondered what had happened. Her long hair was put up but the bun had got disarranged somehow. She did not look as smart as she did at the party at all. She had no lipstick and appeared pale. She had an air of busy-ness about her, but then all Chinese people did, in his opinion.

"Thank you for coming. We met at Carl Sutton's engagement party."

"I know who you are." she said. "Listen, I've got some bad news. My uncle is missing."

"Oh." He couldn't think of anything to say. He looked at her straight. "What do you mean?"

"He has just not come home."

"But... But since when?"

"We saw you at the party on Saturday. His wife says that at around 11am on Sunday, he said he had to leave for a meeting and would be back very soon. She says it couldn't have been a formal meeting as he wasn't wearing a suit. She was making lunch at the time and distracted. She didn't think anything of it."

"He never came back?"

"No. We're all worried. It's been reported. And as I am a cop, I've got my hysterical aunt wanting an update every five minutes." She cupped her face with her palms and shook her head, looking down. "She's been opening and running the restaurant as usual. And by the way, this is a real aunt, my Ah-Yi, not an Ah-Yi aunt."

He nodded briskly, a little bemused at her explanation of the cultural trait. "So she's here at night? Tonight, too?"

"Yes."

"I need to talk to her. I'm supposed to be doing this job." He pointed to the restaurant. "And— well— I am not sure what I am doing next, if I'm still working or how will I and will I be paid, even."

"I understand," she spoke fast. "Why don't you give her a ring at home? I'll give you her number. You might still have to come in an hour or so and meet her. But better ring her first." The girl looked at her watch. She got a card out of her light blue uniform top pocket and a ball-point pen from a different pocket. She had no insignia so she was a junior officer. He had not realized that a uniform was a walking organizer — a compartment for everything, including a gun and probably lunch too.

She wrote down a number. "Go inside and use the telephone."

"Thank you."

"Do you need help with loading?" She asked as she looked at his materials. Seeing the van doors open, she volunteered without being asked. She put the folded drop sheets and the stool in.

"I'd lock the van up first though. Don't want tools to go missing too. Or that brand new van either." She dusted her hands off, as if to say bye. "I'll be in touch if we find out anything."

"Is there no information on Mr Chan at all?"

"We're working on tracing calls made to and from his office, home and restaurant the last week. Someone will be in touch."

He waved to her. She left in quick steps. He wondered if she'd parked nearby or walked to the restaurant, if this was her beat. He hadn't got to bring up the conversation that he'd overheard in the kitchen basement when all he saw had been her shoes and the Art Institute canvas tote bag. What had that been about?

He looked at the card, the number in bright blue ink. He turned the card over.

Emily Chan, written by hand.

On it was printed all the usual information, telephone number of the Chicago PD switchboard and the address of the 9th District Headquarters on South Halsted. No title and no rank. But he was just interested to have discovered her name. He found her easy to communicate with. No hello, no goodbye. No banter or small talk. She was direct and he liked that.

He stared at the card for a long time, before he remembered he had to ring Mrs Chan.

After locking up the van, he went back inside to make the call. It felt strange to stand behind the counter and the bar from the other side.

He dialed the number on the card. Mrs Chan picked up after one ring. She sounded dreadful: anxious, like she had been waiting for the telephone to ring all day. When it was not her husband's voice nor that of someone from the police, she sighed. Her voice was shaky and peppered with gaps. "I don't know what's happened. I keep going back to any conversations we had last week and I just don't understand. Nothing odd had happened at all."

"Really sorry to hear about all this." He swallowed. "But unfortunately I just started working on the restaurant." He said this in a small voice. He did not like bringing it up when she sounded desperate enough herself already.

"I'll be there in half an hour. I talk you through the design. I know what we doing. My husband and I, we have discussed— no, argued— about it for months." Her laugh was gritty.

"Thank you, I'll wait here." He looked at the clock over the bar.

He hung up. There was someone else he had to call.

"Hey, Doll," he said in a low voice, as if anyone was listening. He stared at the bunches of keys in his one free hand: his own, Mr Alfred's and the restaurant's. All these places that he was responsible for and yet somehow, was not.

"What's up? *Where* are you?" She demanded.

"I'm still at the restaurant. Mr Chan's gone missing. Now waiting for his Mrs to come. I need paying. I don't know what's happened to him or what's happening to the job."

"Oh no."

"I'll be back as soon as I can. Okay?"

"Okay. I'm just gonna eat here on my own then."

"Sorry. I have to wait for her to get here."

"Okay, okay. Bye."

"Bye."

She seemed a little pissed with him but then she would be. Nothing had been the same since he found Bones 1 and 2. That discovery had been an omen. He remembered the black and white adventure and mystery movies from his childhood. If you entered a mummy's tomb, you were cursed. How could you not be?

He held his temples with his fingers and massaged the pressure. He sat down on one of those velvety dining chairs where you'd wait for takeout.

A middle-aged Chinese woman came. She was dressed smart, in a silk shirt and black skirt. Heels. She was the owner and liked to look like it for the customers.

"Hi, you must be Jerry Jay Jay," she said. Her eyes were puffy and bloodshot through the multicolored frames of her huge designer glasses. Her skin was a greenish tinge. She must be under a lot of pressure — and makeup. Heavily and poorly applied, it was a mask that just sat on her face. Dallas would be able to transform her into a pretty tomato with her level of cosmetic expertise. After all, they didn't call makeup art an art for nothing. It was the art of transformation.

"I am, how do you do, ma'am."

She entered using her own keys even though he got up to use his. Was that rude in Chinese culture? He oughta consider getting up and appearing busy in the presence of a more senior person, a lady at that.

She took out of her purse a wad of cash. "Here's what you waiting for. I don't know what he give you or don't give you. Mr Sutton he say you keep running bills and tell us later what's what."

"Thank you. He has given me $400 for starters."

She sighed. "Okay, and what we owe you now?"

"Another $300."

She counted the cash. "Not enough," she said. "Only $200."

"That's okay. That'll do for now."

"No, no, no."

She said the three no's in the Chinese way. Jay Jay had heard this usage during countless Saturday afternoons at kung fu training. Yesses were said in the same way too. The first was no — or yes—, the second was to make sure and the third no or yes was for the rhythm only. Mr Chan and Ah-Yi did the same. "There's more in box." She pulled a chair to behind the bar, took off her heels right in front of him and stood on the chair to look for a tin box over all the whiskeys, a dark spot. Only those who knew where things were would find them. She must have trusted him, to look for the cash in front of him.

"Usually very little inside, a hundred at most." She said almost reading his mind. She opened the tin and removed all of the cash. She handed the bunch to him like flowers. "Count."

As she came down, as careful as her skirt forced her to be, she nearly lost her balance as she wasn't built for clambering. He finished counting. "You're right, $100."

"Good."

"Thank you for doing that. I appreciate="

He looked down. She had a strange tattoo on the back of her right heel, not visible when she was wearing shoes. He did not get a good look before she put on her heels.

It was not that he had never seen tattoos. He himself had a

Chinese white crane on his left arm. The crane represented a lasting, soaring spirit. It was considered the prince of all feathered creatures. White crane was a strong-footed kung fu stance with a flexible waist for quick movements, invented by a girl in Southern China about 300 years ago when she shooed away a crane interrupting her work. All the boys from kung fu school had some mythical or real animal tattoo. Dallas would have preferred him to have none, but he had got one anyway in the winter of '69, and since then she had never let him out unless he wore long sleeves.

Mrs Chan did not reply. Her mind was elsewhere. She sat down heavily on the chair to take the weight off her feet. The sight of her shoes made Jay Jay exhausted, as though he had been walking for hours. She sighed and remained staring outside the restaurant window, as if expecting Mr Chan any minute. She looked like she was going to burst into tears.

Mrs Chan grabbed a paper napkin from the bar counter and wiped her eyes.

"And now, the design. I know which wallpaper and what paneling we're doing. We seen this Shanghai club from the 1940s. I think will be very smart. Mr Chan— he— will be very—"

"Okay, we don't have to talk about that now."

"Look. It's in my car. I have written everything down. Wallpaper, paneling photos, carpet... and so on. You will have to just get it done."

"Sure, ma'am."

"Now I must get ready to open the restaurant. The chef is here." She pointed at the door. "He just walked past. You wanna meal? A takeout?"

"Oh no." He checked himself, "no, no, no."

"No, no, no? Oh, you must have meal. What about your wife? What she likes? How about shrimp wonton? I tell chef now," she squeezed past him and rushed to the front door. "Here," she said. "Have look at menu. I will go to car for the information."

So, his no-no-no hadn't worked. He took a quick look at the takeout handbill, alarmed that he didn't know Dallas quite as well as he thought. Did she like shrimp wontons? Or was it spring rolls?

All the while, he kept seeing an image of the heel tattoo, a bird with a long feathery tail.

Mrs Chan came back from her car and handed him the notebook that she and her husband had been using to note down design decisions, suppliers and even some diagrams. "I am now too busy and upset to do this. I'm just waiting for him to be found. I cannot do this. I just cannot."

He wanted to ask her if he could use the telephone to ring Dallas and check what she wanted but then he thought the better of it. Not when Mrs Chan was in this state.

Her panic came in waves. One minute she was okay and the next minute her voice was breaking with emotion. Her eyes were crazed and kept searching. She was repeating herself. "I don't know where he is, what's happened, I don't understand." The same thing over and over.

She inhaled sharply. Straightening her back, she crossed her legs at the ankle and addressed Jay Jay.

"Hope it helps. Please look through," she knocked on the notebook like it was wood. "Price what you're doing and write that all down." She looked sullen. Her fists were clenched and her jaw tense. Now she would have to act all cheerful and normal when the customers arrived.

When his takeout was ready, he was aware that it had already gotten late. He picked up the brown paper bag. He hoped Dallas would like what he'd picked out. She was difficult to please because she was a class act. To him, she was, anyhow. As he was driving, he was struck by the thought that an ordinary object which might seem fine to him, like a jacket, vase or even soap, could cause an emotional uproar. And he had no way of knowing which ones.

-*Can you not see that it's trash?*

-*No, honey, I honestly had no idea.*

That was how he feared the conversation might go, when he

got home with the Jade Palace Garden packages. As soon as he stepped inside he realized his fears were unfounded. She had eaten already. "Don't mind if I have a little treat from the takeout, though," she said. "I'm eating for two hundred," she said. "Did they find him?"

"No, they did not. He's been missing since the Sunday after the party."

"I was waiting for you to ring me."

"I did ring you."

"No. To ask me what I wanted from the restaurant. I knew you'd order something. You always think of food."

"I do?"

"You do."

He paused. "Thought I'd surprise you."

They ate in silence.

The telephone rang. He jumped up, leaving the table.

"We think we have found him," said the voice. "My aunt knows already."

He lowered his voice and put his hand over the receiver. "Who... Who is this?"

"Emily."

"How did you get my number?"

"It was not hard. You're working for my aunt."

She sounded serious. "A body has been found in the lake."

"No!" He whispered. "Is it him?"

"We think so. We will find out later when my aunt identifies the remains."

"Oh God... Okay... Look, I gotta go. Thank you." He hung up.

He looked over and Dallas was enjoying the last shrimp wonton dipped in the sweet sauce. She was either not listening or pretending not to. "Who was it?"

"It... It was the cops."

"Oh! They found him?"

"Oh yes. But it's not good." Stress chemicals could harm the baby. He remembered three of them were in the room at any time, now.

"Oh no. He's dead?"

"He is." He censored the other information. "They are looking into it."

"How?"

"I don't know how he died," he lied. No point giving that kind of bad news to a pregnant woman. He felt protective of the truth, the baby and of Dallas.

"Okay. I gotta look at what work I've got to do now."

"Mrs Chan has told you?"

"She did." He waved the notebook like a little flag. "I have to look through this book and study whatever design they've come up with."

The chair scraped as she stood up to clear away the takeout boxes.

He opened the notebook. The sketches were obviously not professional, but the ideas were interesting. They wanted to open the rear of the building up and make a 1930s Chinese courtyard with a moon gate and a fountain. They wanted pretty feature glass double doors, with woodwork painted and decorated in traditional pre-war style. Diners could enjoy the outside space in good weather. At least, he would be doing a little yard work and not just interiors.

He started to write down a few prices; to "prepare his esti-mate". First the interiors and electrics, then the exterior work: making an opening through the external wall. He made a note of the tools he'd have to hire for that day and the costs involved.

One underlined note said that "Bamboo for planned groves" had been ordered from an address in Englewood. He gripped his ballpoint pen hard and made a dent in the paper. The Garden of friggin' Eden.

CHAPTER 13

H e smiled the Mona Lisa smile again. She glanced up at him. She hadn't been expecting him back so soon. But here he was.

Carl Rodriguez, he'd introduced himself when they parted ways. The name meant nothing. Not in the art world and certainly not in the department store.

"Now, how may I help you today, Sir? I'm afraid we're closing in 5 minutes."

"Yes, I apologize. Thank you, Dallas. I wanted to bring you my drawings to have a look at. My mini oeuvre," he did the universal sign for inverted commas with wiggling index and third fingers. "I'd love some critique."

It was the first time he'd said her name. *Doll-us. Urv-uh. Cr-teek.*

"But I am working now, Sir." Surely he didn't think of Dallas as some kind of guru in the local art scene? He aspired towards having an agent, a gallery show, a talk at the Institute. Something. She wanted to tell him it was impossible. Firstly, he had no art degree. Secondly, neither had she. Thirdly, even if the Professor could be of use to him, he had already helped Jay Jay find work at Mr Alfred's "shatt-oh". She had guessed he wanted something from her a week ago. Anyway, she hardly knew the guy and he'd bought her gifts. He might have thought she was just some dumb broad peddling beauty products.

"I... I'm hoping you'll meet me outside for a few minutes after the store closes." She glanced at the clock over the entrance. "Okay," she sighed. He went outside. She busied herself with spraying and wiping down each glass shelf, the counters, the products and anywhere customers may have touched and left germs and fingerprints. The whole display area must look as sparkling before she left as when the store opened again in the morning.

She checked out at the cash register to record the day's takings. A good day like this meant good commission and good mood. She removed the tray and went to the treasurer's office to clock out. When everything was done, she went to the ladies' staff bathroom to freshen up and to wash her hands. She had always been fastidious before getting pregnant. Sure, he or she'd be covered in mud by age two from playing outside — there was no use in keeping toddlers too clean — but he or she was still living inside her.

She patted her helmet hair. She'd had it cut like Jane Fonda's cute pageboy style. Maybe she'd grow it longer again for the winter; with Stevie Nicks layers, frosted and sprayed. She reapplied her lipstick onto her puffy lips and looked at herself in the staff-room full length mirror for a long time. Was she really pregnant? Her face was still the same, yet she looked like she'd swallowed a cannonball.

He was outside, pacing and taking tokes from his cigarette. The evening was still light.

He cleared this throat. "Do you mind sitting down somewhere with me for a few minutes?"

Jay Jay would probably be late home like he was every night when he was working at the restaurant.

"Well, I am quite tired." She rested her hand on her rounded belly.

He didn't look down at her belly, maybe he hadn't heard. "Would you like a soda? Somewhere quiet to sit down?"

Jay Jay was a regular working guy. You couldn't hold a conversation with him outside "jeet yet? What jeet?"

"What about your kids?" She said.

"Why, my wife is with them." Instinctively, he looked at his left wrist. "They're probably watching TV." She noticed that despite the cheap suit and aftershave, he had a Cartier tank watch on a thin leather strap, the one John F Kennedy was wearing when he was assassinated in Dallas (hah!) nearly a decade ago. They were both enigmas. The President *and* Carl Rodriguez.

As they walked north on State Street, looking at the brightly-colored window displays, well-designed furniture and the latest kitchen appliances, busy people, Dallas knew money and excitement went together, and kept the Windy City going. She'd miss this place when she had her baby. *State Street, the Great Street*, as Sinatra sang in *Chicago*. It was her kind of town too. They turned left.

They sat down in a tiny bar called Portofino on W. Calhoun Street, an ice cream parlor with all kinds of Italian desserts, coffees, sodas. Dallas chose an iced coffee, decorated with strawberries and whipped cream. Elvis Presley was singing *Kentucky Rain* on the jukebox. She couldn't hop on a bar stool to sit at the counter. Instead they found the armchair area where he opened his briefcase and took out a large hardback ring-bound black sketchbook. They looked at his modern art drawings which were less colorful geometric doodles and more Venn diagrams with triangles. Art is not what you see, but what you make others see, Degas had said, and charts and diagrams were what she saw. They were perfectly okay but Dallas was not an art teacher or critic. All she knew was that they were in that 1950s idiom but she wasn't really taking them in. She yawned without stifling. "Yes," she announced. "Very Auguste Herbin. I'm not even sure how to say that name."

"That is *such* a compliment. Thank you. You are very knowl-
edgeable. It's Orgaste Air Bun."

"Okay. Great. Thank you."

"No. I should thank *you*."

She felt wrong calling him Carl. It was nothing personal, but
there was a distance between them that seemed to open and close
like a flower. He was from another world and generation. Too
much to explain to him. She didn't know him. She had been
horribly rude to start yawning rather than gushing over his work,
but she genuinely had had enough. She had been on her feet all
day. She'd like to see him in his white-shoe attorney job standing
for 8 hours a day.

She didn't tell him that she had just started a foundation
course in fine arts when she was waylaid by Jay Jay's job loss, her
pregnancy, their wedding and soon, childbirth, parenthood and
family. She thought back to Carl Rodriguez telling her about his
paintings of Californian industrial abstract landscapes. Pond and
farming equipment. It was as far away from her life as you could
get. He might as well as tell her he was going to the moon.

She already resented having to quit art and work full-time
because Jay Jay was unemployed. Trapped in her cage, she was
now being told this successful father of three was painting what
he loved. Men with money did exactly as they wanted before,
during and after children. Too late for her. What was ahead for
her now? Boredom. Lack of money. Lack of motivation. Life was
inconvenienced by art. Art was inconvenienced by life. Ask any
artist. You want art? Stop living. She tried to bite back her words
before they came out. Her tiredness was talking.

"I still work in art. Kinda. I am a weekend student administrative officer. You could try doing a course." She added, trying to
sound less rude.

He shook his head. "No, I seriously don't have time." He
pointed at a few trapezoids and ellipses. "Do you like this kind of
thing?"

"What, Cubism? Yeah. I s'pose. Look I really gotta go."

"Is it something you usually like?"

"No," a little alarmed but gripped that someone was actually interested in her once artistic passions, now buried, but maybe not six feet under. A little something in her had died when she had to quit the course. "I am an enthusiast, a novice. I like a lot of artists but— I was— I'm just not that into abstract art. I know that's what you do. Sawrrry."

"That's okay. Go on, what's your thing?"

"If I had a style I'm working towards, it would be— I just prefer figurative art. Matisse, Bacon, Freud. People. To me, people is purpose."

"I really enjoy these chats with you, Doll-lass. I can't with my wife. She— she absolutely hates art. And jazz."

Dallas stared glumly at her empty fluted glass. She picked up the straw and stabbed at the leftover crushed ice. The music had changed to John and Yoko's *Power to the People*. Hard to believe The Beatles had only broken up a few months before.

"How will you get home? Shall I give you ride?"

"No, thank you, Sir."

"Carl."

"Carl. Thank you, but I'll take the red line at Monroe."

"Where do you need to go?"

"Armitage. Only a few stops."

"Yeah. Straight up," he pointed to the ceiling to indicate north. "Hope you can show me your paintings too."

"Right," she said, looking out of the cute glass windows. She started fidgeting and twisting her wedding ring.

"I have a little something for you."

"No, no. You've given me plenty. Please don't."

"No, I insist. I'd be offended if you say no."

"Well, I don't—" she looked away. The place was too small to have much to look at. So she looked at him.

"You'll love it." He reached into his briefcase.

CHAPTER 14

"Wait, Jay, c'mon."

"The hell you doing here?"

"I work here, dja forget? Why doncha wanna talk to me?"

"Because I can't help you."

"You don't know that."

"I don't have time to talk now." Jay Jay was next to his van in the parking lot of the Garden of Eden. "I am not working at Mr Alfred's now. I'm shopping for bamboo and some building materials today."

"I can help you with that. Where's your list? You just relax and I'll bring everything out to you."

"No, thank you." He locked the van and walked fast to the entrance.

"Oh good, then wouldn't you like to hear some inner-estin' news I got for ya?"

"Wut?" He turned his head without looking at Ernesto.

"Well. Let's getcha bamboo first. Your list, Sir." He gave his 'professional' smile. "How may I help you today?"

Jay Jay hesitated, gritted his teeth and handed the list over. He didn't want Ernesto in trouble in this job. Times were tough everywhere, and would be getting tougher. Vietnam was not going away anytime soon. Ernesto held his stubby fingers out without taking his eyes off Jay Jay for a second. "Meet me outside the palmhouse after I'm done."

Jay Jay had a cup of Java at the stand outside the parking lot of the Garden of Eden thinking, for the first time, this job was neat. Pretty easy. Plenty of breaks. He was lucky. Many didn't even have work. People said it was the Nixon shock. Supposed to save the American manufacturing industry. But look what happened. He crushed and launched his cup into the trash before he went back to meet Ernesto.

"Okay. You know and you say you know."

Ernesto's Spanglish was meaningless. "Get on with it," said Jay Jay.

"But you know nothing. See this?" He held a pearl earring.

"So? What the hell? 'S not mine."

Ernesto rocked his head back and laughed. "Naw, it don't suit ya. This little beauty was found on the night of 29th August, 1925."

"What the fuck, Nesto. What is the point of this? Don't play games. I don't do games."

"Just wait. It was found in the grounds of Mr Alfred Sutton's property."

"By who?"

"By a little girl."

Jay Jay thought: *Who cares? Why is he telling me this?*

"The girl was the daughter of a servant. The owners were using that exact cabin that is your office now as a wine and gun store. Now. I wonder what is in that room." He nodded, then, tilted his chin to prompt Jay Jay.

Suddenly, Jay Jay felt his hair stand on end. This was about Bones 1 and 2. Had to be. No one else knew, or so he'd thought until now. He kept his cool and listened hard.

"One night, the girl saw a body being dragged from the house to the cabin. The next day, she found this. Just one. In the front yard. There was a dog, barking hard, following them. Then boom. No more barking."

Jay Jay didn't answer. He could only imagine that the dog was Bones 2.

"If you got nothing to say, don't say. But Mr Alfred will know what's happened. He can get me back into the CPD. You can set me up a meeting."

"But... but you have no proof of any of this. How do I know you didn't just find that earring? I mean, whose is it even? We don't know if any of this is true."

"Do you want me to prove it? You want me to come in the cabin? Or do you want to look in the cabin yourself?"

"No, no and no."

"Why? Because it's true. The body went in and never came out again. The barking dog? Same. Went in. Never came out."

"But— who— who was doing the dragging?"

"Yer asking the right things. 'S taken a long time to sink in but yer now in the mode."

Damn.

"I give you your list back, Mr Big Shot Handyman Sir Jerome. Yer gonna tell Mr Alfred somebody here tryna meet him."

"No," he covered his ears. "This is wrong. You're trying to blackmail him? What will you do if he won't and can't help you re-enter the force?"

"I am gonna open the investigation. You been working all this time and you been keeping quiet. Also, you would not let me help ya unload the plants that day— before the party— which means you knew all along, buddy."

Jay Jay shook his head. "This is crazy. But right now I ain't working at that house."

"Bullshit. You are thick with him. You know what I am talking about. He paid for your wedding."

"Who told you that?"

"Never mind who. I am family, ain't I?"

Grandpops, thought Jay Jay. Grandpops always had a soft

spot for Ernesto, and God knew why. He was like the United Nations. He worked at 'encouraging' and fostering better family relations.

"Ernesto."

"Sì."

"You know this is nuts, right? From one earring and a little girl's words? Who is the body even?"

"Now, not so quick. I know it, who it is and you know good that I know it."

"No, I don't." The Spanglish was pretty confusing again and Jay Jay didn't want to waste any more time.

"I must go now."

"Not yet. You have to pay first. Come inside and I will take you to the cashier. You are really helping me with sales commission and don't ask me 'what commission', that is how your pretty wife makes a living too. Gratuities. And you're gonna help me get out of here and I can say adios to this shit job."

Jay Jay marched inside the Garden of Eden's cavernous warehouse. He didn't want to listen to Ernesto's nonsense any more. Ernesto had a mesmeric way of being straight without telling it straight, driving Jay Jay nuts. His mind became the ball in a pinball machine.

"No, I still do not know if any of this is true."

"Is true. You know that it is. Sì."

"No."

"Yes."

Jay Jay was trying to drive off.

"I will go and drop in on Mr Alfred, myself while you are working in the restaurant. Oh yes, I will be eating your chow mein while you eat yours. You ain't gonna forget that!"

"I am not going to do anything. I am not going to talk the talk with Mr Alfred."

"Now who is playing games? Come now, Jerome Lee. Don't be shy. I told you one million times and we goin' round in circles, buddy—"

"I am *not* your buddy."

"No. Worse. You are family. I want you to tell Mr Alfred the truth. His step-nephew needs help to become a cop again. And if he says why? You say to him, a pearl earring was found in August 1925 on his property. It's not just any pearl earring from the market. He will know what that means. You just say that."

"What? This is insane. I am not involved in your crazy mind-fuck schemes. What happened when I last believed you?"

"A good thing happened. You got that job at the steel works. Without me you weren't getting in."

"But I lost it."

"Ain't my fault." He threw his hands in the air and shook his head. "You ain't seeing things are tough around here these days?"

"And if I do nothing?"

"If you do nothing, then I will go myself."

"Yes, you do that."

"You really want me to bring up the cabin? The dog?"

Jay Jay started the engine. He changed from drive to reverse.

"The dog," Ernesto shouted as Jay Jay put it into forward. "A Pekingese. I've given you far too much information, Jerome Lee. How could I bullshit this much detail?"

Jay Jay drove as fast as he could laden with plants, pond liner and bags of cement. Back to the Chinese restaurant. The radio automatically came on and started blaring Three Dog Night.

He felt himself gripping the steering wheel tight. At the lights, he slammed his hands on the wheel and shouted, *Damn!*

———

IN THE EVENING, he left without a takeout. Well, not a full one. Just a couple of char siu buns. That'd do. He was getting too used to Chinese takeout and that was not a good thing. Dallas was hungry. She ate both.

"Hey, that was meant to be for breakfast," he said.

"They eat these for breakfast?" She replied.

"They do!" He had lost his appetite. "It's called dim sum." He was confused. He sighed. He ran his fingers through his sweaty hair and rubbed his mustache roughly. He decided to have a shower instead, since there was no food left. He'd been digging the pond all day. This yard design had to be a showpiece. This was a last attempt at reviving the business now that Mr Chan had been found in the lake tied to a fridge. A fridge, ferchrissake!

He shuddered in the shower even though the water was hot. Homicide. The word roared at him like a huge lion yawn. A lot was going on, with no way of escape. He didn't want to be involved. The police already had come to the restaurant earlier that day and looked at the design notebook left with Jay Jay by Mrs Chan. They declared it worthless after finding no clues about who Mr Chan was meeting or what he was doing right up to the day he went missing.

"Any news about Mr— "

"No," he said.

"Come here, honey." She patted the bed with its garish pink and black sheets she said was the pop art style that was so hot in NYC, if not yet in Chi-Town.

"In a minute."

He took his towel off and got changed.

"Is it because I'm pregnant? Are you okay?"

"I'm okay. This... Job... Is... So... Hard," he whispered. He hoped she didn't ask why.

"Ohhh!" She gasped. Surely he hadn't surprised her that much?

He blew out a sigh as he lay down with the notebook again. He just could not explain to her. He was not articulate. He did not read. He did not talk art. He had no interests but martial arts and songs on the radio. His job was jerking him around like a fairground ride.

———

WHEN HE WOKE UP, he was sticky with sweat. He wondered if he should warn Mr Alfred. He had already finished 2 weeks' work at the restaurant. The yard work after Mr Chan disappeared was extra. A chill slithered down his back. The hairs on his arm were standing up, making his crane tattoo look trippy. The CPD were investigating Mr Chan. Surely that had nothing to do with Ernesto's garbage about the single earring? The police had appealed for witnesses. He hoped Ernesto didn't volunteer just to "bring up the Bones" and the pearl earring. Did Ernesto even watch the news?

Mrs Chan was very keen to keep going as normal. She would *have* to shut for a day or two for the funeral. Bad luck to 'dwell' on death, she said. Maaan, as if anybody wanted to. Mr C was going to have a Taoist funeral, whatever that meant. His ancestors would have been Taoist too, he supposed. Unlike an American funeral, there was no feasting, meal or celebration after the event, according to Mrs Chan. The funeral was the other way round in Chinese families. The wake had already taken place in the family home over a period of up to seven days. Visiting mourners brought white flowers or floral wreaths with banners featuring couplets commemorating the person who had died. White mourning East, black mourning West, and never the twain shall meet.

At the restaurant, he was getting ready to fit the pond liner. Mrs Chan had a ledger and an abacus out at one of the tables. Work was the only thing keeping them both going, from thinking of the tragedy. Jay Jay thought of the two boys and shed a tear too.

"Mr Chan was very fond of you," Mrs Chan said. "He would want you at the funeral."

"Me?" Jay Jay thought. Mr Chan could not want anything. He was dead. Maybe Mrs Chan saw Jay Jay as part of the Jade Garden Palace team.

"Yes. Yes. Of course." He wiped his tears, darkening the back of his mustard-colored corduroy sleeve. Long sleeves kept the sun at bay and Dallas off his back. How sudden. Life and death so close and quick. It had happened with Papa Moriarty, Grandpops' partner in the pond-farming business. Since then no one had wanted to touch a wafflewich, as though there was a direct link to cardiac failure.

A large wreath of flowers arrived. Jay Jay took the delivery. The card said "With Deepest Sympathy from Alfred Sutton". Another two weeks here and he'd be done. He needed to lay the paving and then he would be back at Mr Alfred's.

He was loading the van later that evening, his takeout in a bag already.

"Hey," he said to the visitor he'd just spotted. "What're you doing here?"

"I came to talk to you. You got a nice takeout dinner waiting for you, I see. What? Chow mein? Yum. Is my favorite."

"I can't talk. I am packing up." Jay Jay would not look at him. "Ernesto, please," he said, edging him out of the way while he carried the cement buckets and loaded them into the van.

"Can I help you at all?"

"No."

"Jay Jay, you talked to Mr Alfred yet?"

"No. I haven't even been back. I am here for 2 more weeks. You know that."

"Hey," he said peering into the glass doors at the flowers. "Seen the front page of the Chicago Daily."

"This has nothing to do with me, Nesto. Why you are telling me any of this?"

"Because you and I know something happened in that cabin in 1925. And you want to keep your job, don't you?"

"But I don't friggin' care what happened. It was 1925 for godssake."

"You will care when I talk to Mr Alfred myself. Somebody and a dog went into the cabin and never came out. A little girl found an earring. And a notebook."

"What's all that to you?"

Ernesto pulled the earring out of his pocket, dangled it in

front of Jay Jay. He flashed a small notebook, waving it like a fan. Its blue Chinese brocade fabric cover was faded and torn. "From this notebook, I know who that "somebody" is. Was."

"Who was it, then?"

"Please. Jay Jay. I was good cop. I actually *did* protect some very poor communities. They still talk to me, okay? So I took money, but that was gang pressure. Big deal." He shrugged. "You gotta help me. I was a youth officer. Once."

Jay Jay ignored him. "Just where and how did you find the notebook and the earring?"

Ernesto sighed. This'd better be good, thought Jay Jay.

"A Miss Morales was a servant in the house," said Ernesto. "She lived in a tiny room, now Mr Alfred's room."

Jay Jay reflected upon this. Could be true. Mr Alfred *had* moved to the top floor, where the mould grew on the pizza cartons not on the walls.

Ernesto continued. "In the old days the servants lived in the top floor, so that they could come quickly when the masters rang the bell. Those attic rooms were small and slopin' ceilings weren't no help. Musta been a tight squeeze for Morales and her daughter."

Jay Jay thought about the servant and Mr Alfred. Why had he let his house get so run down? Money? That was usually the reason why these mansions had to be demolished. The family somehow got into financial trouble and the only remedy was to sell the ruined mansion for the land. Ernesto paused to make sure Jay Jay was listening.

"That little girl was my mother."

CHAPTER 15

Dallas opened her closet. She took out and caressed the red pigskin Coach Madison, its tubular handles smooth as metal pipes. She studied the stitching and the lining. Coach was the top American brand of the year. Her eyes had widened in disbelief. Why was he doing this? She was married and looked like a watermelon in a dress. A tussle ensued when she tried to refuse such a generous gift but he'd just laughed it off.

She put the bag down like it was a resting polecat. As she stared at it in amazement, she was thinking of him, unsure whether she wanted to meet him again. At the bottom of all the shoes and bags were the *real* prized possessions. No handbag, no shoes, no perfume compared with them; her sketchbooks.

She had a delicate style. Tiny little pieces of perfection. She studied her verbena sketches. A spray of tiny flowers on long thin spokes which looked like a jail-cell grille. She found drawings of seashells, conches, every dot and speckle applied precisely and in the right place.

She looked at paintings of her own hands and feet, unusual in that she painted them from her own eye angle. Even the nails had that unmistakable red mirror shine finish. They were like little automobiles. Each one fierce and glossy, vying for attention.

She had got married and pregnant since she left art school. Were they done in her last two years of art school?

Now who was he really? She kept thinking that he should be better known than he was. That magnificent Spanish profile, the tan, the art. Here was a cultured man buying her gifts and showing her his abstract art.

Ideally, they would have met on an art course. Unfortunately that wouldn't, couldn't happen for her, as she was having a baby in the fall. If he would have been trained at the Institute, he would have gotten a show and later wall space in one of the smaller, edgier galleries on the North Side, no question. Dallas yawned. The man had given her a sharp look. Surely he was experienced enough, a man with three kids, to know a pregnant woman yawned continuously at the end of every hard day. There was no gas left in her tank. She couldn't wait to get home. She didn't have his telephone number and didn't know if she'd even see him again. The conversation died right there at the table, so they left the Portofino and he walked her to Monroe. He carried her new handbag, re-wrapped, until she said goodbye at the El.

Now she was hiding stuff from Jay Jay. The handbag was the least of it. There was the dress, the earrings and even meeting Carl at all. Though, of course, nothing had 'happened'. He was just a fellow aspiring artist.

———

IN THE APARTMENT, she placed the bag and then her hardback sketchbooks back in the closet. She kept one out, just to look at for a while. He had given her the inspiration to return to art. Some day. After the baby was not a baby any more. She groaned as he or she kicked and turned.

Without any warning, the heavens opened and tears fell at that glimpse of the future. Many years, perhaps even 10, would go by before she would pick up a paintbrush again. She wiped the tears off the cover of the sketchbook alerted by the alarming "plops" as they'd dropped onto it. Was this the pregnancy hormones doing their thing? Already she was having disturbing and vivid dreams. She found a folded towel at the foot of the mountain of bedding she had been on the point of putting away since she got home. This would be an hourly task soon, with diaper washing –

A ringing sound. She realized the telephone had been ringing for a while. What was wrong with her?

"Doll? What're you doing? I've been calling."

"I... I was in the bathroom. Sorry, I didn't—."

"I'm about to leave. Just ordering some chow. Want anything?"

"Naw. I'm good."

She hung up and went back to folding laundry. She dried her tears with the corners of the towel again. She put her hands on her temples. Nobody was perfect. You couldn't have a man who was handy and a man who was candy. A man couldn't be both cultured and refined and still knew how to fix shit, every woman knew that.

Jay Jay got home at last. The whole place stank of grease and sweat as soon as he walked in. He had been in the restaurant kitchen again. She felt nauseous. At first she had enjoyed eating takeout every day but now she could not stomach it. She was kinda glad he'd stop working at the restaurant soon.

"Hon? Jellybeans?"

"Hey. Look. Food." He held up the bags and growled a little at the word "food". He looked wrecked. He *was* working long hours. A hard life now. They hadn't had dinner together for a long time. He ordered takeout that they ate at home. He treated food as a form of payment too. That way she wouldn't stop him from getting his 'party favors'.

"I'm not hungry. I made a sandwich soon as I got in. From yesterday's chicken."

The telephone started ringing. He went to the bright red phone.

"Oh, I got it already," he said, then adding, "thanks." He hung up.

"Who was that?"

"The restaurant," he threw his hands in the air. "About the order. Didn't I just leave with the food?"

"Strange," said Dallas, a little hesitantly. "You goin' to the funeral tomorrow night?"

"Yeah. It's at... wait—" he said. Dallas watched him rummaging in one pocket, and then the other and then his shirt pocket, unable to find the address.

"Never mind," she said, "'S'prob'bly in your tool bag or notebook."

"Somewhere near Cicero anyway," he said, but he still seemed to be thinking about something else.

"Okay, enjoy your takeout. Looks like you need it," she said. "I'm getting a shower now, before you use all the hot water."

"Yeah," he agreed.

She left him and went back into the bedroom to get her towel, thinking about the call from the restaurant.

CHAPTER 16

The blue Camaro was now a rare pleasure. Jay Jay was more likely to be in the van during the week and sometimes weekends, too. It felt great to be back behind the wheel. She was a sporty little number. He'd missed her. He touched the dust on the wooden dashboard which used to be glossy and smart. Embarrassed, he found a cloth from the glove compartment to wipe it down. He didn't want anybody to see it like that.

He felt the warm breeze of a summer evening hit him, a tiny bit relieved that Dallas wasn't with him. She hadn't been invited. "Pregnant woman, unlucky, to attend funeral", Mrs Chan had said the day before. Not a joyous occasion.

The funeral was in a medium-sized hall on N. Cicero Avenue next to Xtreme Auto Body Repairs. Mr Chan seemed to be pally with a lot of business people. Jay Jay had hoped to be offered more work from his connections and recommendations, but who knew now? He'd have to depend on Mrs Chan. He blew out a sigh.

The Thursday night sky was clear.

He had left the restaurant for home an hour earlier than usual to have time to shower and change. He was wearing his wedding shirt, the one he thought he'd never need again. All the while, he dreaded seeing Ernesto. Naturally he'd done nothing with Ernesto's request and time was ticking on. Fact was, Ernesto turning up at the parking lot shared by the funeral services center with Xtreme Auto Body Repairs was highly unlikely. A cop car pulled up. At first he was worried: there had been no siren, but the blue lights had been flashing. He hoped no one got out with a bullhorn.

The door opened. Legs in navy pants climbed out, legs he'd first seen in the restaurant basement when he was eavesdropping a conversation.

"Hi," he said. "I just parked up too. How are you feeling?" He was embarrassed as he was always thinking of food and just then his belly rumbled like a drum roll, which he hoped she hadn't heard.

She shook her head, unable to look at him. She looked like she had been crying. Her skin color was not great. At the same time, she was in uniform and, since she had to look professional, her long hair was in a tight granny-bun.

"The inquest has come through," said Emily, sighing, by way of a greeting.

Jay Jay waited. Didn't seem right to go in before family. More cars pulled up and they watched the family and friends of Mr Chan arrive. Mrs Chan got out of a gold Impala. Mr Chan's shiny Chevrolet seemed wrong in this context. However, he did love it very much. At the sight of the two boys, Jay Jay's eyes filled with tears. Prior to this, Mr Chan's demise was just an awful event, something that happened to people, but seeing the boys made him think. He might make some kinda dad, after all.

"Look, I can't talk now," Emily pointed at the building. "We have to go inside."

———

AFTER THE SERVICE, and some milling around, hugs and tears were exchanged in the parking lot.

"Wanna grab a bite?" He asked Emily, on the off-chance that she'd say yes. After all, the wake had gone on for a week already and there was no more feasting after a funeral. It was really, really the final goodbye to the deceased.

"Are you okay?" He said, seeing that she was not.

"No." She said. "Yes... I mean no. I am *not* okay and yes, let's grab a bite. You must be sick of Chinese food by now."

"Well, I wouldn't say sick."

She stared at the tarmac.

"How about pizza?" He offered.

"Was all my fault. This happened because I didn't do anything."

"About what?"

She didn't reply.

"Let's go. I'll follow you," he said, to which she looked puzzled.

"I am sure you'll clear the traffic." He explained by pointing at the police sign on her car.

"Oh!" She surprised him with a smile.

When you were with a girl in uniform, you could cut to the front of the line. Didn't matter how long the line was outside. As a test of his theory, Jay Jay suggested Johnny's on West 35th in the 60609 neighborhood, which had the longest line in Chicago's history, going round the block. The photographer from the Trib must have waited all day himself to get the shot.

"Originally a guy called Gianni ran this joint," said Jay Jay, offering his best tour guiding to Emily, "and Americanized it to Johnny."

She listened attentively. He was only trying to distract her. He hadn't even mentioned that his own name had been Americanized.

"Ya get a pizza, fries and two cans of coke for about 12 bucks. Johnny's is great for toppings. Whatever toppings. It's all included—" he stopped when he realized he sounded like a douche-bag on a cheap date. Sales nerd. Was probably what poor Dallas had to do all day at work. Talk the talk. Shift the shit.

Was the most he had talked in 3 months. So he'd better shut up. Time to shovel some pepperoni down the skull cave anyway. He was with a VVIP here. Not only had they cut to the front of the line, they were seated and had their order taken within 3 minutes. Now, *that* was fast food.

"I know you were there," she said suddenly.

"Where?"

"In the restaurant."

"Didja?" said Jay Jay, tearing a slice of pizza off. "I *have* been working there for a month."

"No, really?"

"Yes, I have."

"No. That is *not* what I meant. And you know it. The basement in May."

He stopped chewing. He put his Coke down.

"What did you hear?" She asked.

"How did you know I was there?"

She made a face. "Your hair was sticking out. You saw my feet, I saw your head."

"Oh!" He smiled but realized immediately, bad idea. He dropped the grin and looked glum for her sake.

She took more bites of the pizza. Her mouth was huge, but it wasn't unattractive, more like Shirley Bassey or Carly Simon.

"Well?"

"I heard guys giving you something to identify," he said in a lowered voice, "and bring to them. Photographs." Luckily the restaurant was very noisy, thanks to Jim Morrison belting out *Queen of the Highway* over the sound system.

"Let's talk later. Let's just eat now." She stopped chewing and swallowed.

They ate in silence.

Back at the cars, she suggested that they sat in hers. He agreed.

"So you already know who killed my uncle."

"Those guys?"

She nodded.

"How do you know that?"

"They said, if I didn't find out and give them the information they were after, my uncle would simply vanish. He did. To the bottom of the lake."

"What are they after? What was that first photo?"

He hoped he hadn't said anything wrong. She *was* a cop and shouldn't be telling him this.

"That's why I said it was my fault he died."

"Wait. Let's start at the start. Why did they meet you in the basement of the restaurant?"

"My aunt and uncle have given me the spare keys to the office room in the basement, for safekeeping. A few days before you saw me, I was sent a note with a time, place and date, saying *we need to talk to you about your uncle.* I actually thought my uncle had arranged it. But I was tricked. So I turned up and they gave me these photos. If I didn't find her, they would kill my uncle."

"Who? Who were you supposed to look for?"

"We-e-e-ll. The first photo was a spy from the 1920s."

"A spy? Who was he?"

"She. They asked me where she was."

"Why are they looking for her? And why you?"

She stared in that statue-like Chinese way Jay Jay had seen Mrs Chan and even the cleaner Ah-Yi do, as if you'd just asked for fries with chilli sauce.

"She was a Japanese sympathizer from China who went missing in the 1920s," she finally said."The illegal arms trade. Anyway, as I said, nothing to do with you."

"But. You said you caused your unc—"

"Because I didn't help those guys to find her. They are... they seem to be... part of a gang. A triad or tong. One was an American they must have hired. The other two were Chinese guys. One tall and one short."

"So why not just arrest them? They threatened you."

"It's a gang, Jerry. More of them will be back."

"I didn't see them." He said, relieved that it was true. "Just their feet."

Jay Jay was fascinated by their shared culture and the food, even the gang wars. All he was thinking about right at that moment was that she had opened a door into that world. His world. Anything he said might be dumbass, so he shut up and looked smart.

She didn't say anything like it was out of the ordinary. Yet. Her uncle *had* just died. This was a fact. He was sacrificed for something to do with a spy from about 50 years ago. Was that even possible? He was curious but unable to find a way to broach the subject with her without appearing like a knucklehead. What *was* the connection between the uncle and the spy?

He wondered if he would bump into her again out of the blue. Unlikely, as he was near to finishing the restaurant works already. Now it looked like a dreamy courtyard. He wanted to tell her about it: the design, the construction, how *he* had created this lovely outdoor dining area that really *was* a Jade Palace Garden. He was tongue-tied.

She looked at her watch. "I must go now. I'm still on duty. I finagled a couple of hours off for the family funeral but getting the whole evening off was out of the question and I didn't want to try. I don't want to think about this. I'm to blame."

"No, no, you're not." He wondered how the investigations were going. Would they ever find those guys? If the cops did, then she'd be in trouble. If they never found the head of the gang, she'd get away with it.

"I am telling you all this because you and I are the two people who were there that day. We're both witnesses. I may lose my job. Like your cousin, Ernesto."

Ernesto? How did she know they were related. Of course she'd know. A lot more was going on than he dared uncover. "Okay, goodnight, Officer Chan."

"Please," she said. "Emily."

"Emily."

She smiled sadly. She folded her arms and sat back. She looked straight ahead. The conversation was over. He started to climb out of her car.

"Do you understand what I am asking you?" She asked, still staring through the windshield.

"I don't."

"I am asking you not to say a word to anyone about me meeting those guys. We're both in this."

"You have my word."

Emily. A name which you had to close your lips to say, because of the Em. It sounded secretive. He repeated *Emily* a few times in the Camaro on the way home, glad he had wiped down the dashboard even though there had been no one to notice it.

"DOLLS? ARE YOU HOME?" When he got in, a strange scent clung to the air. Perfume. Strong, like night blossoms. Dallas was still dressed. Not in her uniform but a plain black mini dress, and red lip gloss. She was taking off her heels. Heels. At nearly 9 months gone. Really?

"You just got home?"

"Yes I did."

"Where did you go?"

"I went to... dinner." She looked flustered and disoriented, like she had just clicked her heels and returned from Oz.

"Ohh."

"Well doncha act so surprised. You were out too," she said, her voice rising. Maybe it was a question.

"But... I was at the funeral."

"For three hours?"

"Oh no... We went... I went for pizza after the funeral."

"At Johnny's?"

"Yes."

"That's nice... with who?"

"Umm... The guests from the funeral. Where did you go?"

"I went to the Drake Hotel."

"You went to *the* Drake?"

"Yes."

"The *Drake*? Why? With who?"

"Well, honey, calm down. We were celebrating a birthday: Sherylanne's— one of the girls, you know."

"Had fun?"

"Yeah. You?"

"Not so much. It *was* a funeral."

"What pizza?"

"Pepperoni. Double cheese."

They stared at each other like strangers on bus. "Ya didn't have Chinese today, huh."

"Naw. Not today, dollsy."

They got ready for bed. Dallas stretched, yawned and climbed in.

"When we have a new apartment, I'd love a dressing area."

"A dressing area? What's that?"

She huffed. "A room for getting dressed in, just next to the bedroom. A walk-in closet. My clothes are bursting out."

The perfume was new, heavier than her usual, the Estée he'd bought her on vacation in the summer of '68, light and fruity, all American femme, Dallas had called it. Okay, so she'd got it at discount since she'd been on the Estée Lauder counter then. But now, a fragrance he'd never smelt before filled the apartment.

"Dolls, what is that?"

"What is what?"

"The new scent you're wearing?"

CHAPTER 17

The evening had been pre-planned, knowing Jay Jay would be at the funeral, probably for a few hours. She had been worried that not only her hair would be ruined, but so would the portfolio of sketches and small paintings. They were in her black zip-up Marshall Field's nylon bag, along with her black dress and red heels. Why, she couldn't possibly be seen at the Drake wearing a store assistant uniform.

Thankfully it had stopped drizzling, when she got a cab up the 'magnificent mile'. There was no subway station on East Walton Place. She took in all the beautiful hotels and buildings soaring into the sky on N. Michigan Avenue. Their lights and polished glass glittered in the late afternoon sun like the chunky jewelry of a Mafioso's wife. She shut her eyes, inhaling the smog like it was cash.

The landmark Drake Hotel was the grandest place she'd been to since her wedding. Although that wasn't saying much. She'd always taken an interest in design, art and architecture. The Drake was a national treasure, the first urban resort in the country built by the Drake brothers in 1920.

She wanted be an hour early to luxuriate in the Art Deco setting and, of course, change her outfit. She wasn't just making an effort for him. She'd have done the same for anyone who took her to the Drake. She had always fitted right into the rich, artistic glamor of the Drake, like a thick cream card into a thick cream envelope.

She came out of the ladies' powder room in her outfit for the evening and found a high back winged armchair in the legendary bar, the Coq D'Or. The shape of the chair was perfect to observe the entire room from, without anyone observing her. She looked at her red polished nails, pleased that she had done them the night before. She picked up a drinks card. When she looked at the menu, she realized she'd have to buy a drink and make it last all night. Including tips, it would be, like, 20 bucks a drink. She replaced the drinks card.

Dared she say it, in her standard black store bag, she carried a few 3B pencils. She would have time to do quick sketches of the bar and the guests. The opportunity might never come again. Jay Jay would not be seen dead in a place like this, she mourned. Something fluttered in her like a bird in a cage. She was an artist again. She got out one of the pencils and she started sketching the counter, the bar footrail, the bartender and most of all the lights.

Illumination and translucency was something so difficult to achieve in a matt and dull medium like pencil lead and card. Truly that was a skill, a sleight of hand. You conjured up a world within your own. She looked up at the bar clock and 40 minutes had passed so quickly. He would be here soon.

Before she had had no one to paint or draw for. What was the point? Her career? That was too strong. Not a career, nor a profession. A woman like her had neither. Her heart had been crushed by domesticity. Dallas was Dull-ass. She had had no passion, motivation or inspiration for so long. But now she did.

He walked in. He shook his umbrella which he then shoved into the delicate porcelain Chinese umbrella stand next to the bar entrance with full height palms in pots like sentries. He hadn't seen her. His cheap suit was wet. His glasses were steamed up. It must be raining again. And quite hard by the look of it. He got his handkerchief out and tried to dab himself dry, his hands and head of longish-floppy artist-hair.

When he finally spotted her, he came over, smiling his Mona Lisa smile. La Giaconda, the Italians called the painting. Some said the model was really Leonardo's favorite student, Salaì. No reason that smile didn't belong on an enigmatic man. She put down her pencil and sketch card. He took out the handkerchief again, removed his square glasses and his wristwatch and dried each item carefully before setting them down carefully next to the tiny vase of orchids and a spray of baby's breath on the low black marble table.

They studied at each other coolly, like an ice cream that they didn't want to finish.

After what seemed like a long time, he said, "let me buy you a drink and then we'll take a look. What would you like?"

"A cherry martini please."

"Or would you prefer a mai tai? Have a look at the menu. If you are hungry, we can order something." He put his glasses on, straightened his light blue suit and excused himself before getting up to walk to the bar.

She wondered what time it was and whether she should order anything. She was having fun and Jay Jay would probably eat his usual Chinese takeout anyhow.

She noticed he'd forgot to put his Cartier wristwatch back on. She glanced over at the bar to check he wasn't looking back at her. No, he was not. The crowd at the bar was three deep and he was still waiting.

She reached out with her red manicured fingers and picked it up, delicately. The weight was as satisfying as holding a smooth pebble. She turned it over. The words were engraved not in some swirly old fashioned typeface as she'd expected, but in a blocky, modernist font.

"Love is one soul inhabiting two bodies."- Aristotle

She set the wristwatch down on the marble table, the right way up, as carefully as handling a little cake.

He nodded at the sketch. "Let's see," he said. He took off his glasses to do this. Maybe he was older than she'd thought, perhaps at that 'certain' age when eyesight reversed: short-sighted people became more long-sighted — goodbye eye-glasses for the close work.

She handed him her unfinished sketch of the bar and grinned. So did he.

"Very good, really very good. You have just captured perfectly the lighting and the mood. The expression on the barman's face which at first we think of as expressionless— or invisible— as he's behind the bar.... But in fact he's got a look of concentration. He owns the show in Chicago. That *je ne sais quoi* of those in the service industry. Do we own them or do they own us? The customers watching him with feigned interest, their hands resting on each other, on the counter, on their shoulder bags... remark-able! All those hands. You captured all of that in minutes."

She lifted her chin with pride, pleased with his "cr-teek" and the running narrative. He used the word us. Did he mean her too? She was in the service industry, wasn't she? He was articulate and expressive, using his long-fingered hands to gesticulate.

The waiter came and set down the martinis in a fancy display. The silver tray first, then some lace coasters and three little glass bowls, one with nuts, another with olives, the third had some snack she'd never even seen before but didn't dare to ask about. Last of all, he set down the drinks. Carl gave him a big tip.

"Where do you live?" said Dallas.

"I live in the Western Springs area. Stone Avenue?"

She shook her head, unfamiliar with that name.

"That's our nearest station." He shrugged.

Now 'our' didn't include her. It meant his family and him.

"My wife chose the house we're in. We— it's convenient for a few rounds at La Grange Country Club. And... well... it's perfect for families. My kids play in Gilbert Park."

"How old are they?"

"The boys are 9 and 6 and the girl is 2." An entire vista of a warm-as-toast family life opened before Dallas. Middle-class suburb with big yards front and back, swings, a treehouse, two-car garages for him and her, nice good-sized homes with drives, wide tree-lined streets. And children. And the wife who had everything.

"My wife isn't creative at all," he added. "She is an accountant in a big firm. Her idea of creativity is business ideas for the time-poor."

"Oh! That sounds very creative!"

"Yeah, you could say that she is creative and not artistic. That was what I was getting at."

"I understand."

"You do. I know you do. I felt a strong connection with you. The very instant I saw you."

Dallas looked down at her red nails on her lap. The connection between a man and a woman was just that. It was artistic stimulation. Leonardo had connected with Mona Lisa. And now she was known as *the* Mona Lisa.

"I am interested in your husband."

"Oh!" She laughed and her hand flew to her chest. "He is like your wife. Neither creative nor artistic. He's just a handyman." She drained her martini.

"Just? There is no such thing as just."

She didn't reply. Jay Jay was also interested in eating, music, the Cubs and kung fu. So yeah, Carl was right in that: Jay Jay wasn't *just* a handyman.

"I need to grab a cab now." She said.

"How about dinner?"

"No, thank you." She had had enough of the bar snacks.

"Sure?"

"Really." She got up and he did the same.

In the cab, she looked for the bar sketch to have another look at it, but became aware of a gift-wrapped box in her black nylon carry-all. It was even tied up with a fat white satin bow. She pulled the ribbon and opened the box. Inside was a white card she unfolded. She read it.

I know you wouldn't accept any gifts. Just something small. Hope you like it. Sincerely, C.

If she ever saw him again, she'd definitely bring it up. She was married and almost a mom. She wasn't really an artist, not any more. She felt like an impostor. She had misled him into thinking she was any good. It had been her connections to the Institute which caught his attention. She hadn't even mentioned the Professor. That would knock him out.

She was still a part-time, after-hours administrative officer: she handled student enrolments and the Professor's paperwork from home as and when things got busy during the term. got busy. She was also doing a one-off errand on the down-low for the Professor for which she'd be paid $5,000. Two and a half up-front and the rest on completion. That money would certainly be useful for getting back into art school. She had already set up an account for it so that Jay Jay would not find out where it came from.

Still as guiltily excited as a little girl on her birthday, she tore open the crisp white wrapper. Everything was blinding white. She slid the tiny Cubist glass bottle of Chanel No. 19 out of the box. She sprayed it all over herself, making the cab driver wind down the windows. She kept her eyes shut all the way home, inhaling the scents of another world deeply. The South of France. Vineyards. Orange blossoms. Candlelit dinners. White tablecloths.

Obviously his wife *must* adore him, to have given him a Cartier tank watch — with an alligator skin strap — worth thousands of dollars. She recalled the inscription on the back: His wife's name had followed the engraved Aristotle quote:

Catherine.

CHAPTER 18

J ay Jay woke up to the telephone ringing. It must have been going for a long while but the persistent tone had only just registered. He looked at the bedside flip clock. 6:38 am. Must be Grandpops. The hell was going on? He staggered into the kitchen and fumbled to pick up the receiver, even kicking over a chair on the way. Place was looking so scruffy and untidy now. Parcels of baby things had arrived with nowhere to store them.

"He... Hell... Hello?"

"Jerry? You gotta come now. I am sorry to wake you up."

"Oh. Mr Alfred? That you?"

"It is. I need my windows replaced."

"What happened?"

"Someone came an hour ago and fired shots through the front windows. They shattered all the glass. Only two windows left intact."

"Oh God! No!"

"Yes."

"You have any idea who that might be?"

"My enemies," he laughed, but it sounded like me might cry any second.

"I'm coming. Gimme an hour."

He hung up.

Jay Jay immediately thought of Nesto the Pesto. And that would be his fault he had done nothing about talking to Mr Alfred. Now he absolutely had to blow the shit out of Ernesto.

He rang the number, fuming.

"The fuck," said Ernesto in a gravelly, sleep-heavy voice.

"You. What did you do?"

"Whatchu talking about? Didn't do nothing. Fuck! You wake me up at this time. I'm asleep. Ma-aan!"

"I don't believe you. Listena me. An hour ago you were out with your gun. And don't tell me you weren't."

"No! Jeez! I swear. Oh shit! No. Our deal was that this week you were gonna tell him. After you finished with that moon gate restaurant or whatever."

"Jade Pal – never mind." He paused. Ernesto *might* be telling the truth... But, if not Ernesto, then who?

"What happened? I can help. You think I gonna wake up in the night? Who am I shooting?" Ernesto sounding less gravelly.

"Never mind. I don't want your HELP. You can't HELP."

"You in trouble, bro?"

"No! I'm not your bro. D'ya hear what I just said to ya? Oh, forgeddit."

"Jeez, bro — "

He hung up.

Jay Jay righted the chair he'd kicked over and wiped his face down with his palm. He was still not fully awake himself. *Oh God, I need coffee,* he muttered. After a quick breakfast, he got ready faster than Superman in a phone booth. In his white van on the way over to *Catherine* , he thought that Mr Alfred might even look upon Ernesto favorably, if he knew how to protect Mr Alfred from the shooters. That was Nesto's bag, right? Protection racket. But what bothered him was who had shot out Mr Alfred's windows? Had it been done as a warning, and if so, why?

He'd arrived before 8 a.m., bringing with him the tool kit and drop sheets. He rang the bell. The glass transom over the entrance door was damaged too. Only the letters C-A-T remained.

"Good morning Mr Alfred."

"Not so good a morning, but thank you for coming so quickly."

"Did you call the cops already?"

"Yes. They took the usual statements and so on. I know the Chief well. They will keep an eye out. Jay Jay I just don't want trouble. I haven't got long here."

"What do you think they want? Do you know who did this?"

Mr Alfred paused. "No. I don't."

Jay Jay looked at Mr Alfred's light blue eyes which then avoided his. He turned and got on with measuring the glass panels which needed replacing and writing the details in his notebook. So he *didn't* get mixed up, he had numbered each window and made a legend.

After he got back from the glazier, he carried the panels into his cabin. He thought about his old friends, Bones 1 and 2 again. What had actually happened here? He scratched his head and sat on the bench that he made in his first week here. He had not really wanted to take on this job but Dallas said he had no choice. He was straight in. What more could he have asked for? She'd said doors would open for him, and they had, he'd got the Jade job. But now look what had happened.

The windows took almost all day. Cutting out the putty on the glass, sliding the sashes back in, adjusting the weight pulleys. The tedious task was making sure everything taken out fitted back exactly. And boy, he sure wouldn't like to be doing this kind of job again and again. When he'd packed up all the tools and organized the scrap into a pile, he knew it was time time to talk to Mr Alfred. He went through the French windows in the rear garden rather than go round to the front door.

"Sir?" He called out seemingly to no one. He stood in the middle of the expansive hall as if he was in a bad play.

"Hello Jerry," Mr Alfred descended the winding stairs. "I've just been having a nap. Not exactly the wake up call you'd like at my age. Almost gave me a heart attack."

"Is this a good time?"

Mr Alfred didn't say. "Are you finished?"

"Yes."

"Do you want to write me your check?"

"No. No, Sir. I need to talk to you about... about the... the... my Grandpop's stepson."

"Your *what*?"

"My grandfather's wife's son."

"Oh?" My Alfred still looked confused. "Sit down. Come inside."

Jay Jay grunted in reply. Mr Alfred beckoned him into the drawing room. Jay Jay sat down awkwardly on a moth-eaten jacquard couch from about a thousand years ago, which he wasn't sure if he oughta be sitting on. Mr Alfred sat in a velvet high back winged armchair. He looked like a vampire, dressed in his— what was it? A kimono? It looked like a dressing gown with satin lapels. Or was that a smoking jacket?

They said old people feel cold all the time. August 30th was kinda a blistering hot day to be wearing whatever it was he was wearing— one of those glossy wraparound jacket-y things one wore to do nothing but smoke and drink whiskey near a fireplace. He'd watched enough Bela Lugosi movies. On closer inspection it was just as moth eaten and threadbare as the couch. Gold threads pushed out like insects' legs, the cloth all frayed and raw at the sleeve hems.

"His name is Ernesto de la Rua."

"Interesting. *Of the street.*"

"Please could you help return Ernesto to the CPD. He was low in rank. An patrolman. He's been inside. But he's family. In return this will be his beat. I will make sure he will take care of you."

"How?"

"Protection racket was his bag. He'll know what to do."

Mr Alfred nodded, downcast.

"*I'll* be back tomorrow. I need to touch up everything."

"I wasn't at Mr Chan's funeral. Such a good friend, rubbed out."

Jay Jay didn't reply. It wasn't his business. Jay Jay had assumed that Mr Alfred was not well. After all, at his age, he couldn't be expected to make every engagement.

Jay Jay folded his arms. He couldn't understand why this was happening. That heated telephone conversation he'd heard when he first started working was a clue that Mr Alfred had enemies that he either really didn't know or didn't want *him* to find out about.

"Jerry. I really needed you in the last 3 or 4 weeks. I forgot already: you were working with Mr Chan."

"Then you really do need some extra protection. Someone to patrol. Look out for ya. Another pair of eyes. I'll send him along. You can talk. He'll tell you how he's going to fix this. He was a cop, remember."

"Why was he in the slammer?"

"Not his fault. That's what we think. Grandpops and me. It's that neighborhood he's in."

Jay Jay was ad libbing now. He did not like this. It might have been true, and he sure hoped it was. All he wanted was Mr Alfred safe. And Ernesto wanted to be the best-behaved boy there ever was to earn the respect back. He'd better want that, anyway. Whatever reasons there were for Bones 1 and 2 to even be in the cabin, Mr Alfred had never done a thing wrong to Jay Jay. Never a harsh word, never a penny pinched. He'd gotta remember that.

They shook hands and Jay Jay got up. "Well I best go now."

"Tell me again when the baby is due. I forget these things."

"Any day this week."

"Which day?" Mr Alfred laughed his wheezy, rusty hinge laugh.

"No one knows. Not even the doctors."

"You are so right. No one knows. Boy, you have cheered me up." He patted Jay Jay on the back. "I'm counting on ya."

———

WHEN HE GOT BACK HOME to North Kenmore Avenue, something wasn't right. The apartment was eerily silent. "Doll?" His voice echoed. Suddenly, an itch of panic crawled over him. What had happened at Mr Alfred did not mean it would happen here. Where was she? Then he heard her. She was in the bathroom, sitting on the floor. Jay Jay dropped his tool bag and rushed over to her. Oh Jeez, let her be okay.

"I... I... "

Jay Jay wasn't sure if she was trying to say anything or just panting.

"Doll. Oh God. Are you having the baby?"

He wasn't expecting this for another week or so. She had told him as much. She was able to speak in between the contractions. "Time to go, Jay Jay. I counted. 2 minutes and 1 minute."

He picked her up. She was surprisingly heavy. Step by step they trudged, only stopping during contractions, while he supported her under the arms. "The bag," she gasped.

"What bag?"

She cringed, gasped and sighed as the contraction came, waiting before she spoke. Her eyes squeezed shut in pain. "The hospital bag", she said, and pointed to a bag near the bedroom closet door, a leather weekend bag which he'd never seen before. *Another goddamn bag! Didn't she have anough?*

She walked 3 steps during the gaps, doubled over in pain until they got to the van. It was way more roomy than the Camaro. He threw the bag into the front passenger seat. No time to even open the trunk. He put the lights on and drove all the way as steady as possible, no lurching, sharp turns or sudden braking. Dallas slumped in the back seat, groaning, with her eyes shut. The mascara had run all over her eyes. He wished he could have helped her more. He regretted every moment of working 6 days a week and all day long. He hardly had spent any time with her in the last few months. Oh God. He gripped the steering wheel, the leather felt hard, sweaty and cold, like his wife's skin had felt on the way out to the car. The guilt chipped away at him. He kept checking the rear view mirror all the way.

As he checked her in, Dallas was given a wheelchair and she collapsed gratefully into it, leaning forward and panting. A nurse gave him forms to fill, while he sat in a waiting room. The walls were covered in alphabet and number cutouts in bright colors, in between posters about breast feeding and polio vaccines, showing laughing babies and parents. He lion-yawned and tears filled his eyes.

"How is daddy?"

He looked around. "Wut—?" He had been called a daddy by a stranger.

"Yes, you. You're going to be a daddy soon. Whatsmatter?"

"Oh. Yes. That's me. Nothing to eat all day and an incredibly early start," he said.

The nurse took the forms away from him.

"Well, you might have to get used to that. Soon there'll be no night or day."

He didn't think that was meant to be a joke. Dallas talked about sleep-is-for-the-weak all the time, when he tuned out. Nights and days reversed, diaper changes, laundry on the hour. Sleep would soon be for the lucky.

"Is there a telephone, Miss?"

"There is. If you go this way, past the bathrooms, then third door on the right. You'll see a water fountain and telephone booths area."

"Mr Alfred? Hello? Sir, I'm at the hospital now. I know, right?" He tittered nervously, like it was a lame joke, which it wasn't at all. Now it was friggin' real. He was going to be a dad.

"Congratulations, I am so excited for you! You do what you

need to do. No need to come in and be worried. I am so pleased with your work this morning."

"I am just glad I made sure the place was watertight before I left."

"Good."

"I replaced all the window locks too, Sir. You need more security, not less."

"I am sure you are taking care of that, with that relative you mentioned."

Jay Jay grimaced and hung up, searching his pockets for a couple more dimes.

Everything was brimming inside him. Excitement, anxiety, relief. And some mild irritation at having to ring Ernesto now.

"Listen. Nesto."

"The fuck. Two calls in a day."

"Do you want the good shit or not?"

"Jeez. What's up, man? You okay?"

"Dallas is about to have the baby. Yup. I'm at the Children's Hospital right now."

"No way! Shit! Congrats, man! Yo. You're gonna be a daddy."

"Duh. That is usually what happens after you've been in the waiting room."

Ernesto laughed as if the thought had never occurred to him before. "Ya gonna be so great at this shit. You are."

"Listen. I talked to him."

"You did?"

"Yup. 'S in the bag."

"No way! Aw, man! Jeez. What a day."

"But."

"¿Qué más?"

"Keep an eye out please. Tonight. Do what you need to. Round up the boys, whatever. Someone gave him a warning this morning. I replaced all the windows today. But we don't want no more trouble."

"Sure. No problem, Jefe!"

"And one more thing."

"*Dime.*"

"Can you bring me a burrito or something? I am about to pass out."

After he hung up, his mild irritation had turned to tired numbness. He shut his eyes, stretched out his legs on the uncomfortable couch and folded his arms tight, while waiting for Ernesto to appear with his burrito. He shut down, not exactly zombified, but close. Maybe all dads did when they sat here in this very room.

Whilst he'd been wrapping up all the debris, waste and scrap to be taken to the dump in bags, he'd looked up at the transom and felt sad. The plain, clear glass he'd replaced his carefully lettered pane with had robbed the house of its identity, kinda.

He forced himself to nap. He was going to be here for a long time. Could be hours. He was starving. Dallas was always telling him food was all he thought about. And? So what. Now he *was* thinking about it. Why didn't one of those nurses even ask him if he needed something to eat? Dads were always being ignored. The mother was the star. Men labored but were never in labor.

All that retouching he did had been wasted. Jay Jay was no artist, he snickered self-deprecatingly, knowing well Dallas would have done a far greater job of the transom lettering. He pictured her advice on design. Dallas always said *C* must be proud and round, not mean and skinny. She liked high contrast; gold typeface with under-shadows in black.

He imagined her sweet voice to drown out the tortured screaming and shouting in another room somewhere off another corridor. He didn't understand why he was being separated from her at the most crucial point. Was this how civilization kept going and fatherhood began? By preventing dads from seeing the appearance of the next generation and being called "daddy" by a member of staff, a complete stranger?

CHAPTER 19

The next day, just as civilization had dictated, he was a father. Dallas was having a cat nap with their baby girl. He had just settled into a deep, whale coma kind of sleep when he was awoken with the news. The staff nurse, a dead-ringer for Archie Bunker's Cousin Maude, had told him, "Mrs Lee has the the best room. With friggin' views of Chicago." The fuck did she need views for when she was either asleep or awake but looking at the baby? All he thought of was how big the number would be after the dollar sign on the account. Why did she ask for the best room? Still he did not object. Let her be queen for a night. It'd better be "for one night only".

A daddy's heart was like ice cream. Once he held his daughter, it melted and so did the room around him. He couldn't think why he'd ever thought so hard about food, Bones 1 and 2 or anything else. No friggin' view of any great city of the world could compare with the view of your own brand new progeny. THAT was the view that you couldn't buy, the one that would outlast any view your whole life through.

He raised his right arm and wiped his tears on the sleeve while his left still cradled his daughter. He replaced the swaddled baby in the those perspex boxes that they slept in, he wasn't sure what they were call. Were they bassinets? No one had mentioned them by name yet. Bouquets and cards had arrived and were elegantly displayed on the marble window sill over those friggin' views of the Windy City. He took a look at a few of the cards. One from Mr Alfred, of course. No news from Mr Alfred so all must have been okay on the night. Extra vigilance was now necessary. No time to think about that now. Oh gosh, she'd be so happy the Institute had sent a big pink and white bunch of peonies. A mixed bunch from Grandpops and Carmelita. Ernesto must have told his mom after the burrito run. A yellow display of roses too, but they were anonymous. The card said:

To Dallas,

"That which is done with love is well done."-Vincent Van Gogh

And why to her only and not to him also? Someone from the Institute must have sent this. Maybe the Professor. All he was sure of was that Vincent Van Gogh didn't send the flowers. He had once said *Goff*. But she would have said *Go*. Who was right? Very rarely did anyone say it out loud.

When they were both settled, he had to call Grandpops. He thought of making his way to the telephone room and looked for some dimes.

Just then, there was a knock on the door. He replaced the card on the sill.

"You have a visitor, Mr Lee," Cousin Maude's look-alike announced in a low voice.

"Oh! But my wife is asleep." He whispered.

"Could you please come outside?" She whispered. These nurses were so good at volume control, 1 to 10 on the dial was no sweat. Their voices were not even a 1. They made themselves really clear and yet feather soft, more like a 0.5.

He went into the corridor and shut Dallas's room door behind him.

"Oh, Emily!"

"For you guys. Congratulations," she smiled. She was in uniform. He scratched his head. What time was it, exactly? Was she working? She must be. He barely registered when he glanced at his wristwatch. Hospital corridors knew no time. It was daytime on the day after the night before.

She held out a cute little bunch of purple freesias. He had almost forgotten her altogether. They *had* shared a pizza during the distraction phase of impending fatherhood. Guilty, but not as charged.

"What a surprise." He was still whispering.

"No need to whisper now."

"Oh yes," he laughed. "God, I must look like hell."

"You're fine," she smiled. "I look like hell too."

"Everything okay? Are the investigations..." he hesitated, realizing that the second thing he thought of whenever he saw her was Mr Chan.

"They... are ongoing. Can I ask you a question? Are you still working at Mr Alfred's? Is Dallas still doing some paperwork for the Institute?"

"Those are two questions. Yes and yes. But not right now. She's just had a baby." His jaw tightened. She wasn't here to see him. She was here for the job.

"Emily. Just tell me."

"I know what you're going to say."

"What?"

"You are going to say... what are you doing here?"

He managed a small but sincere smile. She said things like what you find inside fortune cookies.

"So what *are* you doing here?" He parroted her.

"Well, you are right. Jay Jay, it's police business, but I need to talk to you somewhere private. Not in a corridor."

He leaned over and buried his face in his hands. "Ugh," he groaned. "I can't. Not now. Not today."

"I didn't say now, or here or today. How about tonight or tomorrow?"

"What? For what?" He jumped.

"For information you may have."

"About what? Who? Not Mr Chan?"

"No. Someone else."

"Who?"

"Your Mr Alfred."

He stared at her, blank. The image of Bones 1 and 2 popped into his head. There were no other secrets he had been keeping from the world. Or maybe this was about Ernesto. Somehow she had found out Ernesto the Pesto was now helping Mr Alfred and vice versa. Or, maybe, this was *actually* about Mr Alfred and the gunshots through his windows. Oh God. He frowned, still confused and red-eyed with tiredness. She did not even blink. He balled up his fingers into tight fists on his lap.

———

IN THE EARLY EVENING, he slipped away. Emily had suggested meeting him at his apartment at 6pm. He said to Dallas he needed to go home for dinner and then go shopping for food and snacks to bring back to the room for her. She asked for some fruit, chocolate milk, cookies, anything that would improve hospital food. He doubted that it would. She had the executive room, the top view, and he was certain, the best meals too.

He went to check at the accounts department before they shut just to see where they were at. If extra luxury was included in the deal, he sure wasn't buying more.

The payment center was on the first floor, just before the exit.

"Why, Sir, of course, we would need to look into your files. Won't be a moment." The cashier disappeared behind the glass. When she came back, she said, "Well, looks like 's all been taken care of."

"Oh! You mean the extra meals? But my wife is hungry. She's breastfeeding round the clock, like every 40 minutes."

"Oh," the cashier laughed. "That's newborns for ya. She's not even a day old. What's her name?"

"Jennifer."

"That's pretty. Aww."

"Please... Tell me, what's included and what's not? This is our first time in maternity."

"Sir," she looked at the alarmingly thick folder of patients' accounts. "The base costs were covered by your insurance, Mr Lee. The rest — the room upgrade, meals, treatments and extras. The jabs and tests Jennifer had. All paid up."

"What do you mean? By who?"

"I'm sorry. An anonymous account holder is all I can say."

"But a person, a company?"

"I can't say. Sir, your bill has been settled."

Mr Alfred must have done this too, as he did for the wedding. He badly wanted to thank Mr Alfred but he only had an hour or so. He would ring from home.

He muttered "thank you" and walked briskly to the Camaro in the hospital parking lot. When he got home it was like the night before the night before. Nothing had changed despite his expectation. He did not even know what day of the week it was. This was now a family home. The cot was ready for Jennifer. The clothes in the closet. The drawers full of mysterious tub things. Sprays, ointments, lotions. The 'drinks station' i.e. the trolley for diapers and formula-making. The gigantic sci-fi baby carriage in the first floor understair area landing. He was on an alien planet. He hadn't noticed until now. For a few months things would be like this until Dallas returned to work. He sure hoped so, anyway.

The bell rang. He opened the door. "Emily."

He showed her in and she sat down. She had an envelope with her. Wasting no time, she opened it. Oh. This was not what he thought.

"A circular is going round the private arms sales. This one." She took out a handbill. It showed a group shot of 20 Asians and below it was a picture of a revolver. "They're called the Black Phoenix. I've been sent this just today. Do you recognize this gun?"

He frowned and stared. "No!"

"Have you ever seen it?"

"No. Never. What is this about? Why are you asking me?"

"The phone number for the sale of this item is yours."

"Wha—? Why? How?"

"That is why I am here."

"Are you sure it's my number?" Jay Jay said, but he knew it was.

"Of course."

"It's just a mistake, a whatchamacallit, a typo," he said. "When they printed the handbill, they typed a wrong number. You can search the apartment if you want."

Jay Jay was thinking it must be the gun the cops found which shot the holes in Mr Alfred's windows. For Jay Jay's money, Nesto the Pesto had found it, and fenced it somewhere. Or taken it to an arms sale himself. But then why would he put Jay Jay's number on the bill? He couldn't think straight. He was most afraid that the bones would be discovered. He tried sending out good vibes: *OK, Bones 1 and 2, nothing to do with us, I hope,* but he was no medium, and neither of them answered. This stupid gun had nothing to do with him.

"Earlier today you said that we were meeting about Mr Alfred."

"Well, we are."

"How?"

"This gun is registered to the Institute. You are well-acquainted with Alfred Sutton and his house."

He did not like her tone, now all official. Emily was in professional mode. He clamped his jaws shut. He stared at her, thinking: "this sure ain't like before, sweetheart. Things they are a-changin'. And not at the turntable."

She stared back at him.

"'S just a gun. I can't even tell the difference between them."

"No, this is a special one, Jerry. Very valuable. An antique. 134 years old."

Suddenly he didn't like her calling him Jerry so much.

"Look." She pointed at the photo, her fingernail over the hilt. It was engraved with an image of a long-tailed bird.

Now where had he seen that before?

"Why is it special?" He asked. "You guys handle guns all day."

"Well, firstly, it is rare, worth $120,000. Easy. Secondly, it was stolen."

"Isn't it an obvious error in the telephone number on the listing?"

She ignored his hypothesis. "Have you received any strange phone calls from collectors?"

"No. Ridiculous. I work 6 days a week, and so did my wife. We never have calls."

"Except from your grandfather and Mr Alfred, am I right?"

"Right. You can search through our AT&T bills for a list of calls made and received if you want. Dallas deals with all that."

"We will."

He kept the bit about Ernesto to himself. Ernesto was not much of a caller. Though from Jay Jay's number, they'd easily trace that on the morning of the window gunshots, he did receive Mr Alfred's call and he did call Ernesto. Was this the gun used to fire those shots? *Please don't let that be the case*, he shuddered. Enough trouble around these days: he'd just had a baby.

Lesson number 1: Never flirt with a cop. Not when you have a pregnant wife, not when you're related to a disgraced cop and— admit it— not ever.

Lesson number 2: Don't keep other people's secrets.

"Mr Alfred talk to you about the Sutton family?"

"No. Never! I'm just fixing shit."

"Jerry. Please. His father was Charles Sutton. You only get as rich as the Sutton family in a few ways, most of them illegal. The Suttons were arms dealers. Charles stole this gun around or after the First World War, from the gang. Or tong, the Black Phoenix. It can never be re-sold. They want it found and returned to them. That was why my uncle was killed. They were looking for the spy who last had the firearms. She's a member of the tong—"

"Was?" Jay Jay interrupted.

"Once you are a tong member, you are forbidden to leave. But I did not help them."

She hung her head.

"They are not after her, they are after just the gun?"

"Find one, find the other. Only in death is she allowed to leave the tong. But now they have seen the arms sales circular, they believe she is alive. If they do find the spy alive after all these years, they will kill her, *and* they'll want the gun too."

"Why do these sales circulars come up?" Asked Jay Jay.

"You see, every time a war starts and ends, you end up with surplus firearms. They have to go somewhere. Hence the dealers, in every state. Private and public sales. And Vietnam won't last for ever."

"And after that?"

"And after that? Someone will be very rich."

He was silent, remembering Nesto's tales of choppers, the rice fields, napalm. He shook his head. He was just a handyman and a new dad. Why was he even being asked these questions?

"You will have a look for the gun, won't you? When you are back at Mr Alfred's."

Jay Jay tried to think back. There were a lot of guns. On walls, in the glass cabinets. Probably under Mr Alfred's bed too. Surely he couldn't go around searching for arms. Shouldn't the cops do that?

"This might sound dumb, but... why... have you thought maybe... that you should actually ask Mr Alfred?"

"Oh we will do that, but no record of his name on the listing exists. Our job is to track down the unlicenced deals. Every couple of months a bulletin of licenced dealers and their deals is updated and sent around the precincts. And this gun was unlicenced here in Illinois or—"

"It probably had been brought in from another state."

"Or another country. Therefore in order to sell, he had to use the Institute's—"

"Have you got proof of any of this?"

"Nope."

They both laughed, like the 'old' days. "Just a hunch," she added with a tinge of anxiety. She did not mind him interrupting. They did that all the time to him. Mr Chan, Mrs Chan. The Ah-Yi. The kung fu boys he trained with. It seemed the ruder the Chinese were to you, the more they liked you. If they were pleasing and thanking you every minute, get ready to scram.

"What is it called?"

"What?"

"The gun, ma'am." *Yes what is this friggin' gun called?* He thought grimly.

"It's a Colt."

"A Colt?"

"From 1837. But its nickname on the sales circular is The Order."

CHAPTER 20

He was just about to pick up the telephone to make sure Ernesto was taking care of things at N. Lakeshore Drive. Then he remembered they might already be checking on his calls.

"Damn! This was shit!" He looked at the kitchen clock. He'd ring Ernesto from the telephone booths at the hospital. He grabbed some yoghurts, oranges and a pear from the fridge and put them in a string bag to take to Dallas. He took them out again. The bag's holes were too big, entangling the items in the string. He grabbed a canvas tote bag from on top of the fridge instead. What he unfolded was the Institute bag, with the printed logo, the same one that Emily had been. That was the beginning of all the trouble, when she was shown a photo of a spy. They killed Mr Chan for that. Who *was* Emily? Was she just a cop?

Only a couple more nights at the hospital in the room with a view and then Dallas'd be back home. He was raw with excitement. His nerves were on fire. A family. He wished he'd never met Emily.

What was Mr Alfred trying to do? He remembered that Mr Alfred had said there were funds 'tied up' which he had to 'free up', at the start of Jay Jay's stint. For people who lived like Jay Jay, from month to month, in a city, with little savings, these words meant nothing. Mouth music. Jay Jay was only interested if *he* was getting paid. Never mind from where.

He loaded the Camaro and drove back to the parking lot at the hospital. He figured this job might not last after all. Was Mr Alfred in trouble? Emily did say she'd be back to update him after they've talked to Mr Alfred. He could almost feel the cops breathing down his neck.

Maybe he should go back to Mr Alfred's and clear the cabin basement. For one thing, if they *did* do a search, they'd find his buddies Bones 1 and 2, and secondly, they might also find the gun. He shouldn't have underestimated Mr Alfred. Something happened in that house as Ernesto had warned him long ago.

Jay Jay almost spilled the contents of the cloth bag when he bowled into Nesto in the corridor outside Dallas's room with a view.

"Nesto! 'Chudoin' here?"

"Ya forgot I work all day at a shit job? I got here, didn't I? Look at the time."

"Yeah. Thanks, man." For the first time Jay Jay was relieved to see the Pesto. How things had changed.

"Yo. Listen. Might be trouble at the farm."

"Oh no, now what?" said Jay Jay.

"My mother says the landlord came. They gonna put pressure on your Grandpops to sell. The landlord is broke himself. Needs the land back. Build new apartments. The farm makes hardly any money."

"Come on. I have no time for all this now, Nesto. I can't take any more bad news. I had a shit day. Thanks for asking."

"Okay, now then, the good news."

"What?"

"My guys, they say all gone okay today. Smooth as silk sheets. Hey! I was just reporting to you. Jeez, no need to go apeshit. 'Samatter. You look like you're mad at something."

"I am. Things ain't what they were."

"'Ssup?"

He shook his head and let out a huge gust of a sigh like he was blowing birthday candles. "Let's go grab a coffee."

"Or two."

"Or two. Just dropped off stuff to Dallas. Turns out she didn't want most of it." He held up the still full bag.

"Yeah. I don't normally do... babies." He shuddered and his giant belly wobbled even under the tight T-shirt which obviously wasn't tight enough to hold him in. "But yours is the cutest li'l punkin."

"You're a step-cousin now."

"I am?"

"Naw, not really. But I couldn't let Jennifer call you the Pesto."

"I am the besto of the pesto."

"Let's go, c'mon."

————

"NOW. THIS MIGHT BE IMPORTANT."

"*Que. Dime.*"

"You gotta gimme a hand. We don't have much time," Jay Jay wanted to put the brakes on but he was speeding off like a released balloon. "I cannot be working *all* the time at Mr Alfred's now. So I just need you with Dallas for a couple of hours while I go back to the cabin. I have to find something before the cops do."

"Whoa, whoa, whoa. Couldja slow down? This the gun to do with the gunshots?"

"Might be."

"What happened tonight? Somethin' must've. Never seen you wettin' your pants like this."

"Emily," said Jay Jay. "She's trouble."

"Uh-oh."

"Yup. The cop."

Jay Jay told him. Bones 1 and 2. Then Emily. Then Mr Chan's death. The day in the restaurant kitchen. Since then

Emily had revealed to him over pizza that the gang members were looking for a female spy. A Chinese girl who disappeared in the 1920s with a valuable gun that she should not have had. Both were the property of the Black Phoenix, you could not take the gun or the girl out of the tong. She had been thought to have been executed after WWII, but the appearance of the gun—

Jay Jay stopped. Emily had also told him to say nothing to anyone about the basement conversation he'd overheard because they, the CPD, were investigating Mr Chan's death. Jay Jay would be a potential witness if that conversation with the tong members got her into trouble about that. You didn't mess with the Chicago gangs. Now both Jay Jay and Emily were in this shit together. Someone had already died. They would not stop until they retrieved the gun. So he skipped telling Ernesto the entire thing. He was trapped, like he was still in the hot-and-stuffy basement kitchen without an outlet. Jay Jay scratched at his forehead which felt like it was burning.

"What does she want? What ya tryna look for?"

"She wants... she is investigating... private arms sales and dealers, that's all I know," he said. It was true. He knew nothing about the market. Maybe he should learn. Hell. Maybe he'd have to. "So I'm looking for a gun. For her."

"I've got a couple. Want one?"

"No!" Jay Jay barked.

"Actually I am gonna try to sell mine, anyway. I don't have much use for them now. But why are *you* looking for one?"

"Not just any gun. A very valuable antique one. The seller had put my telephone number on a hand bill. And... I hope the printer just got the number wrong. There had been that wrong number call one night, too. That was too much of a coincidence. You didn't have to be Columbo to work that out."

"Stay out of it," Ernesto waved his hands. "You ain't heard nothing. If my experience at CPD was anything to go by, they either get or don't get you in the end depending on how you play your cards. The longer you keep 'em close to your chest, the better."

"That's helpful," Jay Jay deadpanned.

"You can't hide evidence." Ernesto was serious. He did not take his eyes off Jay Jay once. His hand on Jay Jay's shoulder was mildly reassuring.

"Stuff happened in that cabin. Toldja already. Imma quit my shit job pretty soon. I never toldya, but I know who that notebook belonged to. The earring too. We decided my abuelita needs to go into a home. We've had to clear her out of her apartment. So we found all this junk of hers. Tons, man. Rooms and rooms to clear out. Most worth nothing. Too old, useless." He pinched his temples, shaking his head slowly. "She was keeping stuff for when she returned to Cuba but no, she never will now."

Jay Jay listened and remembered Papa Moriarty had also done that before he dropped dead. He had been thick with Grandpops, and had been since they were in high school. Set up the farm and so on. Taught Grandpops the basics of seining. He was like an uncle to Jay Jay. All the time he spoke about returning to Ireland, the moment he was this, he was that. The right moment never came.

"A small wooden box nearly got thrown out. Luckily, when my mother opened the box, she kept it all and then remembered the whole story. She had forgotten for all those years. She went to an antique dealer to value the earring." He whistled. "S'worth a lot. Like a laaawwt. Ch-ching!" He sang it out like he was in a show. He rubbed his fingers with the flourish of a magician. "We decided to keep it. Know why? It's my only way to be back with the CPD boys and girls."

"Yeah. Blackmail."

"Stop. Ain't blackmail. S'whitemail. Blackmail is when you want money."

"And you don't?"

"I ever mentioned money to you?" He asked and answered the question himself. "Naw. Never. I got money from my shit job."

Jay Jay nodded and shook his head at the same time, some-thing only an Asian or Latino could do, that a WASP wouldn't be able to.

"Now. The problem is the notebook," added Ernesto. "Which I cannot read. Man! How is your Chinese?"

"Wut?"

"The notebook. S'in Chinese. The name of the person and all the words."

"Right." Jay Jay gritted his teeth.

"Sí. Look."

"Let me," said Jay Jay. He couldn't believe the way Ernesto had carried the museum piece shoved in his grubby jeans back pocket. He handed over the battered silk item. Frayed, delicate silk ties, which had once held it shut, dangled from it.

When Jay Jay opened the front cover, three handwritten char-acters were visible. From watching those kung fu movies, Jay Jay supposed they were the name or the title of the notebook. Had to be a woman's. No man would use a silk brocade notebook. He turned it upside down to look at it from another angle.

"Whatdju lookin' for?"

"I think in Chinese you read from back to front, and right to left."

"That's clever. You're right. Say, know anybody from the restaurant? To translate. The lady? The chefs?"

"No, we can't. 'S important that we don't ask nobody." Jay Jay looked at Ernesto. "Mr Chan's dead. Emily is on my case about this stupid gun. We don't want anything getting back to the cops."

"Looks like dates and times. A diary or some kind of coded thing."

But on the front page or the back page, whichever way, was the symbol again, stamped in black ink. The single bird, its body multi-feathered like serpentine scales.

The bird with the long tail.

CHAPTER 21

S he sensed someone's face coming close. She was already fully awake after breastfeeding and dozing but her eyes were still closed, keeping the world out. Mothers had evolved to sleep lightly and wake quickly, fully functioning and reason intact, in order to continue human civilisation by providing nutrition at all hours in the early days. Or so Dr Spock or someone said. The coming-close face had not yet spoken, but Dallas had instinctively opened her pre-programmed eyes already and said, "Yes?"

"Mrs Lee? You okay to take a telephone call?"

"A call?"

"If you want to rest, I will tell him." She peered at Dallas through her spectacles, the large rounded-edge rectangular frames like twin TV screens.

"Who?"

"The caller."

Groggy, Dallas rose slowly, shuffling her feet into the pink fluffy under her bed.

Where's my husband? She thought but didn't ask. She remembered. Jay Jay had had to dash home to eat something and to bring her fruit and snacks.

"Okay. Who is it?"

"Come with me. You can leave the baby in the bassinet. If she wakes, I'll change her."

She looked at the sleeping baby and hopped off the bed. She never appeared more like a petite little girl than when in a hospital bed, high as the one in that dumb fairy tale about the princess and the pea. If you were really tired, you slept, pea or no pea. She followed the nurse down a corridor to a brightly-lit busy nursing station, a room with desks, other nurses, files, a telephone on each desk and a cluster of blood pressure testing equipment on carts and drip stands stood like trees in a corner.

A black receiver was on one of the desks. "Here," said the nurse, pointing to the telephone.

Dallas picked the receiver up and subconsciously started tidying and uncoiling the tangled cord. "H-hello?"

"Doll-us?"

"Who's this?" She knew the voice. Her heart stopped, waiting for his answer

"Carl."

"Carl?"

"Carl Rodriguez."

"Yes, yes, I know." She even laughed. At his caramel-ly Spanish voice, she melted a little. What did he want?

"You knew I was here?"

"Wasn't hard. I'm no sleuth. I just asked the girls at the store."

"Oh!" She was taken by surprise. "Thank you for the flowers."

"Are you happy with the room? I made sure you had the best view."

"You..? No way. I can't believe it. Why?"

"I just wanted to. Don't say no way. I upped the meal count. When you're feeding the baby, you need proper nutrition. Rich meals."

Her stomach rumbled with hunger when he said the word rich.

"Is your husband around?"

"No. No... he... went home to eat something. I... sorry, my baby brain. I can't... think straight."

"I'd like to meet him."

"Who?"

"Your husband."

"You would?" He wouldn't. Not really. What was he talking about? What would *they* talk about?

"Yes. I have been planning on remodelling my garage into a studio, fix some sky lights to bring light in, fit plumbing so I can have a sink to wash my brushes. Just so I don't have to paint in the corner of my kitchen with all the kids' crap around. If he has any time, I could drop by where he works?"

"That wouldn't be convenient."

"Why?"

"Because he works at his client's home."

"Okaaaay." He sounded unsure, sarcastic, even.

She paused. "I'll tell him. We can arrange something. Maybe he'll be able to help you out on weekends."

"That would be great."

"I've got to go. My legs are weak." Dallas had to lie down again soon. Her thighs quivered, not from the excitement of hearing Carl Rodriguez speak, but from childbirth.

"I just wanted to say hi."

"Hi. Thank you for the call, the room, the flowers."

"My pleasure."

After she replaced the receiver, the nurse came back, smiling, and escorted her back to her room. "Your dinner has arrived. The chef has prepared something special for you."

"What is it?"

"Oh. It's French. I can't even say it," she laughed. "There's a menu card though." The whole corridor had filled with the aroma of garlic, red wine gravy, beef. Dallas returned to her meal trolley and tray, keen to start as the books all said breastfeeding was very calorie-intensive. She *was* hungry all the time. Anyone would be, if they had to use their own body to make food.

When Jay Jay got back, she was full. She hadn't realized exactly how much food was included in "dinner". The fruit bowl was still full of uneaten fruit, too. "Just put it over there. In the little mini fridge. The yogurt. Everything except the fruit. " She explained to him clearly. It felt like she would be giving instructions for a while. She could no longer move or think quickly so she had no choice but to delegate.

Jay Jay was covered in sweat. He looked sick.

"Are you okay?"

"I'm okay. How aboutchu?"

"I'm fine. Saw Ernesto. He popped by with some flowers." She waved vaguely at the window where the bouquets were displayed. "Just had the most incredible French meal. Beef bor-something," she pointed at the menu card.

Jay Jay was sullen. Giving her the 'who cares' look that he was so good at.

"Why do they say jus," she said to make conversation. "Isn't it just juice?"

"Maybe it's not juice," he said. "Did Jennifer wake up?"

"Yes she did have a feed just before 7. I got another 5 minutes before I have to feed again. It seems to come round pretty quickly."

"Did I miss anything?"

She looked out the window. "Just the view," she said. She said nothing about the telephone call. It was a strange call she hadn't had time to think over. She adjusted the pillow, bashing it down flat to how she liked it. She felt naïve suddenly. She was just a young urban mom who liked clothes and art. Was Carl using her to just to find a *handyman*? Or to get gallery space? Images of his paintings floated through her mind again. They drew her in: the tight compositions and the intense contrast of the brightly-colored John Deeres, hay balers and combines against the landscapes.

"What?" Jay Jay had said something. Hormones, that's all.

"I said, Grandpops might be coming into hard times. He

might have to sell up and we'll see. 'S not making money. I haven't had any chance to talk to him at all."

"I'm sorry to hear that!"

"They'll be coming down to see us as soon as we check out of here tomorrow morning."

"I won't talk business. I heard nothing."

"I was just giving you the heads up."

He kissed Jennifer, inhaling her scent deeply. It made his heart flutter like riffled cards. There was something so special about a baby girl that he couldn't explain.

"We got to do the birth certificate."

"No hurry right? You could still change your mind and call her Christopher."

"Or Michelle."

He laughed. "Or Quentin. Enjoy your last evening here, hon."

"I will. I can't wait to go home again."

The baby started to stir and make the stuttering sound which he now knew preceded the full blown yelling. "I'll pick you guys up tomorrow. At about 12, or whenever the checkout is. Well, goodnight." He leant over and kissed her and then the baby.

"You're gonna miss the view and the 60611 zipcode, " he laughed. His first laugh since pizza with Emily.

"Naw, I ain't. 'S just a view."

"But worth every dollar."

She tensed up. She got up and picked up the baby who had started crying.

"I tried to check tonight what our account status was."

"And?"

"And I found that someone has paid up! We must write and thank Mr Alfred."

"Mr Alfred?" She asked.

" 'Course. Whoever did it decided to remain anonymous. But hell, only *he'd* do that. You know it's not Grandpops. He's broke or nearly broke thanks to Carmelita." His expression darkened.

CHAPTER 22

By the time Jay Jay got back, he had never been more tired. He hoped things got better after the first 25 years. *Every year gets quicker. A lifetime of the longest days is still too short.* Now who was thinking like a fortune cookie? He slept deeply after a shower. When he woke up, he remembered to ring Grandpops to arrange their visit.

"Congratulations again. How are they doing?"

"They're doing great. When are you coming to see the baby?"

"Look, you gotta come back to help when you can. With the seining."

"Why? 'Smatter?"

"After I let one guy go, I got that sick guy. And now all I got's Immanuel and he's quitting too."

Like Jay Jay could do anything about that.

"None-a those guys that Carmelita recommended have been great. One after another they've left, either sick, just 'cause they'd had enough, or I had. How 'bout this week?"

"This week? C'mon! Dallas just had a baby."

"That too. But you're off work and I just need a morning, from you. Or an afternoon?"

"How about in two days' time? I just need to settle Dallas back in."

"Sure. That would be so great. The fish really need moving."

"Yes," he sighed. "You said."

He hung up and had breakfast. Nothing much was in the fridge. He needed to fill it for when Dallas came back. She needed help with meals and so on and he wasn't a great cook or even a cook at all, unless you counted omelet. He made a note mentally of the stuff he had to do. He looked at the pile of dirty clothes. The laundry *did* have to be taken care of and she usually did all that. He doubted he had folded anything other than a drop sheet in his life. He opened the window to let some air in, as his head started to spin the more he thought about all the chores to be tackled. When he looked outside, a cop car was parking up on the street. *Oh no.* Emily. What had she found?

"Good morning, Jerry."

He winced at his name. "I am having breakfast." This was code for *this conversation better be important.*

"Well, as you know we are monitoring your telephone line and no calls came in apart from your Grandpops."

"What didja expect?"

"And we've talked to Mr Alfred and Professor Robert Ellesworth. Mind if I come in?"

She was standing on his front steps and thought she was on a lower level than him, he was the one feeling uncomfortable.

He didn't say yes but held the door open for her to enter.

"They claim to know nothing about the gun," she said. "Now we are talking to other executive members. There are quite a few of them."

"Right..." he replied, not sure what else to say.

"The only thing that I am telling you is that if anyone rings up, you need to make a note of where and when to meet up. The spy is a member of a tong. There's no such thing as an ex-member. If you die, your weapons go back to the tong. But here's the big clue: the seller is not Chinese, unaware of the rules nor that the logo engraved is that of the Black Phoenix."

"You did say this before... but the spy was executed."

"Jerry, after my uncle was killed, they had to try the number because they had no choice. They would not do that in the first instance. Protocol. No tong leader rings a number if they can get the information first hand. Too risky for them."

"You mean, the number is a trap?"

"Exactly. First they asked me to help, to save face for all. In the tong, face to face business is conducted, not cold calling. I have to find them this weapon. I am stuck in between two worlds. Slap bang in the middle of OC and the CPD. Do you want to help me?"

He didn't want to but he wanted to. "How?"

"It's not a coincidence."

"What do you mean?"

"I mean your wife. She is the link to the Institute... and the Professor. Hasn't she been working with the Professor for a few years ever since she was an art student? Didn't the Professor make sure Mr Alfred hired you? You think about that, Jerry, until I get back to you."

Jay Jay stocked up the fridge and did the laundry after Emily left. Then he got ready and drove up to Beecher, to Grandpops farm. As he was driving up the farm road, he saw a gleaming white Buick Electra sitting on the drive. The dogs were barking. He recognized the car and then the tanned blond man in an expensive Italian wool sweater coming out of the ranch-house. Grandpops waved goodbye as the man was leaving.

He didn't want to meet the Buick on its way out, so he did a quick detour and turned left into a wooded road where he parked under some trees. He waited ten minutes and drove back to the farm. Terry and Suzanne barked and ran up the road, their tongues and tails wagging.

"That was the landlord," said Grandpops as Jay Jay got out of the Camaro. He patted the dogs as they jumped on him. "Down. Down. C'mon, guys," said Grandpops to them.

"That guy?" Asked Jay Jay. He'd recognized the man: Carl Sutton.

"Yes. We were having the meeting. Not *a* meeting. *The* meeting. We can't be here." He pointed to the house. Jay Jay understood that mean Carmelita was in. "We have to move out."

"Why?"

"Carl Sutton inherited from his father who is in the Bahamas. Carl wants the land back. He's offering and I have to sell the equipment and everything. We have to move. He needs to free up the land to build apartments and he cannot get any more out of the family. Mr Alfred is broke too."

"He can't be," refuted Jay Jay. "He has just spent money on the house and paying our hospital bills and..."

"That's not big ker-ching to a big Kahuna. I mean a lot of money. The house became a ruin in the last 40 years. After what happened with his mother."

"What?"

"Catherine. She drowned in the lake. Tragic."

"Oh jeez." Jay Jay tried to hide his horror.

"Long time ago. Well before you were born. Did he ask you to repaint his mother's name on the glass window over the entrance? I bet he didn't."

Jay Jay's mouth widened in shock.

"The Sutton family made their money in arms and real estate. The Big Guns played with big guns. I hear your Mr Alfred's like his money, almost gone."

No, he couldn't get into that with his grandfather. He shook his head. He remembered that they were investigating right now. Someone had died sure, but they had no proof why *his* number was linked to arms sales. Yet.

"Mr Alfred borrowed money. Someone has lent him money to do these works. He'll have to pay that back. He's probably selling his other assets now. If he sells whatever he has slow and easy, they'll add up considerably. Trust me. I am a businessman too, Jay Jay. What comes around has to go around. It's just the recycling of old money. He couldn't possibly have afforded do the work then nor now: no liquidity. Once done though, he'll sell the land and the house as a hotel or some luxury shit like that and that's how he will survive his last days. Medical care won't be cheap for him. And in case you thought he's spending a lot of money remodeling, no way. He hasn't even hired a team. Why's that? Because he just needs one man make the house the best standard possible. Not luxury. No gold, no marble. Just fixing broken shit."

"Grandpop!" Jay Jay said, slightly deflated. He had done the work with so much pride. "I thought it was a top job."

"It is! Don't get me wrong. It is all he can afford within his budget."

"How do you know what he can afford?"

"Carl Sutton."

"You believe him?"

"No, not everything he says, but it makes sense. Say, whaddabout I come see, when we finish here?"

To see the infamous house? Jay Jay tried to imagine his grandfather riding in his van. The idea was ludicrous.

"They are all broke. This farmland is Ralph Sutton's pride and joy. He wouldn't let Carl redevelop unless they really had to. Ralph's had to move abroad. He's in trouble here. With taxes and so on. He can't come back."

"But they had a big shebang wedding party didn't they? That guy. Carl."

"You didn't even go. What makes you sure they had a big shebang wedding? Don't believe what you hear all the time. Those old families from the old world. 50 years ago they were the richest family in Chi-town. The talk of the town. They built buildings, roads, guns. They ran out of money. They can't even have servants, drivers, cooks, whatever now. Things have changed. The world has changed. Four wars in 60 years. So this is what they have to do. Borrow and sell up and give up on that old world."

Jay Jay listened glumly. He bit his cuticles.

"Sonny, times are harder now. And they were already hard for our family then. Your dad would be—"

His grandpop eyes welled up with tears. The old man couldn't talk.

"This was the real reason you asked me to come," said Jay Jay.

Grandpops nodded his head and buried his face in his hands. His poor grandfather. An incredibly hard life was about to become harder. Papa Moriarty had escaped early through the wafflewich. He was the one who was so into the pond farming as a way to run a business and make money. The truth was, all businesses were finding it hard to survive.

"What will you do when you've done the negotiations?"

"Well, look for a smaller place. An apartment. Look for another business to run until I retire in about 5 years. I have been thinking about this. Maybe a hotel, a guest house, nothing fancy. Just sheets to change and meals to make. I just need more time, that's all. You need a 5-year plan too, Jay Jay. When that old man goes into the box, what will you do? How much work is left?"

Dallas decided all these things while he kept living two weeks at a time. The only time he'd booked work outside of 'Catherine', it had been cut short due to Mr Chan's premature demise.

"I am already working on the second floor. With all the wood-work and cabinetry. Electrics. Plumbing: Spring '72."

"So another floor to go."

"Yes, though the kitchen is last. That'll take a month."

He didn't answer. Time to do the seining. They were still sitting in the tractor. "After this, lunch. Carmelita's making some-thing special. We need to celebrate too."

"Celebrate what?"

"That I'm a great grandfather now."

———

JAY JAY MADE a quick side-trip on his way home. As he'd known, the seining took all day. His Grandpops always told him everything took about half an hour, as if Jay Jay would believe him.

He looked up at the clear glass again.

"Mr Alfred I have to come and fit 4 missing window locks. They were out the other day." He stuttered. He felt awful about misleading Mr Alfred, even if most of what he'd said was true.

"Come in. But isn't it a bit late? It's almost five."

"Naw, September sun. Low but bright. Also I have to measure up the top floor rooms for materials. I sure am going to make a start next week when I'm back full time."

"Don't worry."

"Did they find who fired the shots at the windows?"

"They think it's kids, Jerry. This neighborhood is not what it used to be."

"But we do have to carry on," said Jay Jay. "We've lost time this year with the restaurant. Really sorry about Mr Chan."

"Me too." Mr Alfred hung his head. He was looking even older since his friend was killed and somehow lost, like an old geezer in a department store. "How is the baby?"

"She's great." Jay Jay said. "Anyway, I must get on." He went straight to the second and third floors. He had already started on those rooms and he knew his task was to complete Mr Alfred's room before the Christmas holidays but he did not waste any time on that. He shut the door, throwing a quick glance over his shoulder just to make sure. He started searching through the dust and debris of broken pieces of furniture, torn linen, and stuff in antique closets. He must not take too long. There were still so many rooms.

He wasn't sure how long he was. He took time out to measure the rooms and moved onto the other bedrooms and to do the same search and measure routine. He found plenty of guns but none were *that* one. He wasn't even able to tell if they were real or reproductions. They looked real. Antique ones, modern ones. In cases, boxes, plain and decorated, some lined, some unlined, some lay in a pair like brother and sister. Finally he was in Mr Alfred's room with its semblance of normality. It was relatively clean, just a little dusty. A strong, cloying old person smell masked the pungent scent layers of mothballs and chest rub. At least the bedding was not torn. A small room like this would be warm for the winter months. He hadn't wanted to start with this room when he first got to the house because Mr Alfred believed the grander rooms, which were on the first story, had to be completed first.

Mr Alfred came into the room, silent as a ghost. Jay Jay hadn't heard a thing. He stopped his search and held up his measuring tape, trying to appear "normal".

Mr Alfred sighed. Something about an old person looking sad was unbearable to Jay Jay. He looked away. His grandfather had looked like this sometimes. They did not have the innocence that children had when they were unhappy, on being denied an ice cream or a toy. Old people often did not look sad when they really were.

"Sir, I will leave you with the keys to the window locks. In case of fire or something."

"If there is a fire, I will die here."

Jay Jay ignored the morbid comment. "No, you won't. You have the keys. We've talked through the escape routes. Down onto the flat roof, holding on to the pipes, over the stone porch. A short jump, maybe 3 feet. You can do it. I've been updating the door seals and closers. And your electrics. There won't be a fire."

The sun was setting quickly. The room and its long shadows created an eerie ambience, like the stage set from the last play in a disused theater. Jay Jay wanted to complete his tasks and leave. He took the measurements of Mr Alfred's room and went downstairs.

Dallas and the baby were asleep when he got home. Jay Jay had no way of knowing when they would be up or where they were in the routine. All he knew was that in the early days, sleep cycles were only 45 minutes to 2 hours long. If you got even 3 hours, you'd be laughing. Or you'd think something was wrong and keep checking on the baby.

He opened the fridge and made himself a ham sandwich. He'd have to pick up more groceries in a couple of days. He had just finished eating and washed up his plate when the baby started crying. Dallas woke up and suddenly announced, as if she had been in mid-conversation all along, "She cries all the time because I don't have enough milk. I think I need formula for the night-time. To knock her out. Otherwise we'll be up all night and day."

"I'll pick some up on the next shopping trip."

"Thank you, Lemon Pie. We should take our first walk tomorrow with the baby carriage. I'm excited."

"Whoa, a new vehicle?"

Dallas tried to laugh. She looked so tired and had red-eyes but her laughter melted away her bruise-colored undereye bags and her grayish complexion. Now without any cosmetics she was almost unrecognizable, though he didn't want to say that out loud. That was what happened to women. They became mothers, a far greater achievement than makeup application.

"Doll, are you still working at the Institute?"

Her bloodshot eyes narrowed like a cat's. "I would like to. We need the money."

"We don't. We've saved a lot by... Oh no! I just have... I forgot to thank Mr Alfred."

She didn't answer. "Well, I am sure he knows you have other things on your mind."

"I do. My two girls." He smiled, "Will they still call you? If—"

"They might. They still send the forms for new enrolments which I have to type up and process for the Institute's student files."

He wanted to say what he wanted to say, that their telephone number was on the sales handbill, but again Emily's image popped into his head. His conscience pricked him when Dallas looked away. Her mouth, bare, without lipstick or a swab of gloss, was drawn into a tight line. It was so unlike her.

"I am really hungry," she said in a terse voice. "Could you make some spaghetti? I can't eat any more sandwiches."

"Any *more*?"

"Well, you were out all day today at Grandpops. That was all I ate. I was waiting for you to come back with a hot meal or something. Look at the time," she pointed, at the window and not the clock. "It's dark, must be almost 8. I am starving. And I haven't said anything. You didn't even ask."

The weather change in her was coming. Lightning, and then thunder, then storm. She had turned. And it was his fault for not thinking about her. He spent the entire day with two old men when his young wife needed him at home.

"Of course, let me make you something." He jumped up from sitting on the bed. The pressure of the screws on his skull tightened by a few rounds. He headed in to the kitchen. He grabbed his head, and exhaled, wondering where the hell was the spaghetti?

CHAPTER 23

Dallas looked at the kitchen clock on the wall. She was waiting for Sherylanne and Duane, her pals from work, to visit. She'd been home a week now. She *was* counting. If she didn't, she'd lose track of days, weeks, months, night and day. She washed Jennifer on the diaper station and let her kick around diaper-less and *leaving the* fresh air to dry her bottom. This was another planet in a different galaxy now. A dream. As she scraped the poop into the toilet with her rubber gloved hands and a blunt-bladed tool Jay Jay had called a spackle knife when he'd given it to her, she wondered if she had ever even been at the Drake bar sipping a cherry martini.

She rinsed the diaper and put it into a bucket, now part of an automatic cycle for her, the human washing machine. For pee, straight in the soak bucket. For poop, scrape, then soak. She quietly referred to herself as the "scrapegoat". After a week, she was now able to do this in her sleep, and sometimes did. "Never let it mount up," had been her mother's advice. Not that she ever gave her much else. Advice was *never* needed, only unwanted or too late.

She dressed Jennifer in her best clothes, including a pair of the cutest frilly pants.

The doorbell rang. She buzzed the door open. She screamed and put her hands to mouth, shaking all over. Her colleagues screamed too. They held their arms out and took turns to hug her for a long time.

"We've missed you so much," said Sherylanne.

"You did? I miss you guys too. I can't believe I am now playing mom. I don't even have mascara or lipstick on. I'm a wreck."

"You look beautiful!" Said Duane. "You're glowing like a new mom."

She knew that couldn't be true. She'd seen herself recently. Gaunt cheekbones, blue-gray-green tinged skin, pink-rimmed eyes, piercing and haunted all at once. Holding her poop palette knife, she'd nodded at the stranger in the mirror and thought *hello, you look exactly like Vincent Van Gogh's self-portrait.*

"Where's daddy?"

"He had to go back to work. We need the money."

"Of course. Aww. You're doing great, Dall."

"Where is she?" Asked Sherylanne.

Dallas pointed to the play mat behind her on the floor. She was out of view due to the mountain of domestic clutter and laundry. There was another round of awws and laughter. "I want to pick her up. Can I?"

"Of course, Sherylanne. Please do. How is everything? How is Michael?"

"Well?" She shot a glance at Duane who looked down at his knees in embarrassment. "He might leave his wife or she might leave him. She wants to go back to Singapore. He doesn't. And neither does the girl."

"Oh! That is big news. So... does that mean you'll have a 14-year-old piano whizz living with you soon? What's her name? I forgot."

"Yes. What's-her-name." She rolled her eyes. "Nevermind all that. Now we two kings have brought you gifts!"

"You have?" She joked, seeing that Duane was struggling with a large hamper.

With the excitement of a child, Dallas tore open beautiful parcels which reminded her of the other planet in the other galaxy: the planet with the store, new shiny things, Chicago, State Street. Everything that wasn't her life right now.

"Okay, this big one is from the store. Bill sends his congratulations and he says to tell you we can't wait to have you back."

"The time is coming, yes! I just have to get through a day at a time." She had to remind herself not to talk about poop or pee. They were not exactly her favorite topics but she was measuring out her days and nights in them. Was it any wonder she was pee-brained?

They all sat with her on the carpet as the sofa was covered in towers of stuff. Clothes, books, wrapping paper. Just like Christmas Day. She was surrounded by luxury mom-gifts. Scented candles, bath bubbles, creams. The baby had new clothes, blankets, a fluffy rabbit and a teddy bear, more diapers and several boxes of formula. The sight of the more "luxury" gifts reminded her of Carl. He was her distraction from mundane tasks. She wondered if it was the shared art interest or the costly gifts that he'd showered on her were what made her miss him, slightly.

"Are you okay?"

She realized she was crying and wiped at her tears with the back of her hand.

"Just... I'm just... " She sniffed. "I feel so... touched."

She waved at the mountain of gifts. Sherylanne grabbed the tissues on the sofa's arm rest and handed the box to Dallas. "I miss you guys so much," she repeated.

"You'll be back."

"I know."

Being emotional and alone was a weird place to be in, especially after being surrounded by people all day in a busy job. It was time for her colleagues to return to work. "Sorry but we only had a long lunch break to visit you. Jeff is covering for us both," Duane laughed. "Bill said thank God for Jeff. Imagine if it was Carol."

They shook their heads and burst into laughter though Dallas felt both a little left out and the pain of missing the camaraderie and in-jokes of the store.

Dallas was not crying any more. That was the hormones crying, not her. Anyway, crying was bad. It caused wrinkles. They were having their goodbye hugs when—

"Hey," said Sherylanne, "remember that guy?"

"What guy?"

"That guy came in. Carl."

"He did?"

"Yes. He was looking for a gift."

"Oh. For who?"

"Oh, he didn't say," said Duane. "But... Then... When we told him you were on maternity, he asked if we would be seeing you soon. We said yes. And he bought you this." He pointed at the little trinket box. Dallas opened the box and a tiny necklace with a star on a chain glinted in its satin-lined bed.

"Oh my, isn't it beautiful!"

"What's going on between you guys?" Asked Sherylanne. "C'mon now, spill. I told you all about Michael so now it's your turn," she added.

"Naw," said Dallas, a little red now showing in her regular blue-gray-green complexion. "There's nothing to tell. I'm not you. I'm married and he's married. There is nothing going on." She felt naked as an old piece of raw fish. They were looking at her, wondering who the fuck he was. She scratched her neck absent-mindedly. She wasn't sure herself.

"That's interesting," said Duane. Everybody burst out laughing at the inane statement. Including Duane.

"Thought you might like some news from the store," chuckled Sherylanne.

When they'd left, she shut the door and thought about Carl Rodriguez offering to let Jay come to his house and provide an estimate. She looked at the kitchen clock again. It was her boss now. She loaded the machine with the diapers soaked the day before and rotated the dial to 'start'. She moved Jennifer into the kitchen in her basket and folded fifteen square cloths for diapers. They'd last another 24 hours.

She'd take Jennifer for a walk before the rain later. Maybe that would make her sleep. The sky *was* a little cloudy. She must remember to take the rain cover for the baby carriage.

Jay Jay working on Carl's domestic project would certainly bring income into their household. She felt caged by her new-mom loneliness.

The call supposedly from the restaurant that Jay Jay had inadvertently answered had been *the* call. About "The Order".

The Professor had told her to inform him immediately if a call came from a buyer abroad, somebody famous. And no one was to find out about the sale of the de Weiss sculpture. But Jay Jay had taken the call and hung up because he'd thought it was about the takeout. That had thrown her. Why would he think that? Good job that he had. But she had still messed up and might even lose her job. She was selfishly proud of her only side hustle. It was only art. Yes. Only. A 1957 bronze. Why did anyone have to know about this but the Professor and her? She saw herself as a small-time dealer, a curator, a facilitator for cultured minds that appreciated art.

After folding the dry laundry, she started tidying the crap in the small apartment. She found at the handbill from the hospital advertising a moms' support group in the neighborhood. She crushed it with all the gift packaging and put it in the trash. Except for the necklace gift box, which had fallen open when she put it on the coffee table. She picked up the little card inside.

CHAPTER 24

He looked at his watch. He had overslept. Was he running late? His last dream had been hyper-real and made no sense. Since Jay Jay had started back at Mr Alfred's, he'd had to sleep on the couch unfolded clothes, which of course he had to neaten first to make a big mountain into a smaller one. This was his new bedroom, because of his work: no man could do a solid day's work, if his wife and baby kept him awake all night.

He had dreamt of a party from long ago. He looked down: he was wearing a tux, a winged shirt and was all smart, but as he looked further down, he saw he was barefoot with no idea where his shoes were. He walked through grand rooms into a large, opulent hall where the party was. He was embarrassed by his lack of shoes and tense from looking for them. He went down an ornate corridor with spotted gilt mirrors. He followed the corridor until he reached a dark room lit only by moonlight reflected by the lake outside. It sliced through the room via the expansive French windows.

In the room, a woman was facing the wall and swaying. At first he thought she was dancing. He got closer to her. He did not recognize her. He had never seen her before. She was in a beaded dress. She turned around. A round black gunshot wound was in the middle of her chest, which had actually blown her necklace apart. Tiny glass-shards and gemstones had sprayed her dress and the floor around her, glinting in the moonlight. Her eyes fluttered closed. She fell to the ground. He couldn't find her assailant. He tried to yell but he had no voice. Somebody, *help*. He turned and ran, still barefoot and yelling.

Now he was awake, he was light-headed and cold. He was surprised he remembered so much as he didn't usually remember dreams at all. After getting dressed and eating his breakfast as silently as he could, he took a quick peek at the girls and let them be. The yelling might start at any moment.

The baby did not have any routine yet. She was still in training so not much notice was given before the ear-splitting thunder began. A bit of ecking and ugging was all you got before full-blown crying. Yet when Jennifer wasn't crying he got to stare deeply into her eyes. Brown eyed girl, just like Van Morrison sang. And dark hair, like daddy. His eyes welled up with tears looking at his baby girl. Something was so special about a baby girl. He would never be able to explain why he'd suddenly melt like cheese on a steak. With a kind of sad happiness or happy sadness, he left them asleep.

When he got to Mr Alfred's he had to have another coffee in the kitchenette of his workshop, now all set up comfy and cozy. He sure had missed his own private world. Didn't hurt to check on the room again in case he had missed anything. Like, well, a gun.

He lifted the floor covering and the boards as usual. He hadn't put a lock back on. The flooring was laid tight. Even had a ladder now going down. His safe room was just as he had left it months ago. A little dusty but he'd expect that. He went around the crates and chests, like Ali Baba looking for treasure. "Dja miss me," he said aloud to Bones 1 and 2.

No reply. He kept searching.

Nothing. What he was hoping for? He'd been through the room thoroughly when he first started. even tidied up a little, as though anyone would ever have used the space for anything. He noticed one thing. No ribs. The skeleton's ribcage center was shattered. Just like the woman's in his dream. He shuddered. To think that a woman and her dog had suffered their last moments here and were now giving him nightmares. He thought about the spy who vanished in the '20s. Did someone rub her out because of something she'd found out?

He locked up, left his cabin and checked on the yard, now looking a little rough. No one had been tending it for the month he'd been away. He made a shopping list. Weedkiller. Fertilizer. The lawn needed mowing. At his break time he would have to go to the Garden of Eden. Again.

"Hey, Jay Jay. Listen. Let's grab a coffee. Or two."

"Nesto. Look. I'm in a hurry. I got a lot to do at Mr Alfred's."

"My boys been checking up. Staking out the place. "

"Oh yes?"

Ernesto nodded. "Man. 'S going great. Nobody been back. The old man is safe for now. You talk to him yet?"

"Of course. He said he's taking care of it."

"Cool. I got great news for ya."

"Oh yeah? What?"

"I got that notebook translated," Ernesto gave a tight smug smile. "The anteek notebook?"

"I understand what you're referring to," said Jay Jay. "I get it, okay?"

"Don't get excited, but one of my boys is Chinese. Yup. Nothing to do with the restaurant or anything—."

"Ernesto. I got to tell you something too. But I got all this chemical shit to buy first." He opened his folded piece of paper and pointed.

"Gimme that." Ernesto looked at the scribbles. "Lemme help you find the pesticide, the glyphosate and Pennington's first." He folded and returned the piece of paper to Jay Jay. "Now. We'll be cooking." He nodded and tapped the side of his head like *anything* might be cooking in there.

"I'll meet you at the checkout," said Jay Jay.

Ernesto came back with the cart and helped Jay Jay load his van with 6 bags of various shit. "Die, weeds, die," said Ernesto. "Come on." He beckoned. They walked to the coffee and hotdog stand outside the parking lot.

"So what you do want to say?" Asked Jay Jay.

"Look," pulled out of his pocket the battered silk notebook again and opened the front cover.

葉海花

"The three words. Is her name. The spy's name. Yip Hoi Fa in Cantonese. Leaf. Sea. Flower." Nesto said each word as carefully as he could. The Chinese guy on the surveil team had schooled him on the words.

"I listen. I feel. I speak." Nesto made the gesture of fingers snapping at his ears. He had always been a good copycat. That was why he spoke two languages since he was a kid.

"Sure?"

"Course I'm sure. Asked a Chinese dude, okay?"

"Why d'ya do that?" Said Jay Jay clutching his forehead with the hand not holding the coffee. He'd always thought he was smart guy, landing on his feet. But now he was beginning to doubt himself. He was as dumb as Ernesto. "Didn't you think you might get in trouble?"

"Naw. He's one of our boys."

"What does the rest of the notebook say?"

"Dates, places, times. No more names. My mother, she seen what she seen. The spy and her dog died inside."

"But... Nesto. She didn't. You *said* she saw a body being dragged. And she was a little girl. Are you sure what she is saying is right? I mean, kids imagine things."

He shrugged. "My abuelita agreed with her at the time."

"But she's gone nuts. She has to go into a home. Can you trust—"

"Hey, no old people go nuts about the old days, okay? They

just don't know what is happening to them right now. About the past, their memory is clear."

"That's complete garbage. Their memory is jumbled up. They don't know what is past or present."

Ernesto drank noisily then slurped again. "Hell, forget my abuelita. Whatchu gonna do now?" He slurped.

Jay Jay thought Mrs Chan's life was still in danger. Things were hotting up. The tong members would want Mr Alfred next, and after that... Him. They would not give up hounding Emily until the tong's prized possession, "The Order", was found. That was how their reign of terror had worked, generation after generation. The events on that night in 1925 must be connected to Mr Chan. *Homicide*, he shook at the thought.

So far what had he seen in the notebook, on the gun and Mrs Chan's heel?

The bird.

———

WHEN HE GOT BACK to the mansion, the white Buick Electra was parked at the kerb. As he approached the building, a racket was coming from Mr Alfred's study. He could hear that Mr Alfred was not in a good mood. It was hard not to eavesdrop. Jay Jay had overheard Mr Alfred's telephone conversation clearly enough on this side of the house. This time someone was actually there.

"—that farm."

"Your father— ."

"My father has no control over it. He's in the Bahamas. Broke." That voice. Carl Sutton, that explained the Buick.

"After you fired those shots— ."

"*I* fired those shots? You can't say— ."

"Carl. Come on." Mr Alfred chuckled. "We Suttons know how to squirt metal, Carl. We have been doing it since long before you were born. I'd recognize those slugs anywhere."

"You're lucky to be alive," said Carl.

"You too. I was protecting you. You'd be 'cuffed now if I hadn't."

"No, I wouldn't," Carl refuted, like a child who said no to everything.

"Your Grandma didn't die in the lake for nothing," said Mr Alfred. "You'll have to carry me off in my takeout box first."

"No, I won't. If you are not selling, then why are you having all this work done?"

"To give this treasure the dignity it deserves. Have you ever heard of the word restoration? How about pride?"

"You can't even pay the Professor back."

"You don't know that."

"Oh yeah? You are telling me you have secret assets somewhere?"

"I am not telling you anything, Carl. One thing I learnt from you is that an inch becomes a mile. *That* is why your father had to move abroad. You completely bankrupted him."

"I didn't. Grandma did."

"Your Grandma was sick."

"Sick in the head and in the heart," Carl pointed at his head and chest.

"Carl, stop."

"She never loved him."

"Who?" said Mr Alfred.

"Grandpa."

Mr Alfred was shaking. "Carl, leave them out of this."

"You don't like me saying all this but it's true, Uncle Alfred," said Carl.

Mr Alfred was silent for no more than a second or two.

"It is." Carl hissed and slapped his fist in his palm.

"Well, you still are not going to stick me in a home," said Mr Alfred.

"We're the two Suttons left in Chi-town," said Carl. "Who's staying longer?"

"Carl, stop. Please leave."

Jay Jay knocked loudly and entered. "I'm sorry to interrupt."

"And who are you?"

Carl knew damn well who Jay Jay was.

"I'm... I'm Jerome. Please leave now, Sir. Mr Alfred is not well. He has a medical appointment now that I am taking him to."

"Well... Thaaaat's news. So you are a chauffeur too?" He said show-fer, as in what had he got to show-fer it.

"Yes, Sir. The nurse couldn't make it today."

"You keep your honker out of it," said Carl. "Just fix things up real good here. We want a high price. You keep on doing a great job."

Jay Jay looked Carl in the eye for once and he seemed to be talking with a hard-nosed sincerity. Jay Jay didn't answer. The house wasn't for sale, rather for Mr Alfred's last days, for the sake of his parents and their turbulent life in it. And also for love.

Also, for love.

Carl went back down the front steps and got into his white Buick. He sped off. Jay Jay settled Mr Alfred, made some fancy aromatic English tea for him and gave him his medication.

"Thank you, Jerry. You are a good guy."

"Naw, I am not good, Sir," Jay Jay grinned sadly. He plenty of bad points. Such as stupidity and youth.

"Okay, what I mean is you are good to me, then."

He held Mr Alfred's hands in his for a while.

"I do have to do yard work today. 'S my first day back since Jennifer was born. Oh, I forgot. I wanted to thank you for giving us a room upgrade."

"Where?"

"At the hospital. The first class room with the first class view."

"Oh!"

Jay Jay waited for him to say "You're welcome." But he didn't.

"The additional meals, all French, beauty treatments and services. My wife loved it. And all in the best zip code in Chicago."

"That's wasn't me."

"It wasn't?"

"No. Hmm. Maybe Robert? But certainly not me," he tried to laugh but it turned into a hacking cough.

"I gotta go now." Jay Jay said. The color had returned to Mr Alfred's cheeks and he had cheered up a little." His mind wandered back to the amount of work he had to do. After the yard, he'd carry on with the interiors during the fall and the winter months. Everything would go pretty slow, because he was working alone and there was so much distracting shit going on.

"Since Mr Chan went, I can't help thinking I'll be next."

"What? What did you say, Sir?"

"They are looking for something."

Oh, if only Jay Jay could tell him that he knew that. The whole business had kicked off thanks to Emily.

Mr Alfred beckoned to Jay Jay and they moved towards his leather-covered desk again. He opened the top drawer and pulled out an old photograph of the house when viewed from the front. "There's the sign. Please repaint my mother's name."

He rummaged in the drawer again. Someone like him didn't put photographs in frames. It was beneath him. Jay Jay had noticed that there were no family photographs on display on his first day. Only regular families did that because they could not afford art. They didn't know what art was anyway. So they displayed themselves in frames, as Dallas and Jay Jay did with their wedding photos. Oh, they had other stuff on the walls; a ginormous framed movie poster in the kitchen of *What's New Pussycat.* Woody Allen appealed to Dallas's interest in romantic comedy. Jay Jay didn't think there was much funny about love. A little framed art poster of Vincent Van Gogh's *Starry, Starry Night* in the bedroom next to the closet. Jay Jay thought the posters were enough art for a regular couple. Maybe Dallas did not.

In a house of this size and grandeur, photographs were stored in albums or drawers. Only original art hung on the walls, Paintings, drawings, etchings, woodcuts and all the stuff Jay Jay didn't know about and never would. "Not here," the old man said.

"Ah," he pointed at the wall over the fireplace where the painting of Catherine Sutton hung. "We don't need a photograph. There she is."

"She was unlucky and unhappy," sighed Mr Alfred looking at his mother's portrait, emphasizing the *un* like Jay Jay was a schoolboy learning grammar. "This house was built with blood, sweat and tears of my mother's family's money, not my father's. She made it possible for my father to run all his businesses. As you know, you can't make money from no money."

Jay Jay's hand was half-way to scratching his head, until his boss noticed.

"Let me explain. How do you make a million dollars?"

"Umm..." Jay Jay thought, *it's a test*. He stared at the painting.

"You start with two million dollars."

Luckily he didn't give the dumb-ass answer he'd first thought of. Anyhow, he didn't want to get into talking business with Mr Alfred.

"Sir, I... I will repaint that for you... as per the photograph I found ... lying around in one of the rooms. I kept it after I used it when I redid the lettering the first time." He had decided not to change or update the design after all. That would simply be complicating matters.

"Thank you."

If he hadn't known how she'd died, he might have indulged Mr Alfred in his romanticized reminiscence. The man idolized his mother.

"Sir, has... has everything been... Ernesto has been in charge of this beat in the last two weeks... "

Oh. Mr Alfred suddenly raised his hands, as if in surrender, at the memory. "Of course. He is a good fella. He did come in to say hello with the boys couple times."

Jay Jay waited. "About what we talked about—."

"What did we talk about?"

"The CPD."

"It's in the bag. He should receive a letter soon."

"Oh thank you, Mr Alfred, thank you so much."

"You should keep an eye on Carl Sutton. Whatever you heard stays here. Thank you for coming to the rescue and telling him I have an appointment." He cackled, his laugh still the wheeze of a rusty hinge.

As Jay Jay drove off in his white van, he let out a huge sigh. The radio came blaring on and the local FM station's jock was playing Deep Purple's *Black Night*. When he looked in the rear mirror, he sensed that he was being followed. Whenever he looked in the rear-view mirror, a black Chevy appeared too many times for coincidence and not enough to be sure. Time to find out. He sped up, slowed down and drove badly, but the other car did the same. When he took a sharp left, the Chevy got stuck at the lights.

Back safe in Lincoln Park, Jay Jay turned off the ignition and slammed his sweaty hands on the wheel. He didn't like this at all. He also started to fear for Dallas and Jennifer.

CHAPTER 25

On Friday evening, after work and before sunset, Jay Jay dropped by the attractive suburb of Western Springs on his way home. He parked up and surveyed the wide tree-lined street for his moonlighting gig. He looked around, as he did each time he drove anywhere now, ever since he had been followed by the black Chevy. He demurred when Dallas showed him a card with an address and a telephone number of someone wanting work done. But she was right; as she kept telling him, they could do with the money. Clearly this would be a weekend job if he were to complete all the variety of tasks at Mr Alfred's. He could not fit in any more jobs during the week. He did once for the Jade Palace Garden and look what happened then. Emily. That's what happened. And Mr Chan. He was bumped off because Emily had not given them what they wanted. Boy, that must really stink.

Now *this* job was less likely to be high risk, being in a suburb full of 10- and 20-year-old detached homes for middle-class parents who had liked Ike and Kennedy but weren't sure about Nixon. Boring and safe, just what the doctor ordered. He spotted the house with the garage which the customer— a keen artist— wanted to turn into an art studio. He was plagued by three children under the age of 9 every time he opened his paint box. That was Dallas's brief. The guy was a regular customer at the store, she'd said.

When the customer opened the door, Jay Jay saw a towering figure in "weekend-wear". Slacks, and a T-shirt with collar, buttons and an embroidered logo— so not a tee at all, but a polo shirt. The man seemed very familiar, but he couldn't place him.

"Hello. Carl Rodriguez," he held out his hand, which Jay Jay shook briskly. "Please come in, your wife has told me all about you. I am very honored that you'd consider this project as Dallas said you worked on grand traditional and historic homes— ."

"No problem." He cut Mr Rodriguez short, aware that he'd interrupted, but he didn't need any bouquets or to listen to an award ceremony speech.

"We thought about moving out of Chicago but we— ."

He droned on. We, we, we. They moved as a unit. He was either referring to him and the wife or all five of them. Jay Jay zoned back in as they reached the garage. Mr Rodriguez was still talking. "Now we'd just like to convert the space. A couple of kitchen cabinets to make a sink unit. A skylight, a window facing the side and the rear yard."

"Yes, yes," Jay Jay got it. He scanned the available space, trying to hide his impatience. Flooring. Plumbing for the heating and the sink. Insulate the walls.

"As you know they're bare. 50s standard home. Thin walls, just drywall."

Jay Jay nodded.

"But while you're here, we have a list of things that need fixing too," he smiled. That smile reminded him of someone else. The creases around his eyes and the cheeks which made parentheses, like the smile was just an aside.

He made a few notes of the sizes and lists of tasks to be achieved including stuff he'd have to purchase. He'd need a new sliding sash window to match the other windows, too.

———

HE WAS BARELY through the apartment door when Dallas piped up. "And?"

"Yup. Great. Now I have to prepare the estimate."

"What happened? What was the place like?"

"Regular house in a pretty street. Suburban. Neat."

"What was his wife like?"

"His wife? No idea. I— I didn't actually see anyone else there."

"What about the kids?"

"No one."

"He was alone?"

"Yes. Is that so weird?"

"No," she looked dubious. Jay Jay waited for her to elaborate but she didn't.

"So what's being done?" she said.

"All this stuff. Lighting, heating, electrics, windows," he got his notebook out and held it up, open, like a birthday card. "To turn the garage into his art studio."

"Did he show you his art?"

"He didn't. I saw some canvasses stacked in a pile, some standing against the dining room wall."

"What did you think?"

"Honey. Honey. I didn't even get the chance to look at them. I mean, I saw the first one on the stack, but... " He made jazz hands along with a gesture that was between a slouch and a shrug. "And I was like, okay."

"You really didn't take a look?"

"Well, not everybody is interested in art like you, Doll. Have I ever been to a gallery?"

"You came to my show in first year."

"Well, that was *your* show."

"You oughta show some interest in a customer. Even feign some interest."

"Man. I could care less."

"Why not? Just courtesy."

"Doll. I am working 6 days a week. I am courteous. I showed

interest in Chinese food every night and look what happened there." He pointed randomly at the window.

"That reminds me. Is there anything to eat? I am dying."

"Sure. I made some mac and cheese two seconds before feeding time. I've been with the baby all day. Just look at the diaper mountain." She waved around her and burst into tears without warning. She took one of the diapers she hadn't had time to fold and used the corner to dab at her eyes.

"Oh, I am so sorry, Doll."

"The hormones, not you. Not me." She said, quick to make a joke as usual despite the sudden rogue wave of emotion.

She looked glum and old and she was only 23. What was gonna happen when she was 30? He had no idea how tough this had been on her. What would happen to him? Would they be in a bigger apartment than this? Maybe not if he was still be working 6 days a week as a handyman for wealthy people with problems. There were no prospects for workers. You just got more of the same jobs unless you became a director or contractor with their own business, something like that.

"Let me give you a hand with folding after I eat something." He looked around him and the apartment certainly had the look of a nest now. You could hardly see the walls or the floor any more. He wondered what she was doing if she wasn't tidying but he knew better than to ask. Surely looking after baby wasn't a full-time task? Uh-oh. He'd be in trouble if he said these "guy things". *Are we living in 1917, Jay Jay?* Would be her reply if he even dared mention the mess.

She sniffled and calmed down. She stood up, still cradling the baby with her left arm while she moved plates and cups with one hand. He had only just noticed this new one-handed skill. New mothers acquired it, then kept it for the rest of their lives. "What's next?"

"Next he's checking references. I only have Mrs Chan and Mr Alfred to offer him. He also said he'd like to visit one of my domestic jobs and there's only Mr Alfred's to show him. He said he'd call the referees tonight and come by tomorrow, if it's all okay."

"Oh that's good. That means you'll probably get the job."

"Probably," he said. "Thanks to you, Doll."

"You're welcome, lemon pie." She didn't even look at him. She scratched at the patches of dry skin on her forehead absent-mindedly. Since giving birth, it had been like the plagues of Egypt. Mastitis causing her to be on antibiotics for a week, patches of red inflamed dry skin which the doctor said were psoriasis or dermatitis. And of course sleepless-itis making her despondent and irritable, prone to daydreaming, always thinking of something else, distracted to distraction.

Jay Jay ate quickly, then washed and dried everything that was in the sink too. The bottles, the pots, baby stuff. He was about to help with organizing the wet and dry laundry, an enormous and uplifting task (in the literal sense), when the telephone rang. He looked at the clock, and picked up the receiver.

"Oh, Mr Alfred, good evening," he said, relieved. "I hope you didn't mind—"

"I don't mind, and thank you for using me as a reference. Mr Rodriguez will come by tomorrow. He's an artist. You can show him the fine work you've done in my house. I'll be hanging around if he wants to ask any questions."

"That's very helpful of you."

"Least I can do. I know you need weekend work."

They did. They were feeling the pinch and would have to pay for daycare too, when Dallas went back to work.

They said their goodnights. After he put the telephone down, it rang again. He thought Mr Alfred must have forgotten something, so he answered again.

"Mr Alfred?"

"I am calling about The Order."

The voice was familiar, and one of those he'd heard in the restaurant basement kitchen. It was the taller of the Chinese men, with a high-pitched voice in a Cantonese accent. He could tell.

Most of the boys at kung fu school were Cantonese-speaking from Hong Kong. Only two were from Taiwan. "Yes?" He whispered.

"Is this the Institute of Art?"

"No. My wife works for them, though. May I take a message?"

"Is it ready? Is it there?"

"Nnnn."

He knew that if, as Emily had said, someone was monitoring, she'd get to hear what was said. He had to keep going and obtain as much information as possible. Ernesto had been been told to never ring him at home. They'd just have to meet up at the Garden of Eden or anywhere else if they had to talk.

But the guy just hung up on hearing his "nnnn".

Damn. Jay Jay hand was shaking as he slammed the receiver down so hard it dinged.

"What's happened?"

No point trying to shield Dallas now.

"Someone used our telephone number to advertise a gun."

She said nothing.

Jay Jay stared. "Do you know anything about it?"

"I— ."

"Do you?"

She'd made him raise his voice. He hated that.

"No," she said flatly.

———

As SOON AS he got to N. Lakeshore Drive, he let himself in, ran through the lobby and was knocking on Mr Alfred's study door seconds later.

"Good morning, Mr Alfred."

"Good— ."

"We're going on a quick trip."

"Where?"

"Just into town."

"Why?"

"My treat, Sir. Coffee and uh... cake."

"Oh no, is that really necessary?"

"Yup. I mean, no. But I'd like to."

"This is unlike you, Jerry. What's going on?"

He'd only wanted to make the trip sound attractive. "Okay, truth is... We need to get your photo taken."

"Why?"

He felt himself sounding panicky. He wasn't one for small talk. The big talk was hard enough.

"I'll tell you later. Just trust me. C'mon. I'll... We'll be back in an hour. You can get a ride in the van you paid for." Jay Jay smiled to make light of the subject. "We have to be quick and get back by 10. If you remember, Sir, that potential customer is coming to see my work. And thank you for doing that and helping me."

Mr Alfred waved his hand in his usual "don't mention it" gesture.

When they got to the stand at N. Rush and E. Ontario, Jay Jay parked, got out and opened the passenger door to assist Mr Alfred, but he needed no help. He was a little slow but he was very steady. Jay Jay scanned the immediate vicinity to make sure no one was following, unlikely though that was first thing in the morning. Too hard to keep following a car in rush-hour traffic, but he could never be totally sure now.

"A set of passport photos please," said Jay Jay to the photographer.

CHAPTER 26

When he parked the van and got out to help Mr Alfred again, Carl Rodriguez was already on the front path, his muddy footprints all over Jay Jay's carefully laid tiles. It hand't rained for a couple of days. Jay Jay recently tiled. Rodriguez had his back to them. "Sorry, are we late?" Jay Jay called out, waving.

"No, no. I'm early. This is for Mr Sutton." He gestured at the bouquet. "Thank you for letting me visit your home."

He was wearing a suit and strangely, in Jay Jay's opinion, carried a bunch of mixed aromatic flowers. Oriental lilies, freesias, roses and some other leaf combinations. Since doing yard work and frequent visits to the Garden of Eden, Jay Jay was able to tell some plants apart. Well, plants apart from weeds anyway.

"No problem. Please come in," said Mr Alfred without even looking at Mr Rodriguez because at his age now he had to mind his step. The nurse had said to Jay Jay. "No looking around in wonder or in a daze. No looking at the view, any view. Look at the tiles, look at the ground, look at the lawn, steps, uneven paths. If he trips at his age, which isn't unusual, his recovery'll take months. Might even need surgery." she'd said.

Jay Jay followed after Mr Alfred.

"You did all this?" Mr Rodriguez pointed at the multi-colored decorative and geometric tiling. Period perfect thanks to Jay Jay's hunting through Mr Alfred's books and old photographs.

"Yes. All of this. The tuck pointing into the center of the molded brick joint, new flower beds, stone kerbs." Jay Jay pointed around at each item.

"Beautiful."

"Thank you," said Jay Jay, getting the key out to open the front door. He got Mr Alfred up the steps and they all went inside. Jay Jay shut the door behind them. Mr Alfred said "I'll leave you now. I will be in my study. Jerry will show you what he's done."

"So this is the front—"

"No, stay," said Carl which surprised Jay Jay.

"Well, if you don't mind, I'd rather not. I really do have to sit down. But come into my study to say goodbye later, if you want."

"Yes, thank you. We'll do that, I'm sorry, I should have thought of that," said Carl.

Mr Rodriguez had not taken his eyes off Mr Alfred once since they'd met him outside the door. The house seemed of no interest to Mr Rodriguez after he had seen the tiles. Mesmerized by Mr Alfred, he had seemed anxious to get inside quickly and Jay Jay had no idea why.

Jay Jay cleared his throat. "Yes. Okay, so this is the front hall. I've sanded everything down, fixed the hinges, doorbell, chair rail, wallpaper and this grand staircase, I brought down to the polished wood finish with just a wax coat over that. We're doing electrics now; floor by floor. But pretty much I started with the carpentry in every room and... "

Mr Rodriguez's eyes had already drifted away. Far from looking at the finishes and the woodwork, his gaze had come to rest an apparently random point on the polished stone floor with the heavy Indian rug, probably the ugliest thing in the room.

Jay Jay detected a sudden air of sadness, a ghost that had descended on the room. Was his work upsetting the customer? He began to fret that he may not be hired after all. Oh well, a waste of time doing the estimate. Something was not right but trying to second-guess Mr Rodriguez made him uneasy.

"Umm, let's take a look at the front parlor and next to that Mr Alfred's study. I have also completed that room too. Well, pretty much the first floor, actually." Mr Rodriguez perked up again at this mention of Mr Alfred. Already dispirited, Jay Jay wanted to end this "tour" as soon as possible. He pictured disappointing Dallas, which wasn't hard, admittedly. Either she'd freak out and have hysterics or she might not let her disappointment show and simply turn into a statue. Nowadays any reaction was unpredictable due to hormones, sleep deprivation, endless laundry, poor diet and... the list defeated him.

In the front room, Mr Rodriguez's eyes lifted. He was drawn to the portraits and other paintings. Sure, those were his focus, because he was an artist. Meanwhile Jay Jay droned on about triple-lined curtains just like at the Drake and real crystal chandeliers from Bohemia. That was in "Yerp". He hoped the artist would be impressed with this display of knowledge. He wasn't. Unless ignoring it altogether was his way of showing his approval.

Mr Rodriguez suddenly whizzed around.

"Who painted this?"

"Oh, I painted the whole room, the ceiling, the baseboards, chair rail— ."

"No. This painting."

He pointed to a portrait of a gentleman over the gold and black marble fireplace. Sad eyes, large and blue, looked out at the room. The color of his goatee beard matched that of the polished oak mantel over the hearth.

"Oh. That's... That's... I'm sorry, I'm not entirely sure." Jay Jay said.

He'd never taken any notice of any kind of art in his life and he wouldn't have remembered if Mr Alfred *had* told him who the artist or the model was. Sure, he had seen paintings in the house a few times but never looked closely as, really, he was too busy working. Workmen didn't have time to stare at art. What was the point? All he had to do was make sure none were damaged during the renovations, whether by covering them or, as a last resort, putting them in storage.

Mr Rodriguez nodded slowly.

"Do you want to view any more areas? The yard work I've done? Or the upstairs rooms. But they're all work in progress, really."

"No," he said but quickly changed his mind. "Maybe the top floor if that's allowed?"

"Oh, er, but that's Mr Alfred's living area now. So I'd rather not."

"That's fine. I've seen... a lot. I have to go back to work."

Mr Rodriguez was still carrying the flowers.

"Let me take those from you and put them in a vase," Jay Jay offered.

Mr Rodriguez obediently handed the bunch over like one child giving a toy back to another.

Jay Jay walked through the whole house into the kitchen. He glanced back once and Mr Rodriguez was still staring at the painting. He cut open the strings and paper holding the flowers, filled a vase shaped like a glass urn, or a giant wine glass, with water and put them in it. He carried the vase back to the front of the house.

Back in the front room, Mr Rodriguez was not around. Oh no! As it was, he was not happy leaving the customer alone, even for a minute. Where was he? Where did he go? He figured the man for a gentleman who would *not* wander around without being asked. This was so strange. He set the vase down on the grand piano.

"Mr Rodriguez?" He called in the hall. He rushed from room to room. He went up the stairs to make sure the man was not exploring up there. It was like looking for a child who'd wandered off. "Mr Rodriguez?" He called again.

"Children! They cannot be left for a minute," Carmelita had said once in a rare "heartfelt-advice-giving" mood, when Dallas had been pregnant. God that seemed so far away, though it had been only a few months ago. "They up to no good when is suddenly silent and you can hear no nothing. Is how you know, something is wrong, uh-oh."

Jay Jay knocked on the guest bathroom door on the first floor, off the hall. "Mr Rodriguez? Are you in there?" No reply. He knocked louder as if that would help. The first time had been loud enough already, for such a small room.

Oh my God, he remembered again, Papa Moriarty had keeled over right out of the blue... he tried the handle. The door was locked from the inside. "Mr Rodriguez? Are you okay?"

He listened at the door, pressing his ear hard against the wood. Silence. Jay Jay had no choice but to break the lock. It would take too long to fetch his tool kit to take the handle apart. There was no time, and no time to inform Mr Alfred either. He was young, strong from work. He did it in three.

Mr Rodriguez was on the floor, unmoving. Jay Jay had tiled this beautiful marble floor himself, with a border, baseboard in matching marble, all polished as shiny as the mirror which reflected the bulk that was Mr Rodriguez, like the sea reflects a mountain. He looked like the murder victim in an old black-and-white movie. "Mr Rodriguez," Jay Jay shouted. The man was unconscious. Oh God. He had obviously been using the bathroom when whatever it was had happened. What should he do? He ran back through the hall and corridor again, back to Mr Alfred's study. "Sir! Sir. I need to use the telephone."

"Why? What's happened?"

"Mr Rodriguez. He's collapsed in the bathroom."

They waited around for the ambulance. He didn't know a thing about the poor guy. Jay Jay wrung his hands. "I'll stay with him, Mr Alfred. You go."

"No, I can stay too. This is so unfortunate."

"He... He only came to look at the house."

"Unbelievable," said Mr Alfred. "Who IS he?"

"He's... well... I think he's someone who shops at the departmental store."

"At Marshall Field's?"

"Yes. Dallas met him and recommended me. I am very sorry about this, Sir. I... I will make up the time."

"Nonsense. What time? A man is sick!"

"I know, but the viewing was supposed to take, like, ten minutes."

Mr Alfred remained glum and thoughtful.

The man's thick circular glasses had fallen off and shattered on the marble floor. Without his glasses he looked even more familiar. Jay Jay picked them up and, folding the handles carefully, put them on the generous sized marble sink. The mirror in this bathroom was enormous and reflected how tired and crazy Jay Jay himself looked. That was weird because he actually thought he had slept some and today was the first day he felt like himself.

Mr Alfred kept looking at the figure of Mr Rodriguez on the floor. "You should probably take his watch off too," said Mr Alfred. Jay Jay glanced down. First, he took off the man's highly-polished shoes and laid him out in a recovery position as he'd been taught when he was at the steelworks. The wristwatch was an ordinary square-faced gentleman's watch with a leather strap. It was so tight on the wrist, Rodriguez's fingers had turned purple. Did the wrists swell up or something? His ankles certainly looked like they had. He lined the shoes up neatly in a pair, ignoring the fine leather laces which stuck out like a lobster's antennae.

He also put the wristwatch on the ceramic sink with the eyeglasses, like he was arranging them in a store display for the next customer. When the ambulance got here, he'd just hand them over as a "package".

Mr Alfred said, "wait a minute."

"What?"

Mr Alfred picked the wristwatch and turned it around. What was on the back of the watch made him lose his balance, reeling backwards as though he needed to be as far away as possible. Yet he didn't take his eyes off the watch in his hand.

"What? What's wrong? Mr Alfred?"

Mr Alfred went very pale and his eyes widened.

Oh no, not him too, thought Jay Jay. "Are you okay? Mr Alfred, are you okay?"

But Mr Alfred didn't reply. He was speechless, just kept shaking his head.

"The ambulance is coming, Sir. Just hang in there. We got this." Was Mr Alfred sick too? All his frigging fault bringing a complete stranger to his home. Yet another dumbass thing.

What was on the watch? Besides the time, of course. Now was a "good time" to check. He prised the watch gently from Mr Alfred's hand and turned it around to have a look at whatever was on the back.

Chapter 27

Mr Alfred, still shaky, finally piped up, "I don't understand how he's wearing that watch. It was my father's."

"Wut?" said Jay Jay, unable to take in what he was hearing. "I mean, I beg your pardon, Sir?"

"This watch is— was— my father's," repeated Mr Alfred. "My mother's gift to him."

Jay Jay stared. He read a quotation by somebody beginning with A, followed by the name Catherine... the name that had had to be repainted on the front entrance door's overhead glass panel. That was Mr Alfred's mother.

He kept shaking his head, saying he didn't understand what it was doing on this man's wrist.

"Well, maybe it was sold?"

"No. My father did not sell anything but guns and property." Mr Alfred said, with a joyless laugh.

"No, I mean, maybe it was stolen and sold."

"Okay, I accept that. But by who?"

"Well, maybe your father was robbed."

Mr Alfred did not reply, looking distant and distracted, as if trying to remember what happened to the watch and when.

Just then there was a shuffle and gasp. Mr Rodriguez groaned. "I... am... "

"Don't speak. Just hang in there for a few more minutes."

"I can... speak. I'm feeling... better."

"Are you okay? What happened?" Jay Jay squatted down next to Mr Rodriguez and held his hand.

"I am very sorry about all this. How embarrassing!"

"Don't be sorry."

"I... I'm..." Mr Rodriguez panted and gasped, struggling in between breaths. "Not sure... how to say... this... "

"No, don't," Jay Jay tried to reassure him. "Do you think you might be having some heart problems? I mean, I'm not a doctor, but... " He tried not to think of Papa Moriarty. Again.

Carl Rodriguez was sweaty and looked to be in some pain. He shook his head. "I am Al—"

He kept wanting to say something. But the pain was hitting him in waves and he was finding it difficult to breathe. Jay Jay looked at the top of his head. His hair was thick and black and frankly too long for Jay Jay's taste because the man was not young, maybe in his forties or fifties, get real. Perhaps it was because he was one of those arty types Dallas was always talking about.

"We need to call your wife too."

"No... please... don't. I don't want to worry her."

"We have to," said Jay Jay. "I have your home telephone number in my notebook. I'll call her for you."

"Jerry?"

"Yes, Mr Rodriguez?"

"Thank you." Jay Jay clasped his hand briefly while Mr Alfred went to the door.

The ambulance had arrived.

Jay Jay followed the stretcher out. Best to make sure the guy was okay before calling his wife. Mr Alfred stayed indoors.

"You said he was a painter?" said Mr Alfred.

"Yessir."

"Of what?"

"I have no idea, Sir."

"Like, portraits or... "

"Oh, let me think," said Jay Jay, regretting that he hadn't looked at the art in the customer's house properly.

"We should telephone him at the hospital later, I suppose, to make sure he is okay."

Sometimes, when driving Mr Alfred in the van, or even now, Jay Jay felt close to his boss, felt an honesty between them. But still he could not bring up Bones 1 and 2. Something was not right about this house. He was "only a handyman", as he reminded himself every morning. He didn't ask "inappropriate-to-ask" questions outside of work. Even so, a stranger had just collapsed. The house was cursed.

"I will call him, Sir."

"Send flowers."

"You're too kind. You don't even know him."

"Don't I?"

"You... you don't. Sir."

Jay Jay started to wonder about the expression on Mr Alfred's lined face, which had changed to being flat and unreadable, as still as a painting. They went back into the front parlor and looked at the portrait of Charles Sutton on the fireplace.

"Pardon me," said Jay Jay, "I need to go back to my work now."

"Of course. We've had quite enough drama," said Mr Alfred. He sighed. "Poor guy. Don't forget to call the hospital."

———

THAT NIGHT, Jay Jay had to work a little later. A *lot* later. He felt obliged to make up for all that applesauce in the morning. Oh no. He had forgotten to ring the hospital. He'd had a really busy day. He'd spoken to no one. The day was getting late, or the night was getting early. He'd telephone when he got home. He checked the grandfather clock in the hall and waited patiently: 3 seconds. 8 o'clock and the ding dongs chimed. When he saw its chains, he felt like a prisoner. He was absolutely exhausted. He'd missed his baby girl and Dallas so much but he just had to catch up.

There was a commotion outside on N. Lakeshore Drive. What was going on? Jay Jay was just about to drive off in his van. Luckily he checked the rear view mirror. He had kept checking he was not being followed, ever since that one time. And now there were kooks in the neighborhood. even Lakeshore Drive had changed. Things weren't what they had been ever since Vietnam started.

He wanted to leave. They were blocking his way. He glared at the kooks. He would have recognized that gait and the Garden of Eden combat pants anywhere. What the actual—

Jay Jay had to kill the engine. He got his torch from the glove compartment and got out. "Hey," he shouted. He ran to the guys. "Stop. What are you doing? Nesto?"

Ernesto and two men had some guy pinned.

"My boys rang me, Jay Jay. Look what we got. This guy has been following you." Jay Jay looked at the blond man in a black outfit.

"He's... Oh, shit."

"You know him?"

"He's Carl Sutton. Mr Alfred's nephew."

"What are you doing following me?" Jay Jay growled.

"I am not following you," he snapped, gasping. "Geddoffa me."

"He's been creeping around Mr Alfred's house. Again. See that Chevy?"

Jay Jay tossed his head over his shoulder. The black Chevy. Carl Sutton's other car, or maybe his father owned the white Buick.

"We don't want you making waves here," said Ernesto. "Don't ever come back."

"This was my house too. I grew up here."

"You need to go now," said Ernesto.

"I want it back."

"You're not making any sense," said Jay Jay.

"I am not shutting up. Fuck this!"

He started kicking feebly at Ernesto and his guys.

"We've been looking out for you," said Ernesto, with his knee pressing down harder on the man's stomach. He heard a groan. Then he loosened his grip. "This street ain't safe for you with us around," chuckled Ernesto. Then he hardened his voice into a growl. "Now scram."

"Was my street too." Carl managed to drag himself upright after all the futile kicking. His right fist flew up into Ernesto's ribs, winding him.

"Are you a girl?" One of Ernesto's guys got him square on the jaw. He fell backwards, scrabbled his way back up and ran.

"I *will* be back," he shouted as he sprinted off. "You assholes."

The guys chased after him.

"The hell was that? Dude is just frontin'," Ernesto laughed lightly and shook his head. "He must've come to chuck'em but he ain't dustin' us, no way. Jerk."

"I don't know more than you, Nesto, but it's either pond farm or this house."

"Beecher?"

Jay Jay nodded.

"What do you mean?"

"Didn't your mom tell you anything?" Said Jay Jay. "Carl Sutton wants to sell the land. So Grandpops has to give up the farm."

Carmelita must have kept from Ernesto what wasn't in the bag yet. The deal hadn't been done and Grandpops had been against selling the business for so many years. He and Papa Moriarty had built it up. The pond farm was his pride and joy.

"Grandpops is crazy about it," said Jay Jay. "He works 7 days. What would he do without the farm?"

Ernesto stared at Jay Jay.

"I don't know anything about business. I have no idea how anything works. I just work here fixing shit."

"Okay, let's go guys. You'd better rest, Jay Jay. You look beat."

"Thanks. Pretty long day. And unfortunately a pretty long night too."

Ernesto grinned, understanding or misunderstanding him. Whatever. "Before you go, have this," he reached into his combat pants pocket. He tossed the blue silk notebook which Jay Jay's hand snatched in mid-air like it was a blue-winged butterfly.

CHAPTER 28

Dallas wasn't sure if this was the right street. It was a coolish, drizzly fall day. Every day she had no idea what day or even month it was, until she looked at the calendar. She had a frenzied bout of trying on six different coats before deciding on the one. She was out of touch with herself, seasons, reality. Today was the first time she'd left her own neighborhood since the baby's arrival. Her heart was racing on the subway. She calmed herself down with a jumble of fleeting thoughts of paintings, art and artists. Her favorite daydreams.

She'd only been here once a couple of years ago. But when she saw the door, she recognized the block. She pressed the speaker button and waited.

"Hi! It's me!" She said with an exaggerated nervous cheeriness.

"Come on in."

A long buzz and the door opened. She pushed and propped the heavy chipped door open with her left elbow while she steered the baby's baby carriage in with both hands. What was the alternative? She somehow had to make that one first trip. Hell, she was just a mom in her own city even if she acted like an alien who'd just landed in New York City.

"Good morning, Dallas. Let me help you with that thing."

"Good morning, Professor." He'd called her baby a thing. Or maybe he was referring to the baby carriage. Best not to get hung up about it.

"What've we got?" He said.

"We've got a buyer," she said confidently.

"Great. Wait there. Be careful," he said, adding, "they grow up, you know."

Easy for a man to say that, but they'd never know the truth of it. Only women learned that, thought Dallas, but there was no point telling him so. He turned and disappeared down a darkened corridor.

Dallas sat and waited on a yellow velvet couch. It was like being on a movie set, Cary Grant's place in *Bringing Up Baby*. The high ceilings, peeling wallpaper and stacks of books. Most of all, enormous works of modern art on each wall, and curated too. They all went so well together in shape, size and composition.

He came back with an oblong parcel wrapped in brown paper. "Here's two and a half."

"Thank you. I'll put it in my coat." She said, as though the Professor would care.

"The other two and a half when the job is complete. What is her name?" He pointed at the baby.

"Jennifer."

"That's a pretty name. Are you still doing any art?"

"N... nnn... no. Not right now, Professor. I got my hands full with Jennifer Juniper here," she managed a stupid grin of embarrassment. She shook her head. Suddenly she wanted to burst into tears. She looked down, worried the shutter juice would pop right out of her peepers. And she didn't want him to see. Bringing a baby along on a work gig was silly enough already. But what could she do? Her mother couldn't come and babysit. She had moved to Tulsa with some new guy and there was no "only" about being 24 hours from there. Maybe her mom had moved 'cause of the song. The new guy was no Gene Pitney. Hah!

"Well, little by little. You were one of the best students we had."

"I was?" She looked up. Jennifer had started to fuss. Giving out the ticking, clicking and percussive noises babies made before the full orchestra started.

"Conceptually you came up with a lot of ideas beyond someone your age and experience. You traveled a lot as a child?"

That's him flirting, the voice in her head piped up. Her Inner Self was a striped honey bee. Sweet as honey but with a nice sting. She had a built-in flattery detector, which was now glowing red. She still welcomed his praise as he was an influential and discerning critic. That was how the art world worked. Insincere praise became sincere. Later on. Anyway, she'd had no compliments in about a hundred years. So why put the sting in?

Dallas burst into a cackle, surprising herself as much as him with a crude yet nervous guffaw. She took Jennifer out of the carriage, put her in the vertical and supported the baby on a shoulder. She stood up and started to bounce and jog lightly to soothe her as she'd seen moms do countless times. She'd grown up poor and being bounced like this. Her mom couldn't afford mobiles from Macy's. Who could, apart from the rich?

"I've never been anywhere. Except New York City, once. Tulsa. And our honeymoon, Lake Elkhart—"

"Sorry I... I missed your wedding, but thank you for the invitation."

"That's quite all right," she said. He'd been abroad in Italy on the big day. Some conference. She'd sent him an invitation anyway. It would have arrived long before his trip. But he didn't R.S.V.P.

The crying had started and the volume dial would soon be at painful, before moving up to unbearable.

"Well, you seem to have. You have a natural talent for observation which is basically art. I find that — that piece you worked on — the —"

"Do you mind? I need to feed her?" She cut him off, aware

that she would seem rude. She was very interested to hear his "cr-teek", of course she was, but right now she had to stop the crying. She wanted to cry too. But hey! She was an adult. She *should* be able to control her tears a little better.

She wanted to tell him so much. That she'd met an artist. Carl. How it was important for an artist to find others. How art was lonely. All creative pursuits were. You had to not mind being alone with no one to talk ideas with. No one to look at art with. She had only began to enjoy that and now it was over. That she didn't want to leave art school but had done so quite begrudg-ingly — even Jay Jay had noticed that — and then she got preg-nant. And now she was just a mom who worked in sales. That was her story in fifty words on a postcard to "Ask Ann Landers".

She fumbled for the bottle and uncapped its lid. Her mind could still jump around with speed and verve, but her face, eyes and hands had no focus on — or energy left for — anything except the infant, her own progeny. Jennifer was her work of art now. She exhaled a breathy stream of relief when she sat back down on the yellow couch and inserted the translucent teat into Jennifer's mouth.

"What were you saying, Professor? I am sorry. I don't know where my head is at."

"I said when are you returning to work?"

"In December. Our busiest month. The gifting and all."

"Ooooh yeeeess," he drawled unctuously. "I shall be requiring and acquiring gifts," he smiled.

She wished she'd never let him put his paws all over her when she was in her freshman year.

She had almost blanked out that episode. For a few moments, she gave Jennifer the "house white". She almost fell asleep, she felt so calm, thanks to being in a feeding trance. Closing her eyes wasn't helping her to ward off the unwanted memory. She'd been 17 then. Curious and liberal, yet dumb and traditional. A kaboom combination. She stared glumly but with pride at

Jennifer's cheeks and eyes until her own eyes started to sag with drowsiness.

"Would you like a coffee? Shall I make you a quick cup?"

"Thank you, Professor. That would be lovely." He disappeared into the kitchen. The whoosh of taps and the grinding hum of the machine signaled that the Professor liked his coffee like the Italians made it.

She'd have liked to have quit doing the administration jobs for the Institute, but Jay Jay and her needed the additional income if they were ever going to move to somewhere bigger.

"Here are the keys to my private store room," he said, "two locks," he added, handing her two golden keys on a Golden Gate Bridge key-ring. She took them and shoved them into her handbag.

"I must go now," she announced after she downed the strongest paint-tasting coffee she ever had from the daintiest gold-rimmed cup that she'd ever seen. It looked like a ballerina skirt, turned upside down. She felt as incongruous as an ape holding the cup. "Nap time," she announced more to Jennifer than to the Professor.

"Don't forget how the payment is made."

"I remember."

"Good. I trust you. I'll call a cab. It's safer."

"Thank you."

"You *will* call me when you get home, won't you?"

"Yes. Yes I will."

"And remember," he said, "don't tell anyone. This is the best side-hustle you'll ever get. *Our* gig. You'll be running your own gallery in no time." He winked.

CHAPTER 29

J ay Jay got back too late to call a florist and send flowers to the hospital. What Mr Alfred was asking was just too much. Neither of them knew the guy. Plus, returning to a chaotic home was not great for his state of mind: he wasn't sure if it was Christmas or the 4th of July. And no food. He'd even started to miss the takeouts the chef at the Jade Palace Garden had slipped him on the sly.

The next day, he telephoned the hospital as soon as he was up. After a long wait, he spoke to the receptionist.

"Mr Lee, he's already been discharged. Yesterday evening. If you want to send flowers, you should do so to Mr Rodriguez's home."

"Oh?" He said. "Is he okay?" Jay Jay ran his palm over this forehead and shut his eyes.

"He had a fairly mild heart attack, Mr Lee," said the voice. "We called his wife. She picked him up at... let's see... 8.30pm."

After he hung up, Jay Jay looked up florists in the yellow pages. He rang Mr Alfred to let him know that he'd be late. "I forgot to order the flowers. There's a florist nearby. I'll call them now." He hadn't had a second the day before to organize flowers,

Jay figured it wasn't really his job. Why did Mr Alfred want to send anything to the man?

"Wait," said Mr Alfred.

"What?"

"Jerry," he sighed. "Don't send. "We... Let's... I'd like to go there."

"No. Why? I mean, Sir. We don't know Mr Rodriguez, either of us. Neither does my wife. He's just a customer." And not even that, yet.

"Jerry, listen. I'd like to come with you. Order the flowers then swing by to give me a ride, would you?"

Jay Jay was speechless. Mr Alfred was a kinder man that he'd ever thought. There was no way he'd have been involved in whatever happened to Bones 1 and 2. Sometimes he had talked to the Bones, but only out of habit. It was lonely working alone. "Hey guys! Morning. So what happened to y'all?" Was pretty much all he ever said to them before having his first coffee. Of course there had never been a reply. Jay Jay neither believed in, nor had ever seen ghosts, so ghosts had never talked to him. Anyway, what he found weird was that people claimed to see apparitions. What did they say? Did they have ears, brains and did they hear if you talked back? Made no sense at all. He was no scientist or even an educated guy.

Jay Jay telephoned Mr Rodriguez to say they were coming. Mr Rodriguez answered from the extension in his bedroom, so he must be up and about.

Jay Jay drove out in his Camaro rather than the van. He didn't have any equipment or tools or materials to buy as they were all on site already; the heavy coils and spools of electrical cable had nearly broken his back the day before. He'd carried them two at a time up to the second floor. He cruised to the florist stand at Monroe subway station, hopped out, leaving the motor running and bought a ready-tied mixed bunch, white, pink. Peonies. Something Chinese. He didn't know why he chose them. He just thought the smell was as intoxicating as a woman.

He helped Mr Alfred into the car. Mr Alfred was looking very troubled and frail. "What's wrong, Sir?"

He hoped he wasn't getting too personal, overstepping boundaries they hadn't talked enough to set.

Mr Alfred sighed. "I am not sure. Today I don't feel like I'm myself."

Two statements. Jay Jay wondered if either made any sense at all or if they were the same. The first statement showed that he was himself and the second meant that he wasn't.

Jay Jay shook his head, driving silently, while Mr Alfred stared out of the window at the beautiful views of the beach on the lake. The radio was playing.

"What is this?"

"*Close to You* by the Carpenters. Burt Bacharach wrote it."

Mr Alfred looked stunned. "No. This," he pointed at the compartment under the dashboard for change, ashtrays and whatever else, the flat part. "Oh that's for change, cigarettes, the lighter, the ash— ."

"No," he said. "That."

"Oh. Just a notebook."

Mr Alfred said nothing. They listened to the song, something about birds suddenly appearing, and the stabs in the trumpet solo which Jay Jay found unexpectedly moving. The car was heading West, Mr Alfred continued staring without expression at the scenery. He was too polite, Jay Jay thought. Someone he knew better or more curious would have gone, "wow, what's this thing? Can I? May I?" And immediately picked up whatever it was. He had pushed the notebook into his pocket after he saw Ernesto. Got out of the van without thinking, so this morning, it was still in his pocket. He'd just tossed it in the car because he hadn't wanted to carry some ancient, useless notebook around all day. He couldn't throw it in the trash because it was like... an antique, but what would he do with an antique notebook?

———

"GOOD MORNING. So good of you to come by," an overweight, vaguely Irish-looking woman said as she opened the door. Jay Jay thought she must be Mr Rodriguez's housekeeper or cleaner. She was in chunky men's boots and an apron. She could have be in her forties or fifties but Jay Jay was not so good at guessing people's ages. She had been ginger-haired a long time ago, now her hair was graying and frizzy. Her eyes were small and her mouth pinched.

"You must be Mrs Rodriguez," said Mr Alfred.

"I am. She gave a tight smile. Please come in."

Jay Jay was taken by surprise. Dallas had said the man had gone to the store to buy luxury beauty products for his wife more than once and that she was a very lucky lady. Well that much was true. Lucky but not a looker.

He held up the flowers. "We just want to drop these off. If it's not convenient, we can just go, we don't have to see Mr Rodriguez."

"No, it's fine, please come in," she repeated. "Carl would love visitors. We don't get many. The kids are in school. Excuse the mess. I'm just cleaning up."

"Please go through, he's in his study." Mr Alfred and Jay Jay were shown their way through the dining area and a playroom connected by an expansive toy railway still under construction, complete with hills and lakes. Stuffed bears sat in miniature chairs and children's books teetered in towers or lay discarded in various random locations. There were books everywhere. One wall of the dining room *was* books. Bookcases from from floor to ceiling. What he could see of the polished oak floors gleamed. In an educated family, this was what kids did when they were not in school, played with good toys and looked at books. They did not tear down the street throwing sticks and rocks, making ditch tunnels and mud volcanos, as Jay Jay had grown up doing.

Mr Rodriguez was sitting with his feet up on the couch in his study. A comforter covered him as far as the chest, leaving his hands free, though he didn't seem to be doing anything. Next to him stood a small, industrial-steel bedside table which looked very much like the kind that had been produced from offcuts in the steelworks where Jay Jay had used to work.

"Carl?" Said Mrs Rodriguez. "They are here."

She hadn't asked their names and didn't now. They were just "they".

"Don't," said Mr Alfred, making a stop sign with his hand when Mr Rodriguez tried to move. "We just wanted to say hi."

"Thank you." He shuffled back into his former position, which was by way of being slumped and holding a cup.

"How are you feeling?" said Mr Alfred.

"Would you like coffee?" Said Mrs Rodriguez.

"No, no. We will be going soon," said Mr Alfred.

"Have you met my wife?" said Mr Rodriguez. "Laura."

She gave another tight smile and left the room before Jay Jay and Mr Alfred could speak.

They sat down on a perfectly matched sofa, after moving two Dr Seuss books and a toy truck. They observed him for a few moments like two visiting consultants from a hospital.

On the bedside table was a glass of water, medication with labels, a small time-table with checkmarks showing which medication had been been taken and the date and time that it had. And *that watch.*

Mr Alfred didn't waste time. He never did. That's why he had so much of it. "Mr Rodriguez. Where did you get your watch from?"

Mr Rodriguez stared. Jay Jay simply couldn't make out his expression. Was he excited or afraid?

Mr Rodriguez said, "I... I am... I wanted to say... my... "

He stopped. Jay Jay wondered why wouldn't answer Mr Alfred's question. Surely he hadn't stolen a luxury watch. The atmosphere had changed. Jay Jay reckoned he could have cut it with a kid's Playdoh knife lying on the floor under the Rodriguez couch.

"I am sorry to have to ask," said Mr Alfred. "It's just that... It's my father's, that's all."

"Do you want it back? You can have it back." Mr Rodriguez did not dispute the statement that it was Charles Sutton's. He turned to pick the watch up.

"That's not what I meant. It *is* a very valuable watch but I don't want it back. But where did you— ."

Mr Rodriguez was holding the wristwatch, unsure whether to put it back on the nightstand or not. He said nothing and just stared glumly at its engraved back.

"Well, Jerry, we might as well go," said Mr Alfred. He turned to Rodriguez, "I was curious. And I *am* sorry if I've caused you any anxiety."

"Okay then," said Jay Jay agreed, "we'll be on our way now, Mr Rodriguez. Apologies for dropping by at such short no— ."

"No, wait."

They stood up.

"Don't be mad at me."

"Why would I be mad at you?" Said Mr Alfred.

CHAPTER 30

M r Rodriguez was tearful by the time they sat down again. Firstly, he started by admitting that he wasn't an attorney at all. He was a legal clerk in a realty agency in Chinatown. "I'm just another unsuccessful self-taught artist with an office job, three kids and a wife who earns more than me," he'd said. But that wasn't what he really wanted to tell Mr Alfred.

Carl Rodriguez had taken the trouble to go to N. Lakeshore Drive to see "Jay Jay's work". He admitted, "I *really* wanted to meet Mr Alfred, but unfortunately my heart had other ideas. Just seeing the house, the portraits," He shook his head.

"Why?" Mr Alfred had asked.

Mr Rodriguez scratched his forehead and absent-mindedly pushed his longish hair back. He would have been handsome when he was young like Marlon Brando, but he'd been worn out by work, family and most of all the "crushing delusion that was art". Nowadays, his wife looked at him with resentful tiredness and despair, as *he* did at everything around him. As a last resort, he'd decided to convert his garage so as to have one last stab at art. He was already 51. There might be more pointless years to follow, but he might as well try again.

His fingers reached for his glasses but became aware he didn't have any on. They had been smashed when he fell over. Now he was waiting for a new pair to be ready, he felt naked without them, like people always said you did.

"Me being an artist is not the only reason I visited you," he said to Mr Alfred. "I know you are well-connected with the art industry."

"The portraits interested you."

Mr Rodriguez nodded. "But I am still building up my portfolio right now. Being a weekend painter and a dad, I can't paint three nudes and a still life before lunch like Picasso."

Jay Jay sat with his legs crossed and hands folded. He took in every word but was unable to contribute. He even started to plan his day. Surreptitiously he glanced at the clock on Mr Rodriguez's basic pine desk. What was he getting at?

"I... I'm... "

He shook his head, again unable to speak for a moment. Then he started talking about the watch itself. He was very good at describing objects, or discussing subjects. As long as the subject wasn't him.

"I got the watch from my mother. She just passed away about two months ago. My life has been turned upside down since then."

"Who *was* your mother?" Sutton wanted to know.

"Nobody that you'd have heard of. A nobody. Just an ordinary woman. Isabella Rodriguez. A week before she died she told me I was adopted. So I had no idea. The Rodriguezes were just another poor childless couple of Spanish origin, vineyard workers from New Buffalo, Michigan. On a wine delivery to Chicago they found out from the Sutton staff a baby was available, maybe it was a maid's, my mother didn't say. I grew up in the vineyard. As soon as I could I ran away to New York City. I wanted to study art but my parents said no. They always tried to make me believe you could not make a cent from art and turns out they were right. I still haven't made a cent from it. I've been back in Chicago for the last twelve years. Settled down. I still feel more at home here than I ever did in New Buffalo."

"I remember my parents getting wine deliveries," said Mr Alfred as if the thought was now inconceivable, and it was. No such luxuries at Catherine now, despite its size.

"Before my adoptive mother died, she gave me this watch," Mr Rodriguez rubbed its smooth glass unconsciously like Aladdin's magic lamp. "She said it belonged to someone called Charles Sutton... It was the only thing that my birth mother gave to her. She kept it in a strong box under the floor in the workers' cabin at the vineyard for more than fifty years. That's why it looks like new. I never knew the watch existed."

"One day, I overheard the name Carl Sutton when I was shopping for gifts."

"My wife... " said Jay Jay, nodding.

"Yes. She was chatting about someone's engagement party."

"When I heard the name, and that I was also Carl, I knew there was a connection."

Jay Jay curled his lips and stared straight at Mr Rodriguez, a little skeptical. Usually you could tell if people were related by their surname, not their first.

He didn't think that Dallas had had loose lips. It would all have been small talk. No ships had been sunk yet, as far as he knew. He wrung his hands and looked at his knees. Why had she even mentioned anything about Carl Sutton's party? How was that even related to selling perfume? He didn't really know how a retail job worked but that must be how talking the talk worked. By chatting to customers on which luxury products anybody *who was anybody* in Chicago was using, she must be selling a lot of luxury products.

"From then I was hooked. It was like a scent I had to follow. Somewhere in this city was my birth family if any of them were left. I had to find... you."

"But couldn't you just look up names in the directory?"

"For one thing, Mr Sutton, you are not listed. Yes. Of course. I *did* look. That was the first thing I did when my mother died. There are over four hundred Suttons in this city. I know. I couldn't believe it either. To narrow that down, I'd have had to hire a PI and I am not exactly wealthy. And for another, even if your number was listed, I couldn't just turn up at your doorstep. You'd have called the cops."

And one more thing, Jay Jay thought, he might be just another wannabe artist who wanted a taste of the artist's lifestyle and the way to do that was to get close to someone influential such as Mr Alfred through seemingly natural means. To talk to Dallas, then Jay Jay, and then be welcomed into the house. He wouldn't have wanted to be a stranger knocking on Mr Alfred's gate.

"My birth mother got into a heap of trouble for me. I do not even know her name. She would have lost her job. She must have stolen the watch as revenge. She was a servant in the Sutton house... "

"Where you were born," said Mr Alfred holding his hands together tightly as if to stop them from cracking.

"Yes. Where I was born. In 1920."

"I remember the servant," said Mr Alfred, his voice trembling. "We had quite a few, back then. My memory is not what it is. But only one who became pregnant. Her name was Morales, I think."

Mr Alfred started to weep. He put his face in his hands and Jay Jay put his arm around Mr Alfred. He was hunched and crumpled. Somehow, he looked not older but younger, like someone who had rediscovered emotions that melted away his usual reserve. Until that moment all Jay Jay had seen was a regular, white-haired, elderly man who worried about his various ailments and the medical appointments to fix them.

"Sir, are you okay? What's wrong?"

Mr Alfred shook his head. What was upsetting him so? He held Mr Alfred's hand firmly and looked at him, but he couldn't detect the cause of this sudden reaction.

"She... She... " Mr Alfred whispered.

CHAPTER 31

Midmorning, Dallas took the subway to the Institute with Jennifer, bags of diapers, clothes (hers and Jennifer's just in case of any soiling mishaps), cleaning equipment, cloths, milk (with a spare), all crammed in the baby carriage. Leaving the apartment was an arctic expedition with spares and repairs even though she would probably only be out for two hours. Being a new mother, she was not entirely sure what to take. So she had to take everything.

She'd timed her expedition to coincide with Jennifer's midmorning nap. The three naps a day was all you got to remind you that God existed. They had to have come from somewhere divine because the nights sure came from hell.

She still had her student administrator's card to get past the security guy and inside. She only had to go to the cafeteria to meet a "new student", but via the Professor's personal art storage room first.

She retrieved the wooden box, removed the pillow-wrapped object inside it. She pulled off the grubby cotton material and confirmed that it was the 1957 Eduardo de Weiss bronze. If she wanted to be a curator or dealer in the future, she'd better get this bit right. She carried the box in its pillowcase like a baby since it felt like one. "Hold the head," she told herself. She carried every-thing like it was a baby now. She laid the box in the baby carriage's bottom cart and went back to the cafeteria. She reapplied her lipstick carefully, like a candidate preparing for a job interview.

Dallas sat and waited, pushing the baby carriage back and forth with one hand like her Grandma rocked a cradle. She'd learned the skill of doing it with one foot too, if she needed her hands free. Her other hand held a Harper's Bazaar magazine open and folded over. She'd brought it with her, just one more thing for the arctic explorer's inventory. She glanced at the cafeteria clock a few times. Crowds of students in small groups had arrived at what already seemed like a very busy time, reminding her she was once one of them. Soon she'd be paid her two and a half owing and she'd be free of debt. That would be the highlight of her day.

She was suddenly aware that someone was standing in front of her as a shadow was cast on her magazine. She looked up. She smiled at the well-dressed, middle-aged Chinese woman. She put her magazine down on the table and tried to rise. "Oh, hi!" She said. The woman didn't reply. She'd never seen the woman before. On closer inspection the woman was deathly pale with puffy eyes and makeup that was mis-applied, whether inexpertly or just poorly, Dallas wasn't sure.

The woman handed over a padded Mickey Mouse baby diaper bag. "Take a cab." The voice sounded the same as that of the caller who set up the meeting. Dallas was relieved about that, and she, in turn, got the box from the baby carriage's bottom cart and gave it to the woman. Dallas felt the buzz of doing an art deal!

Before she left, Jennifer woke up. The noise meant changing and a feed would be happening first. That delayed Dallas by at least 50 minutes. New moms couldn't be spontaneous. To do anything required 45 minutes to an hour and a half of getting ready first, including feeding, changing and another lot of changing if a secondary diaper disaster occurred during the 45 minute to an hour and a half period. Finally ready, she went out onto Michigan Avenue and hailed a cab. Viewing the city's sights from the cab, she was a little sad she had missed seeing any art on this errand. She could come back another time: a doable, but lengthy experience.

WHEN SHE GOT to the Professor's apartment, Dallas pressed the buzzer. No reply. Wasn't he expecting her to deliver to him the Mickey Mouse bag? All she had to do was the errand, drop the bag off with him, and receive the balance of the two and a half grand. Hell, just being in the Institute today had underlined how much she wanted to be an art student again, even though it wasn't on the cards right then. But it might be soon, if she played those cards right.

Someone came out of the building, and even held the door open for her as she pushed the baby carriage in. "Thank you," she said. She continued down the corridor and made a turn as before.

The Professor's apartment door, the one with the tarnished brass number 3, was slightly ajar. "Oh, good. He's in," she thought.

"Hell-ow?" She said to the empty hall as she pushed the baby carriage through. "It's me?" She said. Her voice rose at the end, as if she meant to add, *is anybody there?*

"Oh God," she gasped. "Nooooo," she whispered before the screaming started. It took a moment to realize it wasn't Jennifer but herself. Her hands flew to her mouth, as she remembered where she was but forgot how she'd got there. She clamped her mouth shut. Her legs weakened like when the puppet guy let go one half of the strings. Did anyone hear her? Oh Jeez. Before anybody arrived, she got to her feet, pushed Jennifer out of the apartment, the corridor, the communal entrance hall and finally into the street. She almost fell a few times, tripping over her own feet. She was an octopus with eight legs made of jello all colliding with each other and getting tangled with the wheels of the baby carriage. She woman-handled the baby carriage down the few steps of the brick building, bumping over each step. "Taxi!" She shrieked, her tears streaming. "Oh Lord, please send me a taxi, please," she prayed.

When one pulled up, she nearly hugged the driver. He helped her dismantle and put the baby carriage away in the trunk. She kept her beautiful red handbag from Carl, the diaper bag and the Mickey Mouse bag with her: all part of a repetitive 3-act play about luggage-moving. And baby made four. The weight of everything made her feel like luggage too. Lumpen, hardened, clumsy.

"Ma'am, are you all right? Ma'am?"

She could not reply to him. She sobbed. She looked down at the three bags at her feet. She squeezed her eyes shut. She had Jennifer in one arm, her hand automatically petting her in a soothing action. She was aware she was panting with terror. Her other hand reached out and gripped the smooth handles of the red handbag.

Her eyes were still tightly shut. She never trusted older men. She was 8 when daddy had left her and her mom. But... hell, what that meant for Dallas was Psych 101. The Professor had taken advantage of that. But Carl? Carl was a father substitute. Caring, artistic, enjoyed spoiling her. She did not like him in *that* way but in the way that she could be his daughter and yet could *not* be his daughter. Everything was wrong about him. Right down to the wife called Catherine who loved him so much she had given the same antique watch that Jackie Onassis gave JFK. *I miss the old days, Carl. Just beauty and dreams and art. And now look at me.*

The cab driver had been asking her for the address. "Oh! Oh yes, I am so sorry." She forgot her address. Her brain was addled from motherhood and shock. All she could think of was the Professor, once her lecturer and a creep, then her employer and now a corpse. He lay in the sitting room with that yellow couch, completely covered in blood, so much so she couldn't have identified him, couldn't even tell where he'd been shot. His face was a watermelon mess. His size 10 feet were all she recognized. He always wore green and white Stan Smith Adidas tennis sneakers even at home. They were all she was able to focus on without feeling nauseous. His goddamn shoes.

She wanted to believe this was a nightmare. She looked all around the cab, at herself and Jennifer to make sure no blood was visible anywhere. She thought back on the scene of crime. Oh God, what did detectives do all the time? Fingerprints. But she had touched nothing. The baby carriage had been used to push the door further open when she arrived. She hadn't shut it when she fled. No one had seen her except the girl who held the door open for her and so what? Anyone could come and go in that apartment.

But her fingerprint *was* on the buzzer.

CHAPTER 32

"She caused my mother... to... to—" Mr Alfred's eyes took on a stony glaze. "Yes," he whispered. He cleared his throat. "To take her own life."

"No!" Shouted Carl Rodriguez.

From what Jay Jay understood, Mr Alfred's mother, Catherine, had drowned in the lake. On his first day, he had been struck by the name of the house. A woman's name. Strange, when you looked over the entrance at the roof. The top floor windows were punched into the serpentine metal shingles making the house look like a dragon had landed on top of it. CATHERINE: an odd name for a dragon's lair.

"What happened?"

"Ah... a breakdown. My father's fling with the maid, Morales. She wasn't the first and... well, the baby... my mother got worse. The baby had to go. Six months after you were adopted, my mother was gone. Things never did get better. That watch, from her to him, only served as proof that she was trying to mend things."

Rodriguez cut in. "I only wanted to see the art, the house, and you. I never wanted to be discovered or have the watch taken off of me. I wish I hadn't gotten sick in your bathroom. I noticed a miniature painting of Charles Sutton as a boy, with his dog. It shocked me. I look just like Charles Sutton," he trembled, unable to look at anyone.

The two men were thinking what the other was thinking. Jay Jay folded his hands and looked around at the spines of the art books on Mr Rodriguez's shelves.

Mr Alfred was silent during the drive back. So much to take in emotionally and Jay Jay couldn't blame him for not wanting to talk. It had been exhausting morning for a young man like him, never mind a 78-year-old Sir. Here they were again, a pair, a team.

Yet all this had been Mr Alfred's idea: to go to Mr Rodriguez's home in Western Springs. At no point had Jay Jay planned on seeing Mr Rodriguez again. But Mr Alfred and Mr Rodriguez had both suspected all along. Brothers. Even half brothers with 27 years between them. They knew these things.

In the car, Mr Alfred started sniffling. "There are tissues in the glove compartment, Sir." That was all Jay Jay managed to say. He hated seeing the old man like this.

Mr Alfred caught sight of the silky, frayed old notebook and picked it up. He hadn't seemed so interested before. Why now?

"Whose is this?"

"Oh. Not mine," laughed Jay Jay in an effort to make light of it, but his laugh came out like the bark of a nervous dog. Ernesto had already told him the name was Leaf Sea Flower. This might be a tricky moment. The story about the notebook being found on the grounds of the mansion when the spy disappeared, was now third or fourth hand. From a young Carmelita to Morales, who told Ernesto who told Jay Jay. What was the story now? He had so much on his mind, he could easily have forgotten.

"Where did you get it?"

"I..." he sighed. "It was found by Ernesto when he was clearing out his grandmother's apartment. Now she has dementia. She's had to go into a home. It was pretty so we kept it, not even knowing what it says. 'S in Chinese. And we don't know what to do with it."

Mr Alfred did not answer. Was this bad? Jay Jay was really close to bringing up Bones 1 and 2. He gripped the steering hard and kept looking in the rear view mirror.

"You can have it if you want." Jay Jay offered. Mr Alfred opened the notebook and glanced inside. Mr Alfred was thinking. Should he tell Mr Alfred where it was originally found? But shouldn't Ernesto do that?

"I know who this belongs to. 葉海花," he said. "Yip Hoi Fa."

"You read Chinese?"

"Yes," he said.

Mr Alfred shut the notebook and tossed it back into the glove compartment, snapping it shut.

Mr Alfred turned his head and looked out the passenger window, his shoulders shaking. Was he weeping? He thought about giving him a tissue from his own supply, but Mr Alfred reached into his pocket and retrieved a white cotton handkerchief which looked like a man's, until Jay Jay saw its one lace corner. Mr Alfred dabbed at his face and held the fabric against his eyes until they arrived at North Lakeshore Drive around mid-morning.

Jay Jay worked until late afternoon without any breaks. He wanted to complete all the wiring on the landing, second and top floor by five. He heard the doorbell ring repeatedly. and he realized he'd have to answer the door. Where was Mr Alfred?

He ran down the stairs, shouting, "I'm coming."

The mailman made him sign for the parcel.

From the United States Passport Office.

CHAPTER 33

When she got home, Dallas could hardly believe that she and Jennifer were still alive. A new chill seeped into her cozy, safe apartment. They wouldn't come looking for her, would they? They had dealt with the Professor. They had the work of art in the bag. But they had her telephone number too.

She was the only link in the chain who remained unpaid. The Professor was now dead. She would just have to say goodbye to her balance of two and a half. She burst into tears again. She hadn't even taken Jennifer out of the baby carriage. She just sat, fully clothed in her coat, on her couch shared with mountains of clothes, hills of unfolded diapers and rivers of dust. All this was for nothing. A fool's errand.

She unzipped the Mickey Mouse bag. Money. Real money. More than 50 gees easy. She'd seen and weighed cash deals when the Professor bought and sold art. How tempting to just keep this loot. Now they'd be wanting it back, and handing the bag to the cops could turn out to be the better outcome. If only she could talk to Jay Jay, Carl, Dwayne or Sherylanne first. Somebody, anybody.

The minutes went past while she kept thinking they'd be here for her any moment. But they were not. It was quiet. No baby rage. No hammering at the door. She listened to the du-du-du-du of *Mrs Robinson* playing at low volume. They always left the radio on to fool burglars, like as if that worked. "Oh yeah, Simon and Garfunkel, means those guys are out." What burglar would think that?

Still in her coat, shoes and hat, she shut her eyes and tried to sleep hoping to erase the events of the morning. The afternoon came and went, and she hadn't noticed it either. She became part of the furniture, immobilized, inert.

THE SOUND of the door had woken her up. An itch of panic and guilt spread over her face. Jennifer! What? What was the time? She was disoriented and tried to find the clock on the wall but had no idea which wall to look at. She looked around. To her relief Jennifer was still in front of her in the baby carriage, crying, neglected for minutes or hours, she had no idea. She picked her up and Jay Jay came in.

"Thank God, oh my God, thank God you are home, Jay Jay I can't believe it. I've never been so happy to see you." Tears were streaming down her face.

"Oh my God, what happened? Doll, what happened?"

He held her for the longest time. She took a deep breath. It all started with the art sale, she remembered, feeling surprisingly calm. "The Professor said all I needed to do was to take the piece of art to the Institute, be paid half my fee, meet the buyer with the art, take the art payment back to him, and then be paid the next half. That was all. And I hadn't had Jennifer yet. So I thought I would be able to do all that with my eyes closed."

The administrative hustle was a job she handled very well, even though she had another job already. She'd always wanted to keep in close contact with the art school. She believed she'd return there one day as a student because her stint had been cut short, that was thanks to him, too.

"You're already a whizz at two jobs. I don't know how women do it."

"Well, *I* did it for $5,000, sweetie," she was choked up. Her hands were balled up in loose fists. "But I only got 2 and a half. He's dead."

"Wait, slow down."

"I went to the Institute today with keys to the Professor's store room. I got the piece out and waited. I got given money in a bag. I went back to his apartment. And he'd been shot."

"What was it?"

"What was what?" Her shoulders were swaying. She suddenly looked down, aware she was still in the coat she'd been wearing all day.

"What was the work of art that you had to pick up from the store room?"

"Why do you care? What do you know about art?" She snapped, her head tossed back. "A bronze. Abstract Modern. The Order."

"Oh God. No." He said.

"What's wrong?" She said.

"It's not a work of art. Well, it is and it isn't. It's an antique." He said "ant-eek".

"Would you like to explain what you mean, Mr Jerome Lee?"

He paused.

She trembled. "What do you mean?" She shrieked. "Tell me now." Her voice was alien, off-key, unbearable to listen to.

"It's a gun, Doll. A gun called The Order."

"Oh lord. How? Wh— what...?"

The telephone rang. Dallas still had her coat on. But she flew across the room to take the call in the kitchen.

CHAPTER 34

D allas picked the telephone receiver up. Her breath was heavy and steamy. "Hello? Hello? Who's this?"

Silence. She listened, the receiver pressed hard against her ear, allowing herself to breathe deeply just as she had when she was in labor. Five in, five out.

Jay Jay sidled over and they had to share the receiver, the only way they were both able to take the call. She wanted him to listen in. His breathing was heavy too, and she hoped he wouldn't start panting like a dog, nor Jennifer start screaming.

Dallas thought this call was bound to be about the money in the bag, in her keeping yet neither hers nor the Professor's either. She would keep the line on, as long as possible. But the caller wasn't a him. The voice was that of the woman who had delivered the Mickey Mouse bag.

"A reproduction, my dear. A very good one. I am very sorry about the Professor. My husband first and now the Professor." Her voice was very strained and tight.

Dallas became aware that she was not speaking. She was reading... which explained why when they'd met, the woman had said nothing, just took the package in silence, which had seemed strange at the time. Jay Jay put his hand over the receiver's mouth-piece, "That's Mrs Chan."

"Mrs Chan?"

The woman started reading from something with unexpected pauses, indicating she didn't read English well. Why would she? It wasn't her first language.

"Mrs Chan, is that you?"

"At 12 midnight, North Lakeshore Drive. You will bring The Order and the cash. If you do not, then I am next." She stumbled over the time and the address.

The line went dead.

"We need to call Emily," Jay said.

"Who's Emily?"

"A cop. They haven't found Mr Chan's killers yet."

"What did Mrs Chan mean when she said she was next? Jay Jay? Are we next? Oh God, what have I done?" Dallas was on the point of freaking out when Jennifer started to scream. She needed everything. A diaper change, outfit change, food. She was soaked through and through. She was trying to roll. Her little body rotated and twisted in discomfort.

"No, no! Listen, Doll. Why would they come after us? We have nothing. We literally have nothing."

"*We* have the bag of money, Jay Jay. I got us into all this, I am very sorry, please help me think."

"I am trying to! You gotta understand. There's a lot going on at Mr Alfred's—"

"Fuck Mr Alfred. Do you care about this family at all?"

"Yes! Of course I do! Mrs Chan is being held hostage, Doll. Did you not hear it? What about when you went on your art gallery tour this morning?"

His words tasted heavy and bitter on her tongue.

"Get us out of this shit first," she said.

"No," he said. "We gotta save Mr Alfred and Mrs Chan. We gotta call Emily."

Hearing the names, she seethed, her fists clenched. "You

can't help them, Jay Jay. I live for this family." He was so loyal to Mr Alfred but what was happening here? Who was in danger?

He swallowed hard. "If you don't let me call Emily, we will be in danger."

"Don't call the cops, cupcakes," she said. He wasn't thinking right. "If you do, they will kill Mrs Chan."

She almost heard his heart pounding while he was thinking and biting his lip. "Then let me get through to Mr Alfred now."

"Will I be in trouble for being paid by the Professor to run his errand?"

"So that's why you don't want me to call Emily."

Five in, five out. His breath was labored and hard. "Let's think," he said.

"I can't think with all the screaming," said Dallas. "Let me change and feed her first. Shit. I just can't think."

"Neither can I." Jay Jay blew out.

Dallas was confused now. If they called the cops, then she'd probably go to jail for doing the deal with the Professor. If he didn't call the cops, the gang would be back for the cash. She was doomed. It was all her fault for getting Jay Jay the job through the Professor. She shut her eyes and cuddled her baby close, all clean smelling of talc and baby oil. When she opened them, Jay Jay was on the telephone. What? Who was he calling?

He waited. Three rings. Five. Eight. "This is so unlike Mr Alfred," he said. He was *always* there in the evenings, in his study. Jay Jay hung up and repeated the call five minutes later, letting it ring to give Mr Alfred time to answer the telephone in case he was in another room.

Still there was no pick up. He dialed another number.

"Who are you calling now? Jay Jay, I am going nuts here." Her voice was shaky as her left arm cradled Jennifer, bouncing to soothe her.

"Ernesto. Yeah, me. Can you meet me? Yeah. You know where." He hung up and turned to Dallas. His expression looked hard and flat. "I have to go. Doll. I am sorry. I have to go back to see that he's okay."

"You can't leave me here."

"I have to."

She didn't answer. Her mind churned with clashing ideas.

"What are you doing? Oh my cupcakes. What are you doing?" He didn't answer. He strode into the bedroom and she followed, hovering at a distance and watching him.

He pulled open her vanity drawer.

For a second, she thought he was looking for the bottle of French perfume that Carl gave. Would he even recognize which one it was? No. For sure he'd have no idea what the different ones were. She was irrational and clutching at any thoughts. Things in the past. Happy memories. Ideas of art and beauty. Creating. Not destroying.

Underneath all these bottles and jars of cosmetics was his gun. She blinked her tears which fell in great big crystal drops when she glimpsed the gold and freshwater pearl necklace she wore when they went out to celebrate him getting a job. He put his gun in his pocket although she didn't like that he had to carry it. But he had no choice. He slammed the drawer shut so hard she heard the hissing rattle of the necklace.

"What?" He snapped. "The cash," he said. "If they are there, I'll give it back to them. After tonight we will have nothing to do with them."

"Or we'll be dead. Fuck. Help us, God. Oh Jay Jay, you might die tonight." That same itch of panic spread over her face and throat like walking into a cobweb. She hated the Professor and what he'd done. And Carl, too. For bringing her back into the fantasy of the artist life. All that had led to nothing. It was a delusion, just that, and should have remained one. "Oh God, please help us. Oh God."

"Dallas. Will ya calm down? Cut it out." He gripped her shoulders, his fingers like claws. He shook her, glaring, shouting her name.

She stopped praying. God wouldn't be listening, not to someone who hadn't prayed since grade school. She began sobbing again, the *Oh Gods* and the *I'm so sorrys*. She saw him leave the bedroom.

"You can't leave me here," she pleaded in a voice that didn't sound like her own.

He stared at her. "Then come too. Bring Jennifer. You can wait outside. I just have to make sure he's okay. Bring the cash."

"Honey? Where are you going?" Her tears streamed and she knew exactly where, but words spewed out of her mouth like she was speaking in tongues at a pentecostal meeting.

"Get. In. The. Car." Jay Jay said.

CHAPTER 35

J ay Jay left Dallas in the van with Jennifer and the arctic
expedition-sized baby bag. He hoped she'd brought plenty of
blankets. The mercury was falling rapidly, even for a harsh
November night. He parked out of sight of the house, just like on
his first day. Who'd a thunkit? At this house at midnight and for
this kind of no-goodery. At least Dallas could doze in the car. She
wouldn't be sleeping. The baby would take care of that.

The gate and front door had already been opened. He went
in, looking left and right before crossing the threshold. The lights
were on in the lobby and the corridor leading off it but the rest of
the house was a dark cave. The oak floor he'd polished up to a
mirror shine gave the only other light, reflecting a nearby street-
lamp and the corridor light. His fingers reached for his gun. He
slid it out of his pocket and held it close to his chest as he investi-
gated the house he knew so well even in the dim yellow light. "Mr
Alfred? Hello?" He called out. There was a rustling sound, a
shuffle.

"Mr Alfred? Is that you?"

He felt his way around the house, the light fading the further
he went. At the back of the house, he was dazzled by the moonlight glittering on the lake like diamonds scattered on a slab of jet.

He recognized the scene in his dream, and the woman's bloody end. He fixed his gaze on his surroundings. Sweat drenched him. He felt hot and cold at the same time. The November night air was so sharp. He couldn't smell a thing, not even the fragrant bushes he'd planted.

"Put the gun down, " said the voice. Jay Jay turned towards it. The man was tall and well-built. He spoke with a Cantonese accent. The same voice from the basement kitchen. He was wearing a balaclava knitted mask. In front of him was Mrs Chan, shivering and crying. She was barefoot.

Seeing Mrs Chan, Jay Jay dropped his weapon immediately. The man then turned and growled something at her, in Cantonese. Jay Jay understood it to mean shut up, as she attempted to stifle her sobs. He had a ponytail flattened on the back of his neck by the balaclava. He prodded Mrs Chan's back, and repeated his instructions to her.

"The Order. Do you have it?" Said Ponytail.

"I don't. You can have the cash back." Jay Jay said. He almost dropped the bag as he tried to place it on the moth-eaten couch. The first time he'd sat on it, Mr Alfred had offered him the job at *Catherine*. It seemed a long time ago. "Here. That's all of it."

"Just leave it there. Where's Mr Sutton?"

"I don't know. I just arrived. You saw."

"It should not be sold. It belongs to the Hak Fong Tong."

"I don't know anything about that," said Jay Jay.

"The Black Phoenix Gang." He tapped his gun on Mrs Chan again, indicating that she was also one of its members.

"Okay," Jay said, remembering her heel tattoo when she climbed on the chair. She looked less like a manager now.

"You're born a member. You can't join and you can't leave. And you most definitely cannot leave with one of our guns," he exclaimed, like it was part of a speech he'd learned by heart. He gave Mrs Chan a shake to emphasize his point. His voice sounded sad, even though the mask was expressionless. "The spy Yip Hoi Fa did both. She left with The Order."

Emily had said the tong leaders were articulate and learned. They were born into money. Two things they were not short of: dirty money and education. They led and kept the gang going.

"I... I'm just here to keep Mr Alfred... Mr Sutton... safe. I don't... know anything. About the antique gun, I mean. He doesn't neither. Either. Let her go."

Then, a click. Jay Jay couldn't speak. He had felt his voice tremble when he'd made those assumptions about Mr Alfred that even he wasn't convinced about.

The man laughed. "Mr Sutton is in the gun trade. Where do you think this house came from?"

What was so funny? "Come back for it," Jay Jay tried to persuade the man. "Let me talk to him once I've found him. Let Mrs Chan go," he pleaded again. "She's done nothing."

"Mr Chan has."

"What?"

"Mr Chan, the Professor and Mr Sutton. They are all in this."

Ponytail put his arm across Mrs Chan's neck, almost choking her. She gasped for breath. She tried to cry out but couldn't.

"Yip Hoi Fa was hanged after the war for treason after she was tried by the Nationalists. It's taken us 24 years to find a trace of The Order. Imagine! To see that advertisement on the cheap handbill by chance. Finally. Someone had The Order. Not Mr Chan. We threw him in the lake. Not the Professor. He tried to sell us a replica," he stifled a cackle. "It's Mr Alfred. He has the original."

"I am sure he doesn't. Let her go. Let me talk to—"

Suddenly Ponytail was slammed with something from the back. He fell onto his hostage and Mrs Chan screamed as they both hit the floor.

"Ernesto!" Said Jay Jay, distracting the masked man. As he looked around, Ernesto whacked him again with a wooden bar. The man's gun clattered onto the dark floor. Mrs Chan was still pinned to the floor under the man's weight. Mrs Chan wriggled like a butterfly on a board. Jay Jay picked up Ponytail's gun and pointed at him. Ernesto shouted at Mrs Chan. "Run. Run now."

She screamed. She tried to run but tripped over in the dark. Ponytail quickly reacted and grabbed her leg.

"Drop it! Drop it now!" Another voice came in from the lit hall. A short man entered, pointing a gun at Jay Jay. "I got the old man," he tossed his neck to one side, as if it was an afterthought.

Jay Jay recognized the short muscular man: Lucky of Lucky Realtors. Now both the guys he'd overheard in the Jade Palace Garden's basement were here. Suddenly Mrs Chan broke free. "Stop her!" shouted Ponytail. Lucky shot off after her and grabbed her by the throat. Mrs Chan kicked him, screaming and sobbing. She kicked him again, this time harder, right in the balls. The gun fell from his grip, skittering across the oak floor. She flew from the room like a bird freed from its cage.

"Get her," Ponytail screamed. "GET HER." But Lucky was still recovering from her bullseye on his balls.

Ponytail grabbed the other end of Ernesto's bar with his one hand, swinging it in an arc as he tried the reverse rainbow move but was flung against the wall opposite.

Jay Jay scanned the entire room and noted the positions of the two men. Kung Fu: Lesson One. Use your enemy's force against them. He inched closer to the right and Ernesto closed the area to his wing. He settled into his stance right in the middle, one leg steady in front of him and the other behind him, resting paper-light on his toes.

Ponytail cracked his fist into his palm and smiled. Jay Jay flexed his toes.

"We don't wanna fight, buddy," Ponytail said.

Ernesto stood his ground, glaring at Lucky.

"She's gone. So you can leave now," said Lucky, taunting the men with the prospect, "but I know you won't."

Jay Jay tensed his muscles as Ponytail rushed towards him, arm swinging. The heavy-fisted punch swept past his face to the right as he adjusted his entire body to the left. Ponytail danced like a drink, unbalanced by the force of his punch sweeping in the air and a small gap opened. Jay Jay moved quickly.

He whipped his right foot high and landed two heavy blows to the man's leg and hip, before plastering a kick bang on his left ear. Ponytail staggered off in a daze, holding on tightly to his ear.

Ponytail cursed in Cantonese.

Ernesto wasn't quick enough, not even for the short reach of Lucky who dispatched a few blows straight at his jaw. Some of them caught Ernesto in the face. It took a brief scrimmage before he could get out of Lucky's range and realign his posture.

"You had the chance," Lucky spat at Ernesto before turning his attention to Jay Jay.

Lucky's imprecise kick took Jay Jay by surprise. Its force had died off before landing on Jay Jay's side. Jay Jay absorbed it easily, smashing his fist straight into the man's chest. Ernesto took advantage of Jay Jay's help and flew at Lucky, driving his knee straight at Lucky's face.

Lucky ducked. Ernesto sailed right past him, crashing straight into the wall with his knee. Lucky followed with a kick to Ernesto's lower back. Ernesto ricochet-ed off the wall with a loud bang of bone against concrete.

Ernesto yelled.

"You all right?" Jay Jay called out.

"Yeah." Ernesto said. He wasn't. Still rubbing his forehead, where he had come off second best against the wall, he stumbled, his composure half-recovered, back into the brawl. Their opponents were surprisingly clumsy. Brains beat brawn. Mostly. His own split-second decisions and the gang members' disorientation gave him time for a breather. Lucky came back at him, with a one-two combo; one to the right and two to the left just as Jay Jay ducked, stumbling backwards and swinging his head, whilst fending the two guys off.

Jay Jay neatly pointed his toes forward in the Tiger paw move, cracking Lucky on the shin. He fumbled forward and Jay Jay caught him with a dizzying right hook to the bridge of his nose.

He howled like a kicked dog, as he collapsed to the floor to nurse the hurt.

Jay Jay turned, still buzzing from the thrill of the attack, when Ponytail whom he had thought disposed of, caught him unawares with a vase right on the back of his head. Was that one of Mr Alfred's antiques? Jay Jay rolled forward and swung about face, towards the man. He took his stance immediately, touching the back of his head to feel for any injuries. He looked at his pale fingers and thanked the stars there were none. Sensing the onslaught might not cease with the strike, he squared up as Ponytail lunged at him with a shard of the vase.

Jay Jay had been cornered in a small space. He counted a few steps forward, moved his back foot sideways in a feint as though he was opening his body to be struck. Ponytail misread Jay Jay's move and swung the shard. Jay Jay rained blows on Ponytail's ear, jaw and wrist effectively numbing at least three of his five senses. Ponytail, enraged by this, swung sideways, immediately feeding his face to the strong right foot waiting for it. It ran into his face like a train. Jay Jay watched him go down without waiting for the count.

Lucky was watching Ponytail. His look was that of alarm. Ernesto caught his distraction. He launched a vicious attack, raining a half-dozen blows on his already bleeding nose.

Lucky collapsed to the ground. Jay Jay drew a sharp breath, threatened as Ponytail rushed past him and into Lucky's arms, holding his hands over his ears. It was almost a choreographed sequence, only with all the grace of two dancing bears. The Crane move.

"You don't know what you're doing," Ponytail snapped at Ernesto. Ernesto maintained his silence, keeping his eyes on both men.

"You had a choice," Jay Jay said, his voice shaking, "I gave you the money back. Returns. No quibble guarantee. You chose this, instead."

Ponytail helped Lucky to his feet but the man was too

smashed-up from his injury to keep his balance. The man's eyes fluttered open and closed as he lost more and more blood. He could leave, Jay Jay thought, he needed medical care. But some men just did not speak the language of quitting.

Emotions changed when Lucky swung out his gun, waving it unsteadily at the men. Jay Jay moved a few steps but stopped short when Lucky's hand steadied his aim. At him. It had been a terrible move and he did instantly regret it, and even more that he'd stopped after it. He'd realized too late he had placed his life in the hands of a dying man.

"You don't want to use that gun" Jay Jay said, with his hands up.

"You don't get to tell me what I can or cannot use" Lucky rambled, as he took off the weapon's safety.

Jay Jay broke into a sweat when Lucky's finger cradled the trigger. Ponytail backed away with his hand on his ear and Jay Jay said a small prayer of repentance to the Monkey King, Taoist God of Mischief. He shut his eyes.

The gun banged loudly, rattling the french windows.

"No, stop! Please leave him alone. Don't do anything to him please."

Jay Jay knew that voice. He flinched. A piercing cry of someone familiar and recent. He looked around him. Who— ?

He blinked.

The longish floppy hair, the glasses. On top of Lucky.

Jay Jay couldn't believe it. What was he doing here? Why was he even here?

The gun fired again, blowing a neat hole through Carl Rodriguez's shoulder and he shrieked again. He fell off Lucky who started to gasp for breath as Jay Jay tried to work out how Carl had entered the fight.

"Mr Rodriguez!" Jay Jay blurted.

Mr Rodriguez nursed his pain and the gun hung loosely in Lucky's hand.

"Shut up. You brought us on a wild goose chase," said Ponytail, his gaze going from man to gun and from gun back to man, just like Jay Jay's was. Ernesto backed away.

"I did not!" Mr Rodriguez cried out. "I found him for you."

"So?" Said Ponytail.

"Don't hurt him," bleated Carl. "He hasn't got anything. He's an old man."

"Mr Rodriguez?" Shouted Jay Jay. "What are you doing here?"

"I made a mistake. Yet another. I work at the realtors. I thought of them as my brothers... I... helped the Black Phoenix to... to find Mr Sutton for a fee."

Jay Jay could not believe his ears. Mr Rodriguez was in on it? He wouldn't have, would he? He was still buried in this thought when Ponytail sprang sharply towards the gun.

"But now I can't— " Carl shook his head feverishly. "I found out— he's my brother. I have seen him and I can't— I was born in the kitchen of this house."

Seeing that the news threw Ponytail, Jay Jay's feet got one the good foot and dashed towards the gun. He covered the rest of the ground with a desperate slide. The Otter stance. Ponytail's hand reached the gun before his but Jay Jay was swift to kick it out of his reach, creating a no-handicap race for the gun.

Ponytail and Jay Jay dived at the same time. They were face to face on the floor, struggling for the gun. The matter fell to fate's favorite and Jay Jay's finger was first on the trigger.

A distant wail of sirens approached.

Jay Jay pulled it and the gun jumped out of his hand. Ponytail recoiled and his eyes immediately went cold as he lay on his back with blood oozed from his chest.

The blue spinning lights pulsed through the vast windows, casting prismatic shadows on the cut-glass chandeliers.

CHAPTER 36

"Mr Alfred?" Jay Jay called out. Emily shone her flashlight for a few seconds in each direction. They paced the entire cold, wet garden to the cabin. They would be amazed if Mr Alfred was still here in the grounds.

Then, a faint noise, kind of rustling. Mr Alfred would be nearly frozen. He was not moving at all. How had he got here in the dark and cold? He'd even re-sealed the opening to the trap door. "We have to make sure he does not catch pneumonia. Quickly, Emily. Give me a hand. We need to call the ambulance back."

"They're gone. The ambulance took Carl to hospital and Ernesto went with him."

"Please ring for another, Emily," urged Jay Jay. "Now."

"I knew you would come," whispered Mr Alfred, a tremble in his voice. Jay Jay directed the flashlight at him. His face was papery blue. There were no blankets or bedding. Nothing to keep Mr Alfred safe and warm. He must have escaped here when he heard the commotion.

"I have been... playing in here since I was a boy. I can see in the dark, even now." His attempted laugh was the same old wheeze of a weak and rusty hinge.

"Don't speak now," said Jay Jay.

"He's wheezing," said Emily. "The ambulance will be here in two minutes."

"Stay here, Emily. Two minutes. I'll bring some blankets. This cold weather will get to him, if it hasn't already."

Jay Jay ran back to the mansion, up the stairs to the top floor. He switched on all the lights and gathered everything he found on Mr Alfred's bed. On the nightstand, he caught sight of the same family watch that Mr Rodriguez wore.

He got back to Mr Alfred and bundled him up. He carried him out of the cabin and back into the house, where it was much warmer. He was surprisingly light, compared to carrying bags of cement three-at-a-time.

Emily had helped with lighting the way back to the front room of the house. "Please stay with him while I check that Dallas is okay," she said to him.

THREE DAYS later he was sipping coffee.

Bones 1 and 2 was where it began. Now that the crime scene photographs had been taken and the place cleaned up, Jay Jay was back at work. What had brought him back? Only that he had to fix it. The locks blown by the tong members. The glass shattered, furniture broken. Little things. Big things, too. He wanted to press on with the tiling now he'd finished the electrics. He really *was* at the last stage and Mr Alfred had clearly said he did *not* want the kitchen modernized. The original unfitted freestanding 1920s kitchen units had to be kept that way, just like a museum since Mr Alfred doubted he would be doing any cordon bleu cooking. Jay Jay had cupped an ear and said, "Cord on wut?" Something that Dallas should be consulted on, no doubt. Never mind. Mr Alfred had his way of expressing things which went over his head, more often than not. Jay Jay's deep connection with the house, not its occupants, had led him back.

How could a house on the lake have brought him so much joy and so much pain?

———

THE NURSE LEFT THE ROOM, leaving Jay Jay alone with Mr Alfred.

"How are you feeling, Sir?" He said. Mr Alfred was stirring. His eyelids and his fingers twitched.

Mr Alfred opened his eyes.

"I feel better." He was still on a drip, but Jay Jay saw that his blue eyes had come back to life.

"Mr Rodriguez has been discharged already," said Jay Jay.

"How many days have I been here?" Asked Mr Alfred.

"Three. But I have been in and out to check. You'll be out in two days. You just got cold. They were impressed you didn't catch anything."

"Oh I lived in this city without heating. Hadn't worked for decades until you started fixing up the house."

"Mr Alfred, you just get better first."

"I know, Jay Jay. Thank you. You made the cabin so comfortable, I could live in it."

"You mean my workshop? I love having somewhere to store my tools and to—"

"You know, I jumped down into the basement."

Jay Jay felt the urge to mention Bones 1 and 2. Was now the time? Never was. How would he sugar coat the question? Words were his weakness.

"Sir, I... you... " He lowered his voice. "The skeletons."

"Ah yes. Thank you for leaving them where they were. It was thoughtful of you to tidy up..." Mr Alfred broke off and stared at the ceiling.

"No, I mean... Sir. What?" He struggled, as usual, with what to say. "What happened?"

Mr Alfred paused.

Jay Jay dreaded what he had been wanting to find out since Day One. Mr Alfred began with a sigh.

"You see," Mr Alfred said, "on that night, in August 1925, there was a terrible argument in the house between my father and his lawyer. Maxwell Parr had discovered that Yip Hoi Fa was gathering information on the arms trade," Jay Jay listened. He reached his hand out which Mr Alfred held weakly. "She was the most beautiful and intelligent woman you could ever hope to meet." He looked straight at Jay Jay. His eyes glowed like blue flames at the memory of her.

Then he turned to face the ceiling and shut his eyes again. "My father shot Maxwell. When his Pekingnese Fei-Fei wouldn't shut up, my father shot her too." Mr Alfred's tears dropped onto his pillow like rivulets from the creases in his papery skin. "The bodies were never discovered. They were carried into the cabin and buried in the basement. Sealed up in the basement, under a false floor, and the cabin was never used again until–"

"Until I came."

"Yes," he agreed in barely a whisper. "But I didn't think you would find the basement, in such a big cabin, with a false floor so well-fitted, I almost forgot about it."

His hand let go of Jay Jay's. Slowly he tried to wipe his face, struggling with the constricting cannula tubes coming up out of the shunt on the back of his left hand. Jay Jay thought: *Well, Bones 1 and 2, I should start calling you by your real names. Mr Parr and Fei-Fei. I will bury you guys soon. A proper home in the ground.*

"What was the argument about?" He asked Mr Alfred.

Mr Alfred didn't get time to answer before there was a soft knock on the door. He blinked away his silent tears and still more fell. Jay Jay jumped up to retrieve a tissue from a dispenser mounted on the wall behind him.

The door opened very slowly. "I am very sorry, it's me. Visiting hour is nearly up, so I thought I'd better make it now, rather than wait for the next window."

"Emily," said Jay Jay.

"Jerry," she acknowledged.

"What are you doing here?"

"I wanted to talk to Mr Alfred. Is that okay?"

"He is a little weary now." Jay Jay gestured at Mr Alfred, lying with his eyes shut.

"It won't take long. I've got news he might be interested in."

"Would you like me to leave?" Asked Jay Jay.

"No, stay." She looked straight at him, surprising Jay Jay with her tiny cat smile lifting the corners of her mouth. His heart skipped a beat or two. She went back to the door, looked into the corridor left and right to make sure no one was outside, and shut the door gently.

"Mr Sutton, about Yip Hoi Fa."

At the sound of her name, his teary eyes popped open. He blinked and stared at the ceiling, unable to look at Emily. Jay Jay used the tissue and helped wipe his eyes when he raised his hand slowly.

She got out another tissue from one of her many uniform pockets. She dabbed her eyes.

"She is alive."

CHAPTER 37

In the van, a block away, Dallas and Jennifer were asleep until someone tapped on the window. Dallas recognized Mrs Chan from the day she picked up the Mickey Mouse bag. She was sobbing, barefoot and still in her red suit. Dallas hooked her fingers into the car door and opened it. The back seat was kind of crowded but there was always room for a middle-aged Chinese woman. Dallas gave her a blanket and they waited in silence until the sirens and blue flashing lights woke the baby up.

Emily stepped out of her patrol car. Dallas unlocked and opened the car door. Mrs Chan cried out, "I'm fine. Please, my boys, where are they?"

Emily said, "don't worry, Auntie, they are safe." The twins had been with the cleaning lady Ah-Yi since Mrs Chan had been taken hostage. It was difficult being so far away from Hong Kong. They had no relatives or family to depend on. It was something that bugged all immigrants — finding an adoptive new "family", people to trust, to take care of children, and of you when you needed it.

Mrs Chan went home in Emily's car.

BACK IN HER own bed in the early morning, Dallas dreamt that she was back at the brightly-lit store counter, listening to tinkly live piano-playing from the entrance hall, wiping down the glass display cabinets so that they were shiny, displaying a range of lipsticks all half-open to the same height like rows of ammunition.

She distracted herself with bright warm thoughts when Jennifer woke up twice for her night feeds. Never wake a sleeping baby, all the manuals said, the sleeping baby will wake you. While feeding Jennifer, Dallas stared at the poster of *Starry, Starry Night* opposite her bed with its Vincent Van Gogh quote: *I dream my painting, and I paint my dream.* When she thought of Carl, she looked at the poster with a little sadness but also with a sense of achievement. She cuddled her baby closer. This was a moment of magic. There was something to be said about being with your child, alone at night, in silence and warmth. A moment that passed so quickly. She loved the swirling darkness and spiky stars, perfect for a bedroom. We are what we dream.

CHAPTER 38

ONE WEEK LATER

"The tickets." Emily gave him a stash of small rectangular pieces of paper, carbon copies in reds, blues but hard to look at in the blinding sunlight at the end of November, a short sharp day. She was standing outside her cop car. Jay Jay agreed to meet at Johnny's for pizza again. "Give these to Mr Alfred. How is he?"

"He is well," said Jay Jay. "At home and resting."

She did not look at him. "The flight is at 10:40pm. Don't miss it. There isn't another for forty years."

He laughed a sad laugh. He missed the closeness, her punchy directness, their odd friendship. "Long journey ahead for Mr Alfred," he replied. "Two re-fuelling stops, so the travel agent said. Frankfurt and somewhere else in the Arabian Gulf. I forget. He will be at O'Hare on time. I'll take care of that."

"Thanks. I couldn't reveal that my grandmother is Yip Hoi Fa because the Black Phoenix were after her. In protecting her, I caused my uncle's death."

"No, you didn't. Don't say that. They'd have done it anyway."

"She was supposed to have been tried and hanged. But she is looking forward to telling Mr Sutton the whole story of her escape to Hong Kong," she said. "A tale for another evening."

"I am sure. He is pumped up and ready for anything. All packed."

"He'll be picked up when he arrives in Hong Kong. My grand-mother will meet him."

Jay Jay held on to the wad of tickets. More important than cash. But his heart was racing and he had to try hard not to crush it with his tight grip.

———

ON THE DRIVE Mr Alfred held the blue silk notebook with both hands close to his chest. He was silent until the O'Hare exit when he suddenly spoke. "The argument that night was not about Yip Hoi Fa being a spy. There was no argument."

Jay Jay cocked his ears, surprised, but Mr Alfred changed the subject.

"I cannot believe it, Jay Jay. I will meet Hoi Fa in 20 hours. I remember that night in 1925 like it was yesterday."

Jay Jay drove while the cynic in him thought, "so *that* is love?"

Mr Alfred added, "I love her as much as or even more than the moment I first laid eyes on her at the Drake bar in November '24."

Jay Jay drove on. Every word filled him with envy. Had he ever – would he ever – experience that kind of intense love that will drive you crazy and make you give up on everything, business, life, the house? Wasn't love a kind of madness? So that was why Mr Alfred had given up on his house so long ago.

"People will tell you that you can't love someone you don't know. They're wrong. Son, if there is anything you need to know in this life before you grow old, it's that you can and you will fall so hard it changes everything you do, see and say."

Oh no, he didn't question Mr Alfred's conclusion. With some guilt he realized that he wasn't mad about Dallas and never could be. To him, love was a familiar and friendly partnership that was convenient and comfortable, like a favorite pillow or dish. She was his rock. He did not like change, even if he had changed. He would not want to lose sanity or sleep over a woman like Yip Hoi Fa.

Jay Jay listened, not quite believing he was hearing this and still driving calmly. Had Mr Alfred remembered to take his medication before packing it? He had checked Mr Alfred's luggage. Beautiful luxury gifts for the love of his life, his own clothes, his passport. His boss had required Dallas's help in purchasing the gifts. She had started back at work three days a week, while Jennifer was in daycare.

Was love not a cliche, a duty, a sense of self-worth? Or a work of art, intangible and magical as Mr Alfred's Yip Hoi Fa? *Leaf. Sea. Flower.*

Mr Alfred was saying goodbye to Jay Jay and hello to a new life. A love that had never ever died through all the wars, not even after 46 years. He'd never seen Mr Alfred looking so alert and well. Color had returned to his cheeks and he appeared at least 20 years younger. Sure, he couldn't grow more hair overnight, but a fire burned bright in his eyes.

"Not a day goes past when I do not think about her," he went on, now opening the blue silk notebook. "I ruined my whole life, my business, my family, when the news arrived that a Communist, *not* a Japanese, sympathizer had been tried and hanged in Nanking in 1947. I mean, you saw the state of my house. I had given up on everything. Until one day, the Professor said, 'I have Yip Hoi Fa's gun. Let's sell it.'"

"Yes," Jay Jay had been waiting for this. The Professor was bound to come into the conversation about The Order.

"Now, this deep blue," Mr Alfred stroked the notebook, "was the exact deep blue of the sky on that late summer evening. August 17th 1925. My mother was on an evening out downtown. At that time she was already 51."

Jay Jay switched off the radio, something he never did in the car.

"My father was away in New York City on business. Ralph stayed on with him. The air was still, the metallic smell of rain heavy from an afternoon shower. Hoi Fa and I were upstairs in bed," He blushed and Jay Jay looked away.

"But my father came back early. He must have suspected my mother was up to something. The sight of the gun, scarf and leather document case on the couch cooked his blood. My mother's family was wealthy. My father would inherit everything. He sat in the dark waiting for my mother to come home. He almost fell asleep. The clock chimed at 10. As soon as the keys were in the door, he tightened his grip on the gun and the door opened slowly.

"As it opened, someone entered. He fired. The figure collapsed," said Mr Alfred. "But it was not my mother."

"'Max?' My mother screamed. She ran in on hearing the single shot. 'Max?' She called. Her voice became a hiss. 'Oh dear Lord, please, no!'"

"No! What happened next?" said Jay Jay.

"My father ordered her to go upstairs, where I was on the landing looking down. 'I was parking,' she screamed, 'he got out first.' She was getting hysterical. Over and over, she said this, as if she had not made herself heard. When my mother dragged herself upstairs, I comforted her. You know, Jay Jay, even now when I hear someone say *I was parking*, I start trembling; the entire incident returns to me."

Jay Jay put left hand over on Mr Alfred's. What an awful memory, triggered by just three words.

"My father was shaking," Mr Alfred continued. "He just sat on *that* couch. The dog barked and barked. Wouldn't stop. My father went up the stairs and brought a sheet down. He rolled Maxwell up in a sheet. And Jay Jay, I didn't come down the stairs. I went with my mother to her room. We were both shaking, weeping. We heard a bang. At first I thought it was the front door."

"The dog! He shot... " Jay Jay shuddered at Charles's desperate cruelty.

"No, and yes. There were actually two simultaneous bangs. The dog. And... the front door. Hoi Fa had fled. The next day all I could find was the single earring."

"And the other had been found by the little girl," added Jay Jay. "Carmelita."

"Right. In her hurry, Hoi Fa lost her notebook and both earrings one of which the little girl found the next day," he gestured to indicate loss by flinging his hands down. "Hoi Fa was carrying the items loose. Don't forget she did not have her bag."

"The black pocketbook that was on the couch along with the scarf," said Jay Jay. "And the gun too..."

Mr Alfred did not reply about that. He was thinking of his lover again. "Hoi Fa disappeared through the grounds and I never saw her again. She never said goodbye. She had packed hurriedly when I went to the staircase to see what the commotion was about. After the first gunshot, she had jumped off the bed and got dressed. She turned to me and said, 'Alfred, your father knows. I gather information on the arms trade.' She could not have been more wrong. That hadn't even crossed his mind. I will never forget the tears in her eyes, so deep and dark."

Mr Alfred said he'd slept in his mother's room all night, staying with her, shaking, weeping. They'd never mentioned that evening again.

Jay Jay thought about how Catherine's secret date had gone seriously wrong. She had driven downtown with Maxwell Parr and his dog for a summer night out. Jay Jay visualized what Mr Alfred had been saying, how the couple were heading back to his lake house because the proverbial cat was away. But first, they made a quick detour back to North Lakeshore Drive to pick up her overnight essentials. The lake house. Catherine. The dog. The burning heat of summer. Swimming in the lake, it had all sounded perfect.

"She had never known love like this, and you know what they

say, *if it don't hurt, it ain't true, and if it hurts, it's true.* And then, I, too, went through the same thing, like a repeat episode from a TV soap," said Mr Alfred.

Love was generally undefined moments, with the occasional bolt of electricity and a jolt of recognition.

"I did not know it was a reproduction on the couch," said Mr Alfred. "A very good one, even had the Phoenix engraving. We were a team. In 1925 there was no one who didn't know us in this town. A perfect couple."

"What happened to the replica after your father sh... used it ? "

"So. That night my father picked up in the piano room or the library, the Edward de Weiss, and he inserted the gun in—"

"What device is that?"

"De Weiss," said Mr Alfred, separating the syllables patiently. "1957. Never mind. A modern bronze: it was hollow. Twisting cubes? Abstract." He looked at Jay Jay who remembered Dallas had once given him a vaguely similar description. "Anyway. My father sealed it completely with wax and wood and took it to Robert the next day."

"Why?"

"Why what?

"Why the Professor?"

"At the time, Robert was already an art tutor, but not yet a professor. He had access to the secure storage unit at the Institute. My father said to Robert, 'I need you to keep this. This... Edward de Weiss for me.' And Robert owed my father, for financially helping him to enter the art school in the first place and then to acquire his PhD. His father worked in a meat-packing plant. They lived on the South Side."

"Well, he must have been a little talented. He is a Professor. *The* Professor."

Mr Alfred shrugged and made a kind of expression that was almost Chinese. He nodded, while his mouth became not quite a smile but a line. "Let's just say he made it. That was his dream. So he helped my father by storing it at the Institute. Until now."

Jay Jay nodded politely. And then wondered, thinking why ever had the Professor waited so long to retrieve it?

"My father never went back for it. Robert found it again a few months ago buried under other pieces."

"But why?" Asked Jay Jay. "Why did he go back to it after these years?"

"He told me, *Alfred, it's your father's.* And I knew the art was far less valuable than the gun encased in it. So we took it apart and sold both. I needed funds. I can't even pay my medical bills any more. He was doing this to help me. And then, since I realized the works would finally go ahead. I hired you."

Jay Jay was thinking, *I got hired because of this Professor guy, and I'd known that since day zero. They were Dallas's exact words, and then bam, the guy's dead.*

"I'm sorry you sold the sculpture *and* the replica gun in order to fund the building works and your medical care," said Jay Jay, being practical, as he always *had* been. He cleared his throat. "You'll be well taken care of in Hong Kong. Emily tells me everything is so much cheaper there. Especially medical care."

"So he said he got both valued," said Mr Alfred, "and suggested we could split the profit."

Jay Jay took a deep breath and sighed. He didn't know what to make of the gun within a work of art by that guy, the artist, Edward "Device". He had no juice for names and dates, numbers and music were his thing. He remembered all the telephone numbers he rang even if he only rang them once or twice.

TRAFFIC HAD BEEN heavy due to some accident. He had listened to the whole tense story. They finally arrived at Chicago O'Hare. They sat in the car and Mr Alfred spoke again.

"I didn't know you were not allowed to leave the tong or to sell their property," said Mr Alfred. "I owe Robert so much. I've been in financial trouble for decades."

Jay Jay thought for a moment, then asked. "So what happened to it?"

"To what?"

"The original. The Order."

CHAPTER 39

The Piano Girl was playing *Winter Wonderland* on the white Steinway, next to a decorated white bushy tree about ten times the size of the girl. At the busiest time of year for sales, Dallas was pleased she was back at work *and* on top of it. For Jennifer's first Christmas, Dallas had already prepared some cute brand new outfits to spoil her, or yes, maybe herself.

SHE SAW THE HANDS FIRST. They were on the glass counter adorned with white and gold tinsel. She looked up. The floppy black hair.

He gave a slow, sad smile. He looked older. She was not surprised. He'd only just recovered from being shot. This wasn't Hollywood. You didn't recover by the next scene. She looked straight into the window frames of his gold-rimmed glasses. He was wearing a suit in that Van Gogh's *Starry Night* deep midnight blue.

She widened her eyes in the customer stare as she'd been trained to do and gave her widest professional smile.

"Hi," he said, a little shakily. She wondered what she'd be like thirty years into the future.

Dallas steeled herself. Her bland and pleasant porcelain appearance disguised what she was: a working mom with curled hair, tired out by standing all day in heels.

"How may I help you today, Sir? Something for your wife?"

"I went to visit my birth mother. Morales. She lives in a care home," he said. "I was getting something for her from upstairs, so I thought I'd drop in on you first."

Her grinning mask slipped. The store was loud with the sounds of tinkly piano, holiday bells, angelic choir voices harmonizing to *sleigh bells ring, are you lis'ning*, store announcements, crowds with money and crowds with no money. "How is she?"

"She remembers everything. The instant she laid eyes on me she said, 'Oh Carl. You're back.' "

Dallas laughed, just like the first time she'd laughed, describing the Halston silver crescent-moon earrings to him when he came in to buy his wife's birthday gift; a thrilled childish laugh and not one to cover an awkward gap. "She hadn't seen you since—"

"Since 1920. My half-sister Carmelita hadn't seen me since she was two. She didn't remember me."

"She was born in the house?"

"No. My birth mother had Carmelita in 1918 before she came to work as a servant in the Sutton household."

A quick mental calculation and Dallas blinked. Grandpop's wife was only 54? Jay Jay never talked about her. All that bad makeup, poor skin and diet, and garish dress sense made her look about 70.

"I just wanted... I *have* enrolled at the Institute of Art, thanks to you," he added awkwardly, seemingly forgetting they'd been talking about his mother. "I start in January after the holidays."

"I am waiting to go back there as a student myself. When Jennifer is bigger."

"Which is when?"

She gave him the mom-stare, to silence him. She became aware that shutter juice was quickly filling her eyes up faster than a cup under a tap. Astounded by her own emotion, she pulled a couple of tissues from under the counter and surreptitiously dabbed at her tears. She didn't want to look up at him.

There were customers hovering, two women were chatting and distracting themselves with the new range of holiday eye makeup palettes, all shiny and frosted party colors. They seemed cheerful and not bothered about waiting their turn. There were plenty of new products to keep them occupied. Dallas cleared her throat, "I won't be a moment, I'll be with you shortly," she said to the women.

"You're busy," he said. "I'll head upstairs now."

"Bye," she said, then added, "Have a nice evening." She said, but she didn't mean it.

He paused. He didn't reply or say bye or thank you. Dallas wished he would go. What was he waiting for?

He slid a white envelope and a small white box across the counter. "I miss you. This is for you. Merry Christmas." She scooped both up and tossed them on the shelf under the counter like a hot bun without a second glance or a 'thank you'. She turned immediately to the two waiting women. *The customer comes first, right?*

He turned and walked away. She watched him on the crowded escalator going up until the deep midnight blue vanished.

CHAPTER 40

The party was on the edge of town. Ernesto had organized the catering. Jay Jay and Grandpops went. Mostly for the Cuban food on Jay Jay's part. Twice fried plantain, seasoned shrimp and moros y cristianos, Moors and Christians. Rice and beans. The light and the dark. When they'd arrived, Nesto was introducing Carl to his own abuelita, Granny Morales, and his mother Carmelita, too.

CARL RODRIGUEZ HAD FOUND his Chicago family at last. He looked like he belonged to the Windy City and not the vineyards. Granny Morales wasn't as demented as people said. She called out "Carl!" immediately when she saw him.

"First time in 51 years, huh?" said Jay Jay.

Granny Morales went silent. Grandpops and Jay Jay looked at each other wondering the same thing. If she was confused, again.

She suddenly said, "never loved her." Who was "her"? And who never loved "her"? Everyone looked around, not understanding at all what she meant, or if indeed this was part of "her illness" and her brain was talking horsefeathers.

"Is no true. *Almost* 51 years," she said, looking straight at Carl, after a long pause. "I was jus' working out the math." Carl looked around the room, then at Ernesto as though seeking more explanation but Ernesto looked blank.

"One darkest night in November 1925," she said. "In the evening at around six, I am working in the kitchen, preparing the dinner for Mr Charles and family. Then comes a visit from Isabella Rodriguez. I was surprised as I never see she doing the delivery for years. Usually, is her husband. I say in Spanish to she: 'Is wine delivery day? Today?' And she say, 'no.' So I says, 'why you come?' She say, 'I have very bad news. I really don't want to bother you, but Carl is very sick.' 'The boy?' I ask she. I stop peeling the potatoes. I stare at my hands, not at she. And she say, 'Sí. El niño.' Now this is my baby too, that I could not keep, remember. We are both crying as we don't know what to do. I also have no money, is why I work there. We talk and talk and then we decided we gonna ask Sir for help."

Carl took a tissue and started dabbing his eyes. He chewed his lip to stop himself from weeping aloud. He sniffed and everybody looked away.

"I remember I knock on his study door. I see that big desk with the green leather top," said Granny Morales. "I ask he for money but he didn't believe me that his own son is sick. I got very angry as is my son too. But I keep myself calm though my tears keep coming. At first I was planning to get the money from he, then meet Isabella at the Foster Beach Pier and give her the money but he says he won't just hand over money. But after I say, to he, Carl is our child," she thumped on her chest with her right fist. "My baby. Is very sick. Is urgent. I beg him. Por supuesto, needs medicine, treatment, hospital. They come to the city just for the top hospital. They are waiting for a bed. Por favor. Why he won't just give me the money to give Isabella? No, he says, a finalmente. He wants to see his son. He does not believe me. How does he know I am not just asking for the money for something else? So he say, he will see the boy, only one time, never again. I tell him midnight so no one will see him. Or her or the boy. Because Sir is an important man in this city. No one must know."

She stopped, the whole room spellbound by her story. Ernesto gently putting down an empty plate with its cutlery on it sounded like a clap of thunder. Señora Morales continued. Her voice was monotonous yet enthralling, like she was simply reciting step-by-step what she had made for dinner.

"At midnight he goes to the Pier. Mi pequeña, Carmelita is seven, and I have left her in the house with the driver, Albert. Freezing rain start coming down, like bits of glass, but the moon is bright. I follow Sir. Because I am not sure I trust that he will give her the money and also Carl is my son. Sir is heading for the pier. He is tall with his longish black hair, just like you," she faced Carl, "The wind turn it into millions of spiders. He is wearing his big wool gray coat which I just cleaned two days before. I stay quite near the truck, only a couple yards away, but behind long grass, so sharp and cold they are like needles. The Rodriguez delivery truck is park in the area with huge trees, bushes and a sandy path. Isabella's husband opens the big back doors. The boy is lying there, no moving, on Isabella's lap wrapped in blanket. Two lamps are on. When I saw my boy, I am sobbing too." She pressed the heels of her palms into her eye sockets as if pushing back the tears into her eyeballs.

At this point, Carmelita handed her a tissue and kept one herself. Granny Morales's seemingly flat voice broke. Tears welled up in her eyes at the astonishing clarity of the memory. She wiped them away quickly.

"Carl... Carl, you did not open your eyes once," she wept. "Every part of me is breaking... " Carmelita put her arm around her mother. Jay Jay felt bad, guilty for what he'd thought of Grandpop's wife. "No one can hear nothing. The wind, he is howling. My tears they are hot, but icy rain wash them away just like that. When Sir he see the boy, he cried too. His hands cover his mouth. Then he touch the boy's forehead. Isabella is also crying. He take out of his inside pocket some money, must be a thousand. I cannot truly see. But is big, is a few inches thick. He put it in Isabella's hand."

Carl listened, one hand on his throat to still himself, the other clutching the tissue tightly in a fist.

"Just as the boy's father shut the truck door, Mr Charles he turn around. He seem to have remembered something. He take off his watch from his left hand and he give it to Isabella."

She paused. "And then?" asked Ernesto after a few seconds. His grandmother's eyes remained downcast, with an unreadable expression. Jay Jay thought, *has she just lost the thread?*

"We watch the truck drive off in a hurry. Sir with his hands in the pocket and me in the grass. I know I will never see the boy again so I may as well watch until the truck is gone. As Sir turns to walk back, suddenly someone appears from behind him from the large bushes. An attacker. I see the figure dressed in black. They are shouting and I cannot hear the words but is a woman's voice. She starts swinging at Sir with something in both hands. No guns, no nothing, just a long stick and some kung fu kicks. She is strong. Could it be... it must be! Yip Hoi Fa. The Chinese woman who used to come to the house. She is back? For a second, I am very excited. I am thinking how to tell Mr Alfred. But I was distracted when she drops the stick. His hands are around her neck. She kicks, she hits but he does not let go. He is taking her, guiding her, going further and further away, until they on the pier. Here is completely dark. I cannot see any more. I wait and I wait. No sound except the screaming winds and the rain."

They wait.

"He comes back alone," she said.

Jay Jay put his hand on his forehead.

"But why didn't you tell anyone this before?" asked Carl.

"What? And lose my job?" she answered. "After giving a child away?"

"No, why didn't you tell anyone more recently," prompted Jay Jay.

"I have no idea what I did today or yesterday," she said.

Ernesto and Carl sympathetically shook their heads, thinking uh-oh, she *was* having a senile moment. But then she added, "I don't know what I have or not said. I just know I have forgotten everything until today, when I see my boy Carl here. You." She held out her hand, and he firmly took it.

Jay Jay looked around at the cheerful yellow "party room" which Carmelita had booked in the care home. There was a chill in the air. The "party room" certainly bore no difference to the one at the daycare center that Jennifer attended.

"No," Granny Morales gripped the chair arms. "Is no the Chinese woman. She ain't back. It was Mrs Charles. She was following him too. She did not like the idea that Sir gave away money and the watch that was her recent gift to him. That the boy was her husband's son. Or that Maxwell Parr was gone. She didn't like it one bit. I don't know why, but she used to talk to herself 'I was parking, I was parking' a few times a day. She was 51 years old."

———

DECEMBER 1972

"PLEASE SIGN HERE. Registered mail for you," said the mailman. He was wearing thick gloves. He handed Jay Jay a cheap pen.

He had been just about to walk out his apartment door on a freezing, still dark morning. He had an early start that day, like most days and quite a few tasks to complete before the holidays.

His current job was a little further away than usual. Since meeting Carl, he'd been recommended to some new customers in those Western family suburbs a little further out of the city. Bigger homes, none with as much character or history as North Lakeshore Drive, natch. But knowing a few realtors had helped get him to a better place.

The postmark was from Hong Kong. He rubbed his thumb

over the glossy, pretty postage stamp. The padded airmail envelope had the blue and red stripes on all four edges. Mr Alfred had been gone for nearly a year. Jay Jay had been working on the empty house as and when he could. He finished the house on Lakeshore Drive at last, a few months ago. He'd sent photos to Mr Alfred. He guessed that Mr Alfred wouldn't be back because he said he liked living abroad. Now that Carl Sutton was selling the farmland and was off his back, Mr Alfred had written to realtors inviting them to value the house.

But mostly, Jay Jay went just to check on what had been his baby before Jennifer came.

MR ALFRED HAD WRITTEN a few times since he left. In the first letter, he wrote:

> Jerry,
>
> I didn't get to explain this at the airport because we ran out of time the day you gave me a lift. I don't know the whole truth, not even now I have talked to Hoi Fa. We have no proof, but it wouldn't surprise me if The Order was in the Bahamas. Ralph. He blew the whistle. It was he, not Maxwell, who had discovered her involvement with the arms trade.
>
> On the night she heard the gunshot, Hoi Fa had rushed back to her apartment to pack. But it had been raided. And that was the night Ralph was supposedly in NYC. The next day, the cops got her. I very much doubt that he will, but if Ralph ever sends you a plane ticket to work on his property there, would you please look for The Order?
>
> Alfred.

In other letters, Mr Alfred wrote about exotic places and scenes Jay Jay had only seen in kung fu movies. The Peak. Kowloon Tong. The ferry. One of the postcards from Mr Alfred was of high tea at the famous historic Peninsula Hotel. He sent photographs of misty limestone cave mountains in Guilin. They were just like a painting. Junks with red sails in Hong Kong harbor. Art Deco skyscrapers in Shanghai, which looked kind of like the New York City of the East.

Jay Jay was curious and excited as any boy looking at a picture book of places far away. His experience beyond Beecher extended as far as the steel works, the warm domestic womb of North Kenmore Avenue and the faded grandeur of North Lakeshore Drive. The most "for'n" place he had ever been to was the Garden of Eden in Englewood. He needed to return one day to China, or more specifically Canton, from where his grandmother Lee Cha had fled. Receiving Mr Alfred's letters gave Jay Jay a feeling of contentment; a certain buzz which was about nothing but meant something. That was the 'nothing' that people cared about, craved, needed.

HAPPINESS WAS A BLANK PAGE. Mr Alfred was reunited with the love of his life in Hong Kong. His previous letter had said he would be back in Chicago for the Christmas and New Year holidays with Yip Hoi Fa. He planned to take her round all their old haunts.

MR ALFRED HAD NEVER SENT his letters registered, not to Jay Jay, anyhow. Was this about their imminent trip? When Jay Jay turned the envelope around, the sender's name was Marshall, Lee, Kwong and Rajan: Advocates and Solicitors.

Whoa. Who dat? He went into the kitchen and brought back a butter knife. He slid the bulky envelope open. Oh my, he thought, shaking as he held the letter. Heavy. Keys. Mr Alfred's original bunch. His key ring.

Mr Alfred had passed away peacefully. "Oh my god. Oh. My. God." He whispered. The letter was regarding the will. As a formality, Jay Jay would have to meet a lawyer hired by the local bank to sign some papers organized by Mr Alfred. There was a telephone number and address downtown to make the appointment. Re-reading the letter over and over, Jay Jay thought of Grandpops and his dream to run a little city hotel or bed and breakfast business. He really did need to do something now he no longer had the pond farm.

All he could see was his name. Clearly. Jerome Siracuse Lee. That, and "sole beneficiary".

"Doll? Honey! Wake up. You won't believe it."

Dallas opened her eyes. "What? What time is it?"

"Never mind what time. We're rich."

"What are you talking about?"

"You know how you always said we should find somewhere bigger?"

"What do you mean? Right now?"

"Right now, baby."

"Where are we going, lemon pie?"

"How about 1020, North Lakeshore Drive?"

―――――

WHEN SHE MEETS DALLAS AGAIN, Li-an is still a Chicago piano whizz. She's not a kid anymore, and she's in trouble. How will Dallas help her? From semitones to Semillon Blanc, Li-an's luck changes when she's offered a job abroad. But what's the catch? She is. *Heart of Glass* is a suspense thriller set in the disco era of the 1980s in Chicago and Macau. As a young, naive and impoverished American Asian musician, her ambition gets the better of her. Read the heart-pounding sequel to White Crane Strikes, *Heart of Glass*, coming soon.

DO YOU LOVE SHORT STORIES? **Fascinated by Asian culture?** Crocodiles in the city, street food fandom, a psychic club meeting in a Penang beach resort. *Asian Anthology: New Writing*

Vol. 1 is a showcase of short stories and place writing by both new and more established prize-winning writers. Some unexpected, a few surreal and others traditional, these are 23 compelling stories of irony, humanity and satire, exploring a range of subject matter to reveal a glimpse of modern Asian society and culture. Read Asian Anthology New Writing Vol. 1.

THE JUNGLE KNOWS the truth and will follow you to the city. What lies behind the secrets of the Iban tattoo? Winner of an international award, the 2016 International Proverse Prize, *Cry of the Flying Rhino* is a post-colonial Malaysian suspense thriller set in the plantations of Johor and the jungles of Borneo about injustice, climate change, class and colonial guilt. Read *Cry of the Flying Rhino*.

Before you go

The book you are holding in your hand is the result of my dream to be an author. I hope you enjoyed it as much as I enjoyed writing it. I am slowly building my author brand, ranking and profile. As you probably suspected, it takes weeks, months or years to write a book. It exists through dedication, passion and love. Reviews help persuade the reading community to give my books a shot. Please take *less than a minute* to leave me a one-liner review on Goodreads or a major online retailer in USA or UK. A big thank you. *Ivy*

FREE BOOK

Thank you for reading *White Crane Strikes*. Here is your free gift, *The Power Ballads & Other Stories*, a short story collection. Scan code above or type this into your browser:

https://BookHip.com/LQWBRJ

You will be joining my VIP fan club, receiving a monthly newsletter and be among the first to know about exciting new books and tour merch. Unsubscribe at any time. We can break up; no hard feelings, lol. You won't receive spam. I know. I hate spam too. I will only keep in touch with you with news. If you would like to write to me, please use my online form. You can also email me:

ivy_ngeow AT yahoo DOT com

About the Author

Ivy Ngeow was born and raised in Johor Bahru, Malaysia. A graduate of the Middlesex University Writing MA programme, Ivy won the 2005 Middlesex University Literary Press Prize out of almost 1500 entrants worldwide. Her debut *Cry of the Flying Rhino* (2017) won the 2016 International Proverse Prize.

Ivy is a regular suburban London mum who likes dogs, cake, wine and piano-pounding. She has had a passion for creative writing since she was a child, winning her first national competition at 16. She lives in London. You can find her here:

writengeow (www.writengeow.com)
Twitter (twitter.com/ivyngeow)
Facebook (facebook.com/ivyngeowwriter)
Instagram (www.instagram.com/ivyngeow)
Email: ivy_ngeow AT yahoo DOT com

ALSO BY IVY NGEOW

NOVELS

Overboard

White Crane Strikes

Heart of Glass

Cry of the Flying Rhino

SHORT STORIES

Asian Anthology New Writing Vol. 1

The Power Ballads and Other Stories

Printed in Great Britain
by Amazon

81903299R00164